AT RISK OF WINNING

Mark E. Becker

PUBLISHING

DEBUT
BOOKS

AT RISK OF WINNING

For information on distribution rights, royalties, derivative works or licensing opportunities on behalf of this content or work, please contact the Publisher at the address below or via email info@nolimitpublishinggroup.com.

COMPANIES, ORGANIZATIONS, INSTITUTIONS, AND INDUSTRY PUBLICATIONS: Quantity discounts are available on bulk purchases of this book for reselling, educational purposes, subscription incentives, gifts, sponsorship, or fundraising. Special books or book excerpts can also be created to fit specific needs such as private labeling with your logo on the cover and a message from a VIP printed inside.

No Limit Publishing Group
123 E Baseline Road, D-108
Tempe AZ 85283
info@nolimitpublishinggroup.com

This book was printed in the United States of America

No Limit Publishing
No Limit Enterprises, LLC
1601 E 69th Street, Suite 200
Sioux Falls, SD 57108

PART ONE

A FATHER FINDS A SON

Chapter One

Across the river and behind the towering oaks that lined its banks, the nation's capitol stood proud. The white limestone monuments maintained their grandeur by law, for no structure could exceed the height of the Capitol Dome. There were no skyscrapers and no towering condos to dwarf the Washington Monument. The Jefferson Memorial could be seen from a distance across the tidal basin once a visitor ventured inside the beltway, but from the senator's vantage point, the political world was as far away as he could make it.

Along the top of the bluffs that line the Potomac River is the beltway, representing the border between the political center of the nation and the rest of the world. There are no gates or signs designating this border. To all but veterans of national politics, it is invisible, but it has a strange effect on people. In the course of the transition from the rolling hills of the Virginia countryside into the gut of our country, Washington D.C., the mind changes in unique and subtle ways.

The senator had lived that surreal life for as long as he could stand it, and although he had been out of the Washington scene for ten years, the draw of the famous and important people of the world brought him back inside the beltway. He would visit for a flash in time—a public appearance or party here or there—and then return to the insular world he had created.

There are only forty minutes each day when the light is right to take photographs outdoors; twenty minutes in the morning when the sun comes up and twenty minutes each late afternoon when the golden glow of light exaggerates the shadows. Each moment during that fleeting passage from dawn to day and from day to dusk is special in time and transforms everyday objects into visual art.

During those windows of opportunity, the senator chose to set his medium format camera on the bluff overlooking the Potomac and wait for the time when the shadows transformed the river into a strip of gold passing between the ochre bluffs. It was a tedious process; first, the tripod had to be erected and leveled. Then came the process of removing the heavy camera from the leather case that had housed it for one hundred and fifty years and focusing the lens. Finally, the film was carefully placed in the back, exposed inside a dark box that would be opened for less than a second. When it was done right, the image exposed on the film showed all the detail of the panorama that his eyes could see.

He tried to capture the perfect photograph but perfection is fleeting, and his failures far exceeded his successes. In the rare moments when the light was golden, his choice of subject was right, and the time of year brought out the colors of the wildflowers, he was satisfied for the moment. Then, his mind began formulating ways to improve his fleeting perfection. He launched himself into making it better, and the process started from the beginning.

It seemed that his whole life was filled with big efforts, striving for perfection, coming close but never quite getting there, contemplating, scheming, and tackling it again. It didn't matter much whether he was politicking or taking the perfect shot. He had to get it right.

Following his retirement from the United States Senate after four terms of meritorious service, John Masterson was rich, bored, and less than satisfied with his life. He was alone and felt like he had been put out to pasture. It was his own fault, he realized. His solitude was self-imposed, and his retirement was the result of a career-long frustration with the American way of running the country.

He had never bothered to marry. He came close a few times, but there was always that nagging thought that he was too busy to settle down. Despite the attention and adoration he had received over the years from more than a few glamorous women, he chose career over family. But when he watched his colleagues pose for pictures in front of the Capitol with family in tow, all smiling and clean and happy, he wondered whether he had made a huge error of judgment in his life's plans. He had no family. He was an only child, the son of hard-working middle class parents. Both his mother and his father had encouraged him to settle down and make a family life for himself, but he was driven.

He had chosen a path that many strive to follow but few attain, and his years of public service were spent as the curmudgeon of the Washington establishment. He delighted in following the long, grand, glorious speeches of his fellow senators with a short, to the point analysis that reduced their words to an understandable essence. Most times, the analysis provoked laughter. Once the smoke screen of words that surrounded the message was lifted, he left the message bare for the public to hear, and it was seen with all of its logical flaws. Images of the senator throughout his career revealed his trademark distant expression. This aloof persona was interpreted as the face of a man who was thinking lofty and powerful thoughts that mere mortals could not attain. While his face portrayed a deep thinker, his mind was primarily occupied with regret. Since his retirement, the regrets had transformed into a profound sadness. He had forsaken family for politics, and now there was nothing to show for his life except some old photographs, a plaque or certificate that nobody saw or remembered, and his memories of days spent in public service. Posterity, they called it.

"My life is almost gone, and all I have to show for it is money and a gap in my heart," he lamented, an ache spreading through his chest. The time for being a family man had passed him by. In his retirement, he could afford to go anywhere in the world and do whatever he pleased, but he had no heir, no children to pass his legacy to.

Masterson moved the camera to eliminate Tuscarora Road from the bottom of the frame. He sought to create an illusion of timelessness from the real panorama that spread before him, without telephone poles, buildings, or roads. He wanted nothing in the scene that would allow the viewer to date the image by time or era.

As he looked through the viewfinder, he heard the faint sound of an engine, with squealing tires at intervals indicating that the driver's speed was much faster than the car was meant to handle. He knew it well. Many of his Sunday afternoons were spent trying to navigate the winding turns of Tuscarora Road at the maximum possible speed without losing control. His Jaguar could do that turn at nearly 52 miles per hour, but the car that produced the sounds below was an ancient Pontiac Firebird, and its oversized engine and narrow tires were better suited for a drag race than a winding road rally. Through the viewfinder, he saw the car skid across the turn, overcorrect, and crash sideways into a large live oak that somehow had survived for hundreds of years. The tree never even shuddered. It wasn't going anywhere.

The car began to smoke, and Masterson launched his geriatric legs down the hill toward the tragic scene. As he reached the last hill before the roadway, he could smell it. The smoke was now pouring out from under the hood, and the horrid smell of burning gasoline, rubber, and plastic rolled in his direction. "I hope I can make it in time," he thought, wondering what he would do when he got there. Flames began to lap at the edges of the hood, and the windshield blackened from the smoke billowing from the broken windows.

As he came within the last 100 yards, lungs burning and legs failing, he thought he heard a baby cry. The driver's side of the car was crunched against the bark of the huge tree. He had better access to the passenger's side. He skidded to a stop at the bottom of the hill and crossed the road in a semicrouch, trying to hold his head below the black poisonous plumes. There were no sounds, just a slight hissing as the flames grew taller. Again, the sound of a baby, its voice barely a peep, but he was sure of it now.

He reached the passenger door. As he yanked it open, a woman fell to the ground, her neck twisted at a strange angle. The white/gray color of her skin revealed that she was already dead. He looked across at the dark-haired man in the driver's seat. His bloody head was slumped over the steering wheel. He had to find that baby…

The smoke billowed in his face, blocking his sight, but when it thinned for a moment, he saw a white car seat in the back. A small child was gasping for breath, his little hands and legs thrashing frantically. He flipped the passenger seat forward and, closing his eyes to the smoke, groped for the buckle that held the baby seat. His fingers finally found the familiar shape and he pressed the center, relieved at the click and release that he sought. Reaching into the black plume, he pulled the plastic shell from the seatbelt and yanked the car seat toward him. It popped forward, and he fell onto his back on the pavement, clutching his prize to his chest.

Seconds later, the car erupted into flames, and he crab-walked backwards, balancing the car seat on his chest. The heat was intense as the flames roared 20 feet above his head. There was nothing more he could do.

When he had crawled far enough that the heat no longer scorched his face, he rolled to his knees and opened the car seat. A small boy, no more than six months old, lay on his back. He was wide-eyed and panicky, trying to escape the car seat, but the straps bound him tightly. The senator unfastened the restraints and held the child at arm's length. "He doesn't seem hurt, and his hair isn't even singed," he surmised. "A close call for this little guy, but a tragedy for those poor souls." He turned briefly to face the burning car, but the heat was too intense.

He struggled to catch his breath as sirens wailed on the parkway. Within a minute, the lights appeared, and a police cruiser and ambulance followed by a fire truck surrounded the accident scene. By the time the heat from the fire had been doused enough to approach the car, the old Firebird was a charred black husk. Masterson kept his back to the heat until it no longer warmed the back of his neck, and then he turned, clutching the small boy to his chest. A young police officer walked up, clipboard in hand.

"Excuse me sir, but is this baby yours?"

He couldn't respond. The question, as insipid as it was, pushed his mind deeper. He looked down at the little face. The baby smiled and grasped his index finger in his tiny hands, squeezing tightly.

"Sir?" The police officer looked directly at the child and then blushed as he turned his attention to Masterson's smoke-smudged face and recognized the famous senator. "Senator Masterson? Is this little boy yours?"

The baby looked directly into his eyes and captured the old man's heart. "Yes, I suppose he is," he finally replied.

Chapter Two

When word reached the office of Hamilton Bennett that his highest retainer client wanted to adopt an infant orphaned in a car wreck, the ambitious lawyer thought the old man was nuts. But when his oldest and best friend outlined each step to complete the appropriate paperwork, file the lawsuit, and call his friend Judge Hopkins to finalize the transaction, Bennett realized that what he had initially perceived as eccentricity was more a scene of true genius in action. He admired John Masterson for his accomplishments in the political and business world. Who wouldn't admire one of the richest self-made men in the last part of the twentieth century? "There are those who are blessed, and then there are the rest of us," he thought, looking across at Masterson, who sat in the red leather chair, a seat he had occupied many times before, but only to discuss matters he seemed to believe now were far less important than the issue at hand. "I'm a damn power lawyer, John! I don't know squat about adopting babies. I have spent the past two decades doing everything you wanted me to do, but this…" he finally said, feeling the flush threaten to rise from his neck to his cheeks.

Masterson raised his hand to quiet him. "High blood pressure will be the end of you, Ham! Whatever happened to the fearless young barrister who wasn't afraid to take on the entire U.S. Congress, the Supreme Court, and anybody who had the stupidity to stand in your way?"

"I'm not young, I've never been fearless, and you're asking me to do something that I have never done before. I'm referring you to someone who knows what they're doing, and I'll get you the best in the business for this sort of thing." He felt his expression sour at the thought of having to take on a family law case. He'd rather sell used cars to the Amish. He looked away and then back at his scowling friend. "You old fart! I pegged you for many amazing accomplishments in your retirement, but I figured they would mainly revolve around something like circumnavigation of the Pacific Ocean in a sea kayak rather than taking on something as scary as parenthood. Can't you act your age?"

"Never!" Masterson replied, clenching and unclenching his fist. "I want to leave this world with an heir." His tone was sad, but determined. When an old politician is confronted, conversational tone converts to a voice broadcast from the diaphragm, loud enough to be heard by those sleeping in the back row. Ham knew his old friend was serious in his intentions, but he couldn't pass up the chance to render advice.

"I hope you know what you're doing. By the time the press finds out, I want this adoption to be final. I don't want to be subjected to endless months of so-called experts spouting their opinions about how what you're doing is wrong," Ham said in a conspiratorial tone.

"I don't care what they think. Never did, never will. A man has to follow his heart, and that's exactly what I'm gonna do." The senator smiled. Hamilton Bennett knew when someone had dug in his heels and the look on his old friend's face showed a determination he hadn't seen in a long time. Still, he couldn't resist the opportunity to needle a buddy who had prevailed in every major battle of his life at a time when he was most vulnerable.

"I suppose this means that come tarpon season, you'll wimp out and tell me that you can't come down to the beach house because you're too busy changing poopy diapers."

"Mr. Bennett, our conversation is nearing an end. I know how much you charge by the hour and, being the fiscal conservative that I am, I'm not going to dignify that statement with a response on my dime. Get to work and make this happen. Oh, and don't get any funny ideas about sending any of your lady friends over to assist in my time of need." He grinned.

Senator John "Minuteman" Masterson looked younger than his years. It was a contented visage, the kind a person acquires when they have accomplished a lofty goal. He rose from the chair and shook the hand of his old friend and advisor, who peered at him over the top of his reading glasses. The lawyer looked deep into his eyes and found a glint that he hadn't seen in many years. "Maybe he has finally found what he's been searching for," he thought.

Chapter Three

"I knew when I took on this responsibility that it would be tough, but this is a job for a young guy, who can get up in the middle of the night without being trashed from sleep deprivation the next day," he kept telling himself. He paced the floor with baby Max, who he had named Maximum in line with his approach toward life: Maximum effort yields maximum results. This night, though, he was dragging. The nanny had retired for the night, and he had heard Max stirring in the nursery. It was situated down a short hallway from the library, a throwback to the days when educated aristocrats prided themselves on the number of books they possessed. He called it a den, but it was really a research facility with wireless access to a state of the art mind-controlled computer, where he could display results on a large holographic screen situated on the opposite wall of the room.

Despite the room's ability to allow him to focus on his millions of thoughts and ideas, the sound of a baby's tiny voice was enough to direct his attention to his new son. He pulled the young boy from his crib and held him close, feeling the warm pounding of his heart against his chest. Even though Max was an infant, he had already learned how to get the attention of a retired United States Senator, a task at which older and mightier men had never succeeded when he was on the Hill. Little Max had bonded with the nanny from the first day, and when he wasn't being fed or bathed by the nanny, he was with the lovely Adrianna.

"Just when I need her, my girlfriend takes off to visit her mother," he commented to the baby, who was gleefully pulling his hair. Adrianna was more than a girlfriend, and if she had heard his description of her place in his life, there would have been hell to pay, but he was confident that Max wouldn't tattle. A certified teacher, she spent several hours each day with the little boy, who already displayed high intelligence. At eighteen months, the little manipulator constantly sought the comfort of his new father and Adrianna. When the nanny and Adrianna weren't around, the senator assumed parenting duties by default.

"Did you miss me?" He looked down at the little guy, who smiled at the sound of his voice. "You heard me working, didn't you?" He carried Max tenderly down the hall and placed him on his lap in front of the screen. Before them flashed images of colorful Sesame Street characters, who talked directly to the little boy conjured from the senator's previously stored memory. "Hi, Max!" said Ernie. Max laughed, clapped his hands in delight and immediately threw up in the lap of his esteemed father. As the fetid liquid dripped from his lap onto the Persian rug, the senator jumped up and ran in search of a towel, holding his baby boy in front of him at arm's length. As he dashed down the hall toward the pantry, Max giggled at the game he had created.

"What do they use to clean this stuff up? Powder? No! The white bottle!" He sniffed, and the ammonia fumes nearly took his head off. "That ought to do." He placed Max in his crib and ran down the hall to the waiting mess. The leak on the leather chair was easy to wipe away. It was the puddle on the rug that took some rubbing. He poured more of the liquid onto the stain.

The next morning, when the nanny arrived to assume her matronly duties, she found the old man in his bathrobe, the little boy asleep in his arms in the plush leather recliner of the den. The boy's head rested against his chest. She looked down at the white oval on the rug and shook her head. "That spot won't be coming out anytime soon," she thought, shaking her head. Tenderly, she pulled Max from his father's arms, while the senator slept in apparent bliss. After his son left his arms, his forehead creased. "A bad dream again," she thought as she stared at the screen in front of the recliner. Images of men in identical suits, milling in the Senate chamber with angry faces, filled the screen. She tiptoed back to the nursery, the little boy sleeping openmouthed, his head on her breast.

Chapter Four

In the plush comfort of the recliner, Masterson's mind slipped back to his Washington years. The dream was as clear as if it was happening in real life. The voices were distinct, and the colorful details of the setting were real. The monitor flickered for a moment, and then the scene was vividly displayed on the screen before him, recorded from his brain waves. The neural monitor was still tracking his brain waves in his sleep, and although the event was ten years in the past, his memories brought the details back to life.

The senator conducted all of his life's activities on the hour principle. If any activity took more than an hour of his time, Masterson's patience ground to a halt. During his term in the Senate, many years ago, the idea of a filibuster to block a bill was so repugnant to him that he voted against his own party just to avoid sitting through the long hours of monotony. He earned the nickname "Minuteman Masterson." Although the description lacked the accuracy he would have required if he had coined the phrase, the name stuck. His friends from the Senate, old colleagues from the press, and even the president of the United States referred to him as Minuteman.

In his meetings of the Senate Intelligence Committee years before, the senator could see the writing on the wall. Anyone who used the Internet, drove a car, voted, talked on a cell phone, or went to the doctor was subject to surveillance by the government and the agencies that were created for that purpose. Privacy for Americans was disappearing. He sat through day after day of classified briefings by law enforcement and national security agencies, all designed to erode the freedoms of the people who had voted him into office. The legislation before his committee expanded the type and amount of information that government could squeeze from records, extract from conversations, and extrapolate from everyday activities in the search for terrorists.

"I have heard all of this talk about how you need to root out these terrorists in our midst, Director." The senator addressed Adam Wirtep, Director of Homeland Security, as he had on hundreds of previous occasions, and his disdain for the man was legendary among his peers.

"What I want to know, for the umpteenth time, is how do you decide who you gather information about. From what I've heard, that big computer in that big building in my home state of Florida is busily gathering information on every man, woman, and child in our great country, and then it filters out the bad guys based upon profiles of the words they use, isn't that right, Mr. Director?" He had long ago stopped masking his tone to temper his words.

"Well, Senator, we don't use the information we gather against law-abiding Americans." Minuteman Masterson had his opponent on the ropes, blissfully aware that Wirtep would never be comfortable with his persistent grilling, and the director was obviously weary of the subpoenas generated by the committee chairman.

"Well, once again, we have gone full circle. You gather the information about law-abiding citizens. You never throw it away because you don't know when down the road you might need it, and I'm supposed to sit here and take your word that somebody in government won't abuse this invasion of my privacy…"

"Senator, I only meant—"

"Don't talk while I'm summarizing your testimony, or I will have you bound and gagged. Do you understand me?" He leaned back in his chair and continued, "…and the privacy of all Americans, because the government would never do that sort of thing, is that your testimony?"

"Senator, I am here under subpoena, I have been sworn to tell the truth, and as God is my witness, I—"

"Don't bring God into this. You will someday meet your maker, but today, you're mine, and I don't trust you or any of the people who have their security clearance to tap into that information, to steal my words and use them against me, and neither should anyone who has had their privacy stolen by their own government," he pronounced loudly. "You are excused from this subpoena, but you are subject to recall at any time I decide to have your sorry ass back in this committee room." Masterson slammed his large notebook shut with a bang. The other committee members jumped at the sound but sat speechless.

This memory was now displayed on the large screen before him, and even though he was dreaming, the experience was as real as if it had happened seconds before. The sound of the notebook startled him awake, as he wondered for a moment where he was and sat in silence for a long time. Rising at last, he directed the machine to sign off and walked down the hall for his morning coffee.

Chapter Five

Masterson rowed his titanium and carbon rowing shell on the mirror-smooth surface of the Potomac as had done many times before. He thought back over the years in which he had presided over the Senate Intelligence Committee, its constant challenges, triumphs, and disappointments. His fitness regimen called for three times on the water each week, but he was lucky to get in two with his busy schedule. The graphite oars feathered the surface into ripples that quickly disappeared, a repetition that lulled his mind into a state of alert relaxation. He took a mental inventory of the path that had brought his beloved country to the precipice. In one decade, beginning with the terrorist attacks of 9/11, a series of "government reforms" were launched. Over the ensuing years, the massive intelligence and military community gained the ability to hear and see anyone at any time or place. They had access to medical and psychiatric records, sealed court files, Internet data galore, even library cards. They knew where you were going, who traveled with you, what you charged on your credit card, and what you ate for dinner. They developed devices that could see through walls, and made surveillance devices standard equipment in all home electronics. The intelligence community was massive and eminently capable of intruding into the lives of Americans, and did so on a continuous basis.

By the time he left Congress, Masterson had voted against thirty bills that gave the Department of Homeland Security increased powers to intrude, but his nemesis, Wirtep, had prevailed. Masterson was a member of a small minority who refused to rubber stamp the new laws. His terms in the Senate saw the president's National Security Advisor morph into the Secretary of Intelligence, a position that controlled the combined might of the FBI, NSA, and CIA. All of it was legislated into existence to deter terrorism and promote national security, but the unintended effect was that they could direct their attention to anyone anywhere, and law-abiding Americans lost their right to be left alone. He steered the rowing shell toward the dock. It happened every time; each time he thought back over his gradual loss of control of the committee, his own domain, he rowed faster until he reached his maximum heart rate, and the day's exercise came to an end. He seethed at the thought that he had presided over the stealthy erosion of a right he had taken an oath to uphold.

After twenty-four years of distinguished service representing the State of Florida from Pensacola to Miami, he had finally reached the point where he had enough of politics. It resulted mainly from his failed attempts at passing legislation to protect the privacy rights of Americans. Every man, woman, and child in the nation lost the ability to be free from random surveillance by the government, and as long as he had a good breath in his body, he would not give up.

He pulled the rowing shell into his private boathouse and activated the sling that raised it out of the water. As he cleaned his gear with fresh water sprayed from the hose and stowed the oars and rowing vest into their assigned spots, he thought of the big picture: It was insidious how Congress had done the unthinkable, but over a period of years, they had stolen a basic right from the American people, the right to be left alone.

Chapter Six

The senator drove his classic Jaguar XKR convertible slowly down the long driveway toward the house. Although the car was designed for high speed touring on winding roads, he liked to savor his return to sanity by driving at little more than an idle, searching for wildlife and shedding the effects of urban clutter that he felt whenever he drove to the Capitol. While a trip into the city gave him the feeling of being closed in, the approach to home had the opposite effect. By the time he pulled the Jag into its pampered space in the garage, he had decompressed enough to let out a sigh that only comfortable surroundings can induce.

He walked through the private tunnel from the garage to the house and considered the news of the day. During his return from the confines of D.C., his ever-active mind had conjured up a strategy for protecting Max from the ravages of society, and while it was hot in his mind, he was anxious to sit for ideas.

The concept of sitting for ideas is not new to brilliant, productive people. It involves a process of withdrawing from distractions and entering the mind, where the journey begins. Inside the mind, the creative, ever-active state, once achieved, produces thoughts that flow continuously. Seemingly random ideas can frequently provide the solutions to problems, strategies for complex accomplishments, and new inventions. Depending on the creative bent of the traveler, sitting for ideas can lead the mind down an expected path or shoot off into the realm of the unknown.

The senator's journey of sitting for ideas took place in a small room off the study, where a small unadorned desk and a chair faced a blank wall. On the desk, a pen and a legal pad were the only items necessary. He sat in the chair and focused his thoughts. Microprocessors in the chair detected his brain waves and projected his thoughts on the wall in front of the desk. He had to focus, and the first ten or fifteen minutes were spent getting rid of the "garbage" as he called the fragments of thoughts and memories that were irrelevant to the issues he chose to focus upon. Even childhood memories bubbled to the surface and were soon gone. When he focused, his mind eventually got to the items he was interested in dealing with.

Max was his focus today. He had just left a think tank meeting of the Patriot Group, a secret society of sorts, whose primary cause was the preservation and promotion of the American way of life. Their discussion that morning was the extent to which the right to privacy had been eroded by technology and security fears. The consensus of the group was that individual rights had disappeared through the use of technology in society. Privacy, the right to be left alone, was gone. By accessing records indexed by social security numbers, street addresses, cell phones, and credit card statements, almost anything that had been recorded could be brought to one location. Anything that had ever been entered into a computer database or the Internet was accessible in a micro-second, to be sorted and used for any purpose, and there were no secrets outside the electronic grasp of government surveillance.

His child was going to need protection from unwanted intrusion into his life. He resolved that he would never ask for nor allow Max to have a social security number or ID card. His medical needs would be met by a personal physician who made house calls and signed a strict confidentiality agreement. The doctor would be paid handsomely for providing exclusive medical care to the Masterson family, but it was necessary to maintain the privacy of their lives. No computer records were to be kept. Blood tests would be performed in-house, and the results anonymously maintained in the doctor's excellent mind. No driver's license, either, although he suspected that Max would rebel against this idea when he became old enough to drive. No purchases by credit in his name or Max's. Those duties would be performed by a proxy shopper, who would purchase anything from razors to plane tickets. He planned all of it, his mind reaching forward to the day when Max would be an adult and subjected to the microscope of scrutiny that accompanies any venture into the political world.

Chapter Seven

His office in the Congressional Office Building had been adorned with artifacts and mementoes from the Jefferson administration; various inventions were on display in the outer office. Jefferson's hunting rifle and powder flask hung over the expansive fireplace in his comfortable study.

As a result of his long term in the Senate and his chairmanship of the Intelligence Committee, his office also displayed numerous handshake pictures and awards. A thorough review of this wealth of acclaim, though, did not reveal partisanship. Democrats and Republicans, American Indians and Indira Gandhi, Martin Luther King and Muhammad Ali, John Grisham and Lady Diana, all adorned his walls. All of the photographs were basically the same; the senator stood smiling next to each famous person, shaking hands.

The day after Senator Masterson announced his retirement, the entire office was cleared, its contents packed in large wooden crates and transported to the Smithsonian for public display. A special room was meticulously prepared duplicating his office at the Capitol, and three days later, went on public display to become a part of the enormous collection of national memories too important to discard.

Masterson declined to appear at the public dedication. He couldn't be located at his Virginia estate, and messages from friends on his cell phone went unanswered. Finally, the storage capacity of his answering service was reached, and callers were met with a video image of the former senator in casual clothes, explaining that he was unavailable for the foreseeable future and would not be returning any calls until he had completed a little project. John Masterson had a plan to take all of it back, and he considered it as devout an act of patriotism as his mind could conceive. If he succeeded, he would save the country he loved from a tyranny worse than any dictatorship, and he wasn't willing to waste a single minute setting it in motion. The project was named Closed Door, a reference to the ambitious goal of protecting the right of citizens to be left alone. They had a right, he reasoned, to disclose information only to those who had their permission and to deny access to the snoopers, who had the unlimited ability to use their private information to hurt them. Most times, the information gathered was innocuous, the indicia of living in a technological society. But it was the mass of it, the sheer volume of information that was mindlessly stored on databases that had the potential to intrude and hurt.

"I brought you all here for a noble purpose," he announced to the fifty information technology experts he had assembled in a large conference room, all of whom were well aware of his reputation as a straight shooter. "I am paying you big bucks to save the ability of Americans to be Americans, to hold themselves apart from the rest of the world."

They drank coffee as they listened to the legendary Minuteman, who had retired with his head held high, unlike most of his colleagues who had either been carried out feet first or slunk away in hushed disgrace after resigning "to spend more time with my family."

"You are the best people I could find to make this project a success. I want to build a way to extract private citizens' information from the Internet and give them the right to decide when and with whom they are going to share it." His words were met with a brief silence as the technicians pondered the problem and the solution, followed by a low muttering as several of them began to frantically scribble notes on yellow legal pads. Masterson waited and watched as their collective minds began to work.

Eventually, a small man in the center of the room stood. He was obviously the de facto leader of the group, and all deferred to him. It was the familiar face of Martin Hilliard, a physicist who had gained fame in artificial intelligence. Years earlier, he developed a program that improved the odds of winning at blackjack as each card was dealt. His idea caused a temporary loss at casinos around the world until the casino operators discovered signaling devices implanted in the ear canals of the winners. By that time, hundreds of millions of dollars had been won, which was shared 50/50 with Hilliard. He was fabulously wealthy, but he hadn't taken his wealth and gone home. He was now using his brilliance to solve more important problems, and today he was in his element.

"Senator, we know of ways to keep new information from being released, and we know how to construct safeguards in a program that will prevent hackers from getting to it, but whatever is already out there can't be retrieved and protected." He paused for effect, letting his words sink in.

"You need to understand that we're talking about millions of databases containing information that can be filtered and sorted. Hell, the collective information of the human race is spread out over computers all over the world, and once it's out there, it can't be retrieved and secured. It's like detonating a nuclear bomb and then trying to put all of the radiation back into the metal shell it was contained in. We can probably start with medical records and psychiatric records, because they have a certain degree of protection, but criminal records, driving records, credit card transactions, phone records…"

Masterson stopped him before he rattled off all of the "can't do's." "Let's talk about this prospectively. I want a clear-cut system to which people can surrender their private information. I can't protect what is already out there, but I'm going to try to protect what I can," he said. "This will be funded by a transaction fee. Authorization codes must be created, and all of the safeguards need to be in place to prevent access to information once it is in the system, and that includes the government, the press, and terror organizations. I don't want some bureaucrat downtown to be able to scan through my medical records and find out my blood type or prescriptions, know who I vote for, or what my fears may reveal."

The senator's mind was erupting with thoughts that came from years of frustration. It had all started in 2007, after a quantum shift began in the government propaganda machine. To answer complaints that government was invading the privacy of law-abiding Americans, a move began to change the definition of privacy. The old meaning, the right to be left alone, free from prying eyes and ears, had surrendered to technology.

The mass of information about anyone could be sifted and sorted to intrude into every aspect of life, and he had sworn an oath to uphold the Constitution, something he considered a sacred trust placed upon him by all Americans. He had no intention of keeping government from pursuing terror suspects and enemies of the United States, but the information to be disclosed would be a matter for the courts to decide on an individual basis. It was no longer possible to keep any information private if that information was transmitted electronically, and Senator Masterson had created a mechanism to become the gatekeeper of privacy, or as much of it as could be shielded from those who sought to invade it.

The irony of it all was that once he had sold the concept to Congress and had used his clout to have Gatekeeper become law, he acquired a monopoly, and for privacy's sake, it could not be undone. He amassed enormous wealth from the one cause that had defined his career. Now privacy meant any information an individual would pay to protect, and that gave him a financial stake in every transaction placed in the Gatekeeper system. Nobody, with the possible exception of his infant son, whom he had kept off the grid by design, would be able to protect information from the eyes and ears of the rest of the world without Gatekeeper.

Chapter Eight

Max progressed rapidly. From the time he could talk, he read. At five years of age, his reading level was the equivalent of a fifth grader, and by the time he was eight, he regularly read the Wall Street Journal and had begun regular discussions with Adrianna and his father on world affairs.

Home schooling with Adrianna involved a daily ritual of one-on-one instruction, followed by three hours of Internet learning, followed by life instructions and outdoor sports. In the evening, Max read while the senator attended social events. Rather than the typical Saturday and Sunday off enjoyed by other school-aged children, Max adhered to his schedule seven days a week.

He never got to sleep in on a Saturday morning, but since he had never done that, he didn't miss it. Even though his friends were constantly puzzled by his lack of desire for time off, his life was normal in most respects, and he was developing well. Adrianna was an accomplished teacher and dedicated her life to Max's education until his studies at home were complete.

He wasn't so much pushed as encouraged to excel, and he accomplished much in his studies. He was given the choice of a variety of new subjects to learn each day, all part of a list prepared to give him a broad education. Each day's teachings also involved one subject that had been previously covered. Tests allowed him to cover subjects for a third time, and by the time he had completed the learning cycle, it had been reinforced in his mind as a complete idea. Adrianna had pioneered the technique in college, and the senator came across her thesis in his search to find Max an instructor and mentor.

Adrianna McVeigh was not only brilliant, she also was stunningly beautiful. Her long raven hair and light green eyes had a transfixing ability to simultaneously attract the attention of every man in the room and quickly neutralize their planned mating rituals. She acted as though they were invisible. Her eyes never strayed from her path, for to do so would acknowledge their presence. A woman of her intelligence and beauty should have been surrounded by eligible young bachelors, all vying for her attention, but she didn't seem to notice their efforts. She was single-minded in her approach to life, and it resulted in the perception by those men she encountered that she was cold. It wasn't a coldness that she felt, though. It was a defense mechanism. Her inner purpose was to convey unattainability, and at that she was an expert.

On the rare occasions that she appeared at social events, she came with the same escort, her employer and clandestine lover, retired senator John "Minuteman" Masterson. With Adrianna at his side, women shied away, melting into the scenery. Her beauty served as a barrier that also made the senator unattainable, and he liked it that way. Throughout his life, he did the choosing and resented the efforts of those who sought to pierce his cloak of privacy without his permission.

Alone, John Masterson and Adrianna McVeigh were able to be themselves. "It's nice that we don't need to bother with clothes if we don't want to," purred Adrianna as she combed her long dark hair. Its length obscured her full breasts. The senator, standing behind her, held her in a tight embrace. Not wanting to be deprived of the delight of her nakedness, he pulled her long hair behind her shoulders. "I want to admire you," he growled in his low baritone. "Until my dying day, I will never get tired of looking at you."

Adrianna dropped the brush and turned toward her man. "You have me, lock, stock and barrel," she replied.

"I want you, heart, mind and body," he said, suddenly turning serious. "There are some things I need to say to you." He led her to two plush wingback chairs in the corner of the master suite, where they sat for several minutes without saying a word, comfortable in their nudity and understanding that important messages come in their own time. They sipped coffee and looked into each other's eyes until the focus became intense and their connection excluded all distractions.

"You know me." He swallowed, his throat suddenly dry. He reached for his coffee and took a long sip before continuing. He suddenly seemed nervous. Adrianna sat in silence, knowing that it wasn't his habit to prolong a conversation beyond its essence.

"Adrianna, we have been together for a long time..."

"Seventeen years, three months and fourteen days, to be exact..." She smirked as he blushed. She began to calculate the last time she had seen John Masterson—or any politician—blush, but his quiet voice brought her back to the present.

"I know my fear of commitment and the Washington social calendar have kept me from making our relationship exclusive..."

She frowned. Maybe he was cutting her loose. "Johnny, first you surprise me by blushing, and now you're beating around the bush. That isn't like you, and if you don't get to the point, I'm going to conclude that you don't like me anymore." She crossed her arms and legs in a defensive posture and stared directly into his grey eyes. She wasn't going to let up on him until he capitulated, and the retired United States senator was unaccustomed to backing down on anything. She saw him swallow hard.

"I'm not speaking clearly, because I have never told this to a woman before."

Adrianna knew when to keep silent, despite her fleeting fantasy of placing a front kick squarely between his legs. The suspense in the room was not lessened by the sweat that was forming on his battle-hardened forehead, either. She maintained her dignity, having no clue as to his next words.

"I love you."

"I love you too, darlin', is that so hard to say?"

"No, you don't understand. I really love you, and I don't want to spend another day without…" He was clearly on the verge of becoming speechless. Abruptly, he jumped up and ran out of the room.

She decided not to budge. He was rummaging around the dressing room, and in the reflection of the large mirror, she could see his frantic search through the pockets of his suits. Finally, he slapped his forehead and ran over to a wool topcoat. He smiled broadly when he found the object of his efforts.

The sight of a naked man carrying a velvet box reverently in his outstretched hands was too much for her to maintain her composure, and she ran to him, laughing delightedly. The diamond ring seemed to take on a life of its own. The round stone was large, but not so ostentatious as to make it unwieldy on her slender finger. Without a word, he dropped to his knee and slid the ring onto her waiting hand. She thought of her years of devotion to him and to Max and nodded gently when he said, "I have waited too long to do this."

Chapter Nine

"You can do it, Son! Falling is easy. It's the climb that's the scary part!"

The senator stood at the bottom of the high dive as Max, fully eight years of age, stood shivering at the end of the diving board. He had been up there for about ten minutes now, his legs shaking so much that the board swayed up and down. This motion only compounded his fear to the point that he began looking for an escape. Anything to avoid the jump. Any route that wouldn't involve losing face. He turned and looked at the thirty steps that transported him to the top. It was the only other way out, but to go back down those steps of shame would only result in another challenge from the senator. Next time, it might be worse. At the moment, he couldn't imagine what that might be, but his father had a vivid imagination. Each challenge was a lesson, and for as long as he could remember, Max was challenged almost on a daily basis. Max considered his choices. He jumped.

Dad was right. It wasn't so bad. In fact, it was fun, hurtling through the air with that elevator feeling in your gut. Hitting the water didn't hurt either, if you pointed your toes.

"I want to do it again!"

"That's my boy. This time, do a cannonball and see if you can splash me."

The lesson at the pool lasted exactly one hour. Every lesson lasted the same length of time. His tutor had one hour per subject, no more, no less. Daily exercise was an intense nonstop activity for those sixty minutes. Reading after dinner was one hour. Access to television and video games was the same. He learned early on that most worthwhile activities lasted one hour and declined in intensity if extended beyond that time. Anything longer could not be completed or be of enough benefit to suit the senator. One hour was just right, and he had no more patience than that. Adrianna continued to tutor Max under the Minuteman Principle, realizing the important lesson of living life under the senator's guidance. He always got his way.

During his life in politics, before he retired to create the business that made him famous and defined his life, the senator was "Minuteman." To Max, he was father, teacher, philosopher, playmate, motivator and friend. Life on the estate with the senator was Max's total existence, and it was all-consuming. It was all he knew, but the bounty of his existence far surpassed all that was available to anyone else and was designed for one purpose: Max was going to be president of the United States.

Chapter Ten

Senator Masterson was being interviewed by a reporter for the weekly edition of Meet the Press, flanked by the Director of Homeland Security, Adam Wirtep, his nemesis during his years in Congress.

"Senator Masterson, may I refer to you by your nickname, 'Minuteman' or would you prefer I just call you 'Smiley'? The moderator, Charles Axeson, was teasing him for the overt joy he was displaying over the recent vote of Congress in adopting the American Privacy Bill, which guaranteed the right of U.S. citizens to be exempted from wholesale surveillance by government.

"You can call me anything you want as long as you don't attach my medical records to the transcript of the show," joked Masterson. He was referring to the practice of the National Security Agency to include irrelevant information about surveillance suspects in their reports in an effort to pad the information obtained through unlimited access to private records.

Wirtep, not known for sitting idly by while his agency was being publicly vilified, responded swiftly. "I resent the implication that the government would use information obtained lawfully to harm law abiding citizens. We acted within the law in effect at the time to ensure that patriotic Americans are not harmed by the terrorists who are planning to destroy U.S. facilities."

"I am sick and tired of politicians telling me that it's unpatriotic to not want to turn over every detail of my life to them, so they can do what they please with it. I can understand their surveillance of foreigners. Hellfire, I'd be the first in line to say that some foreign national with a terrorist profile should be brain scanned, fingerprinted, and picked apart like buzzards do to road kill. But I am not going to sit back and let them do it to law-abiding Americans."

"Mr. Masterson is merely trying to make money off of this issue, and he doesn't give a hoot about privacy." This outburst by Wirtep was the culmination of years of acrimonious exchanges between Minuteman and his adversaries, and the effect of his words could be seen in detail on Masterson's face. As the camera closed in on Minuteman's angry expression, Axeson sought to temper the fury by asking a question.

"Senator, I understand that information will now be filtered through a program that locks personal information away from prying eyes and will only be made available to those who have permission, and they have to pay a fee, is that right?"

"Charles, my company will make a dollar off of every request. The rest of the five dollar fee goes to administrative expenses, and is paid by the requester, including Mr. Wirtep here. He doesn't want to pay for the cost of protecting Americans from the government, and he's here today to whine about it just like he has for the past decade. But he can't rain on my parade. He lost, I won, and now Congress has voted that he has to have permission from lawabiding citizens to pry into their private lives."

Wirtep stood, his microphone falling from its perch on his collar. As he faced Masterson, the senator rose, not quite reaching the chin of the taller man. Wirtep grabbed the lapels of his adversary, realizing only too late that he was challenging a lifelong practitioner of the martial arts. With one movement, Wirtep was rendered unconscious with simultaneous blows to the groin and the trachea. As Wirtep fell to the floor, Masterson calmly faced the cameras and said, "Charles, this is how Americans should respond to attacks, and today we regained the right to protect ourselves." Minuteman Masterson calmly unclipped his microphone and walked offstage to the silence of the stunned commentator, content that he had made his point, and within the allotted time.

Chapter Eleven

Adrianna had pushed Max in his Baby Jogger from the time he came to live in the Masterson estate, Fairlane, until he was four years old. She ran on the winding trails through the woods that provided a cushioned respite from the hard concrete of paved roads, and the shadows felt cool on her perspiring skin. She taught Max the ABCs and how to count to one hundred. He learned the names of the dinosaurs and words that would not be learned by other children until they were well into high school. When Max began to ask adult questions and discuss adult issues, she allowed the conversations to expand. He became her running partner, his little legs strengthening daily and his endurance peaking. By age six, he was able to carry on their conversations while running an eight-minute mile pace.

"Mommy?"

"Max, we talked about this last week. I'm not your mommy. I'm just a lady who wants to be your mommy." They had discussed the death of Max's parents in the car wreck on many of their runs, but Max needed someone to be there for him and Adrianna supplied all of the emotional support that a boy could want from his mother.

"Mommy," Max continued, ignoring yet another correction on her status in his young life. "I love you."

"I love you, too, Sweetie," she replied as she sprinted to the top of a small rise along the Potomac. When Max caught up seconds later, she put her arms around the boy and held him close, inhaling the sweet scent that only young children can produce. "You can call me mommy anytime." She realized that young children describe their world and the people around them in the most honest of ways, and it didn't matter to the little boy that she had yet to obtain the legal status of wife or mother. To him she was mommy, and for her, that was good enough.

Chapter Twelve

As they sat on the huge rock at the top of Soaring Cliffs, Max and the senator watched the clouds turn from orange to lavender. Eagles and hawks soared on the updrafts around the ancient volcanic dome. For as long as he could remember, his father had taken him to this spot, and they had free climbed to the top, past the "Do Not Climb" signs posted in the years following the falling deaths of tourists who had no reason to go there. There was a secret grotto at the top, an outdoor cathedral open to the sky. It was encircled by enormous boulders, which reflected the firelight and stood as silent sentinels from the rest of the world. Their refuge was hidden from the path below, where they would set up a nylon hiking tent just big enough for the two of them. Max loved the tent and the freedom it offered with its screen top open to the sky. He could lie next to the senator and look at the stars bright in the evening sky, closer to God. The sky came down to greet them, the early stars shining before the sunset.

At 16, Max realized that their special trip would likely be the last to this private spot. He could see the toll the hike was taking on the senator. It wasn't that he wasn't nimble; his father had had a lifetime of athletic accomplishments as a gymnast and triathlete in his younger years. But the rasping sound he made upon exertion was new, and it foretold an underlying illness that the senator had hidden from everyone except his personal doctors.

His father was slowly dying.

In the year since his diagnosis, the senator had aged in subtle but distinct ways. His once proud mane of dark brown hair was gradually turning white. The color of his skin had taken on a yellow tint, not the robust golden tan of days spent rowing on the Potomac. His wrinkles, which started as crow's feet, now extended across his forehead, and the dimples that he had endured since childhood as "dents" were now deep creases that extended from his cheekbones to his chin. Adrianna knew, and his doctor knew, and others only suspected. If he revealed his condition to the public, he would be deluged with unwanted attention, and Max would know. He would do anything to spare his son that pain.

Max grew worried as he waited near the top of the climb. He had the backpack and busied himself setting up the tent while the old man brought up the rear. It was taking too long, and he decided to run down to the edge of the mountain where he could peer over the side of a large boulder and view part of the trail.

Hundreds of yards below, in a small clearing, sat the senator. He seemed smaller than Max remembered. He was staring off into the distance, his back to the trail, and Max was almost tempted to toss a stone at his feet to get his attention. He decided that it was better to approach quietly from the rear and try to surprise him.

"Come sit next to me, son." He hadn't turned his head, but his ears were still sharp. Max sat without saying a word.

"I need to talk with you. We may not have too many opportunities to do this again, and there are some words that need to be said." He appeared to be out of breath, but after a moment of silence, his breathing returned to normal.

The young man broke the silence. "Did I do something wrong?"

"Oh, no," he smiled and pulled him closer. Max felt the familiar arm around his shoulders. It had always calmed him; no matter how excited or aggravated he was, his father's touch had an almost hypnotic effect on him. They snuggled a little and held each other in silence for a long time. An osprey circled on the updrafts 20 yards away.

"My boy, for the rest of your life, people will try to push and pull you in every direction except the way you want to go…" His voice trailed off, his face showed that his mind was far away. The past, present, and future are places where the mind can go, and it wasn't apparent where he had gone, but Max was sure he wasn't in the present at the moment. He was somewhere else, that was certain, and Max watched his face intently, waiting for him to continue.

"From the day I took you in, I have tried to keep you on course."

"What course?"

"The path that is your destiny."

Max creased his forehead, trying to comprehend the meaning of his father's simple statement.

"The difference between those of us who succeed in life and the rest of the world is a basic truth. If you stick to your ideals, you will eliminate regret from the distractions that can hold you back."

The young man looked even more mystified.

"Do you know what wisdom is, son?"

He thought for a moment and tried to answer the question, as if the question could be answered.

"Listen, don't speak. I need to share my wisdom, or it will be lost. You don't have the time to make the mistakes I have made in order to achieve wisdom. I have a gift for you." He pulled his fanny pack up from between his feet and tossed it to Max, who had begun pacing nervously in front of him. "Look inside."

Max unzipped the waterproof pouch. Inside was an audio viewer and what looked like hundreds of flash drives, each capable of holding billions of bytes of information.

"I made these for you."

"What are they?"

"Wisdom."

Max pulled the flash drives from the pouch. Each one was inscribed with descriptive words and phrases along with a number.

"The first time you watch these, I want you to watch them in order. There are written instructions in the bag. Listen to one for an hour each day. They will provide you with the base that you need. After that, when you are in a situation that requires guidance, you can come back to the lesson that applies to your situation. After I'm gone, you will have the comfort of my thoughts. My wisdom."

"But I don't want you to leave. Where are you going?"

The senator faced him, his eyes exploring every detail of his young face as if it would be his last. His smile was kind; the glowing warmth of true love passed between them. He reached out and ran his fingers through his son's thick mane, his strong hand resting on the side of his smooth face. "Look at me."

Tears welled up in Max's eyes. He felt overwhelmed. He wanted to run, but his father held him tight.

"Let's make this a game. I won't be going anywhere for a long time. I don't know when I'll leave this world, but I want you to be ready to get along without me. Pull out some of the flash drives and read them to me, and I'll tell you a little bit of what's on there. Some of them might make you laugh." He sneaked his hand under his son's left arm to a spot he knew was ticklish, and his fingers immediately found their mark.

"Stop! Stop!" Max rolled off the rock and the contents of the bag spilled out on the ground. He stared at the scattered flash drives. Each had inscriptions etched into the side in gold, lending a special permanence to an everyday information storage device. The effect it had on Max was what an explorer must feel when encountering an abandoned temple in the Amazon rainforest, or when a treasure hunter opens a chest after it has lain beneath the ocean for centuries. Excitement was followed by serious scrutiny.

The father waited for the adolescent son to gather his focus before speaking. "I want you to spend an hour each day going through these in order. There is a number assigned to each. One to 1,001, and I don't want you to skip one simply because you think you don't need it. That was decided by me when I began this quest, and I will always be older and wiser than you. Understand?"

Max looked at the inscriptions. "Okay, I'll play. What do you want me to know?" His response bordered on insolence, but the senator dismissed it as the bravado of youth. In Max's teenage mind, the attainment of his father's knowledge was low on his list of priorities.

He picked up the one closest to him and made a sour face. "Love? You want to tell me about love?"

Ignoring the embarrassment a young man feels when talking about personal issues, Masterson explained. "You will fall in love. You might not know it at the time, but you will, and it will sneak up on you. There are two types of love. Crazy love and joyful love. Choose joyful love and reject crazy love."

"Okay." Max picked up the second at random. "Worry."

"People worry about two things. The first is the unknown. The second is that which we can't control. Both are things that you shouldn't waste your time about. Live in the present."

"Responsibility."

"In the back of your mind, whatever you do, think about the consequences of your actions on those you love and those you serve. They come first, and everyone else is beyond your control."

"Innocence."

"Always protect the innocents. Little children can't be sinister. They haven't lived long enough to be cynical. If you protect them, you will always be their hero."

"The Core? What's that?" Max was intrigued.

He continued. "Your 'core' is who you are and what you stand for and it requires no apology. State your opinion and your position clearly. If people agree with you, they will support your cause. If they disagree with you, they will still respect your opinion."

"Fame."

"Don't seek it. There is no good to come from it. If it finds you, use it responsibly to do good or it will never improve your life or those of the ones who rely on you."

"Wealth."

"Wealthy people will always tell you that they are merely comfortable. In their reality, there is always someone wealthier. Never confuse wealth with being rich. Money never did anything more than keep people from worrying about money. The danger is that when you have money, you might think you are better than someone who doesn't have it. The reality is that because of money, you may lose sight of the values that make a person rich."

"Nothing." He looked at his father expecting a joke but found a serious look. He laughed anyway, and the more he laughed the funnier it seemed, until tears were streaming down his face. Now he was getting silly.

"What are you laughing about? Did you think I was going to talk about nothing?"

Max smirked. "How can you tell me about nothing?" As he said the word, he broke out laughing again, and the old man waited patiently while he got it out of his system. Finally, Max paused to take a deep breath, giving his father the opportunity to explain.

"My point is, you can't think about nothing. There is always something. Something to see, something to hear, a memory that fills your mind. You'll find out some day that everything is connected. Every thought. What you think is a coincidence is really just a part of your life. There are no ordinary moments. Nothing happens without purpose. You may not understand how it all connects, but believe me, somehow, some way, it all fits together." Leaning over, he grabbed the bag and scanned the contents that hadn't scattered on the ground, searching for the right message. Politics. Joy. Tradition. Intelligence. Freedom. Religion. Family. America. Privacy. Fear. Loyalty. Faith. Then he found it. "Work and Play," he announced.

Max was on his feet and grabbed the bag from his hands. He backed out of reach, expecting that the treasures would be ripped from his grasp. "I want to play, and you want to work, and I didn't come up here to do nothing…" Masterson paused and stared, deep in thought. His hands were gathering the remaining flash drives and gently placing them back in the bag. He continued the serious look until he got the desired response.

"What are you thinking about?"

"Oh, nothing." This got Max laughing again, and he chuckled all the way up the trail, pushing the old man from behind and forcing him to complete the trek to the top.

By the time they reached the clearing where Max had erected the tent, the fire was crackling. Max fed dry kindling to the flames until the firelight illuminated the boulders that surrounded their refuge. They remained silent until the darkness was complete, content in the solitude. When the time was right, they ate hotdogs cooked on green sticks suspended over the fire, not bothering to smother them with condiments. Camping was a time to return to basics.

Continuing with their serious conversation, Minuteman took up where he had left off.

"Most people go their entire lives not knowing. You are different. You have greatness in you. I felt it from the time I first held you in my arms, and I feel it now."

"Greatness? You mean I'll be famous someday?" His face contorted slightly. He had no idea what his father was talking about, but he thought that if he focused hard enough and long enough, maybe the meaning of the words would pop into his mind. He wasn't having much success, and after ten minutes he became distracted by an owl, which silently swooped into the clearing and snatched a field mouse with its claws not fifteen feet from where they sat.

Until the owl forced Max to return his mind to the present, Minuteman sat waiting patiently. The interruption gave him the opportunity to speak. "Max, you don't have any idea what I mean, do you?"

"Not really." He felt frightened, unsure of what he should say. "I always knew you had plans for me. All the lessons, and the people you introduced me to. We never really go on a vacation and do nothing…" He smiled at the thought, but was able to hold back the laughter. "I just knew that someday it would all be clear to me, but that day never seemed to come." He looked into the old man's eyes for guidance, but found none. Instead, the senator rose to his feet and spoke in the voice he reserved for the Senate floor.

"The time has come." He paused to scan Max's eyes. Clearly, he didn't want Max to assume what he was about to say was anything other than serious. Seemingly satisfied by Max's countenance, he slipped a gold card into Max's hand. "Take this." It was heavy and warm and substantial. The gold was real, not a plastic stamped imitation. Deeply engraved on the surface was a list:

MAXIMS
No speeches.
No fund-raising events.
No messages over two minutes long.
If you bore the listener, they can't hear you.
Keep each message simple.
Every statement is a sound bite.
The message is available 24/7.
It is better to say nothing than to say something stupid.
It is better to confess you don't know than to lie about it.
The message is more important than the image.
The image is more important than the candidate.
Don't quote a statistic unless you can back it up with facts.
Educate people before asking them to decide on an issue.
American interests must prevail over world interests.
Never lie to promote the interests of the minority.

Always present an idea in a positive way.
If you can't commit to an idea, quit trying to sell it.
The perception of reality is more important than reality.
It's not what you say. It's how you say it.

Max looked at the words and tried to absorb their meaning. "I guess I should say thank you, but I…" The senator held up his hand, commanding his son to listen. "You, my son, will be president of the United States someday, and these are the rules."

Chapter Thirteen

"Okay, boys and girls. Take your seats," proclaimed Luke Postlewaite in a loud voice. "I need to give you the general concept of successful political efforts, and then we will discuss the campaigns of successful candidates through history." The class was composed of twenty of the best and brightest sixteen-year-olds from elite American families who, by inheritance or guile, had developed the networking and name recognition to place their most photogenic offspring into the political pool. The payoff for these families was enormous. By getting a child elected, a family tapped directly into the power supply of capitalism: money and connections.

"I will give it to you in a few words, and then we won't talk about it until you understand how the process works. I don't expect you to have an opinion, and I'm not interested in it anyway. That's not my job. My job is to train you to get elected. I'm sure you understand," he shouted.

"Yes, sir!" They had been trained at the outset to respond with enthusiasm, and they did it well. Twenty young voices shouted with enthusiasm. Max sat next to an attractive young redhead named Scarlett, and he was enthralled by her genteel demeanor contained in a cheerleader's body. Between classes, he flirted with the young girl from Charleston, who responded with the appropriate amount of disdain. Her years of cotillions and Junior League social contact had created a cultured young woman. "Good breeding," as they say in the South.

Scarlett Conroy was a well-bred product of Charleston society, and her close proximity was making his male hormones work overtime.

"Here it is," spoke Postlewaite, dressed in the formal attire of the successful political advisor. "All campaigns start out the same. You must look the part. When people speak your name, everyone must know who they are talking about, and most of all, they must have a favorable opinion of you on a subject that you agree about. Do you understand?"

The shout was louder this time. "Yes sir!"

Postlewaite was a veteran of political campaigns beginning with the demise of Richard Nixon and throughout the nine Presidential campaigns that followed, and he was highly regarded by each politician who had attained public office, whether they had hired him and won or hired his competition and lost.

Luke had been on the losing side of an election only once since the 1980s, when he worked on the campaign of John Anderson during Reagan's first run for the Presidency. Of all the campaigns his candidates had won, that one loss had taught him the most, and now his wisdom was called upon full time for huge compensation. Today, he was running a camp for baby politicians, and he looked at it as recreation. Someday, these kids were going to be the people he worked for.

"Elected officials are, first and foremost, narcissists who surround themselves with yes men and women, and by doing so, they isolate themselves from the pulse of the American public. Issues that inflame the voter sometimes fail to reach the level of attention necessary to prompt a politician to action, and when the voice of the voter is not heard and heeded, a certain form of helpless alienation grows." He scanned the classroom for recognition on their faces. Feeling that he had achieved partial success, he continued.

"If it persists, the voter's interest wanes and apathy sets in. With apathy comes a disconnect that becomes impenetrable for the politician when they run for reelection. If you let this happen, you stand a good chance of losing when it comes time for reelection. This invisible wall of discontent is the barrier between the person in office and the vote that keeps them there." He knew he was talking over their heads, but he was speaking more for himself than teaching something they would retain and use.

"This isolation gradually leads to widespread discontent among the voters until the alienation is nearly universal. The irony of it all is that politicians inside the beltway don't have a clue. It is only when the voice of the American public becomes louder than the whispers of the lobbyists that the legislators will begin to listen. I am counting on you to make a difference."

Postlewaite was speaking to a group of privileged children, but among them were two types that held his fascination: the children of politicians, and a scattering of those poised and talented offspring of parents of average status, whose presence was made possible by their genius. They had no reason for being there other than their ability to work a room and speak their minds. It was in these prodigies that he privately maintained the most hope. Out of this class of possibilities, he had identified two young hopes for the future. Max Masterson, the son of his friend Senator John Masterson, was the first offspring of notice, and a fiery girl from South Carolina, Scarlett Conroy, was the other. They were bright, savvy, and promising, and his private focus was on them. The other kids were destined to hold positions of high office, but they didn't possess that gusto that would propel them to the top.

Chapter Fourteen

A visit to the Masterson estate, named Fairlane after automaker Henry Ford's nineteenth-century estate home in Dearborn, Michigan, was a journey into the finer aspects of the past. Luke Postlewaite had driven this path hundreds of times, but he never stopped marveling at how entering through the automated gate made him feel like he was entering a nineteenth-century utopian fantasy. The red brick driveway wound between huge live oaks, the Spanish moss dripping in light green swatches from the lower branches. In each direction, the natural beauty of the wildlife preserve was enhanced by trees and plants indigenous to the eastern United States.

The home of John Masterson, a massive stone castle designed by a team of architects trained in their youth by Frank Lloyd Wright and Buckminster Fuller, spread over a full acre. Perched at the top of a cliff above the Potomac River, the house was surpassed only by the beauty that could be seen through each massive window.

The grandeur of the home was enhanced by the use of state of the art computer controlled imagery that projected the art of the masters on the walls at preprogrammed intervals. In the foyer, a waterfall flowed under the stairs from the second floor sleeping quarters, giving the impression that the visitor was walking into a Maxfield Parrish inspired paradise. The entire back of the home was glass and opened onto a grotto surrounded by tropical flowering plants. A geodesic dome allowed natural light to enter each room and could be adjusted to allow more or less light at the whim of the owner. Holographic sculptures appeared to talk as the visitor moved from room to room, quoting inspirational phrases in an intimate whisper that changed on each pass. The effect was a seductive invitation to a sanctuary where the troubles of the world were left behind, and as traditional as the façade appeared, the technological innovations of the interior afforded each visitor a unique experience.

The senator had spent the early years of his ownership of the property restoring the land to the condition it enjoyed before the first Europeans set foot in the region. His knowledge of native flora and fauna had reached the point where local biology professors at the surrounding universities could no longer answer his questions, and he resorted to spending occasional afternoons in their online research libraries to satisfy his urge to learn. The plants that he found had been removed from the landscape over centuries of urban development and were rare. A wild turkey ran ahead of Postlewaite's Cadillac Escalade, wary of his intrusion. It ran in a zigzag pattern until it spotted a gap in the sparkleberry bushes and then disappeared as fast as it had come into his path. He slowed, not because he needed to, but because he wanted to savor the feeling of calm escape that the approach provided. He crossed a small bridge over a rocky stream. Then the driveway straightened out, and the pillars appeared. The white of the house contrasted with the green of the trees.

There was no lawn. The senator saw no utility in copying the high maintenance English tradition of converting natural space into a golf course. Instead, he had planted wildflowers, the seeds spread by the sack load, and in the 32 years since he had bought the house, they spread to fill the space previously occupied by a manicured green lawn. It had been replaced with the special colors that only those wild seeds could provide. The effect was a palette of colors out of a Monet painting, and at any season of the year, even winter, the colors greeted the eyes of visitors with a special flourish.

He drove past the front entrance and circled around to a large parking garage hidden by a grove of sugar maples. Their leaves had turned bright red with the approaching autumn, providing a flashback to the days he'd spent in college in Ann Arbor, where the smell of burning leaves combined with the distant roar of football fans at Wolverine stadium. But that was over fifty years ago, and he had to attend to the task at hand. Minuteman Masterson had summoned him to Fairlane for a reason, and he didn't have the luxury of living in his memories for long.

"Postlewaite, you old goat! You're late!" he senator stood behind him with his camera equipment slung over his shoulder. He seemed to delight in sneaking up on people, and his bemused smile betrayed his amusement at surprising his longtime friend and campaign advisor.

"You're the old goat! Have you looked in the mirror lately? You look like you just slept under the bridge!" Masterson stood in front of him, dressed in bib overalls, flannel shirt, and work boots. By contrast, Postlewaite's trademark three-piece suit and bow tie were definitely out of place, and he shed his gold silk tie in one smooth movement, tossing it on the passenger seat as he retrieved his briefcase.

"Come on in! I was about to have some brandy and cider to take the chill out of my bones. Care to join me?" He didn't bother to wait for a response. He knew that Luke had a weakness for good brandy, and he kept the liquor cabinet well stocked with vintage Armagnac varieties, collected over fifty years by his favorite vintner at the Capitol.

The senator poured, and Postlewaite settled into a chair near the wood fire roaring in the cavernous fireplace. He wasted no time in formalities, as if he was in a hurry to get on with his retirement. On the Senate floor, he was known to go into a rage at filibusters, moving to end discussion and calling the vote within minutes of any long-winded speech. If the words continued beyond his patience, he would storm out of the chamber and instruct his legislative assistant to page him on his communicator when the "blowhards," as he loudly called them, were done "wasting my time and the taxpayers' money."

Postlewaite knew that their meeting would be short, direct, and no-nonsense, and he would be out of there within an hour. It must have been important for his old friend to call him out to speak to him in person, he thought, or it would have been handled in summary fashion over the phone.

"Luke, I have been thinking about my own demise." He paused, and waited for Postlewaite's bushy brown eyebrows to settle back into their customary position.

"Ten years ago, I was diagnosed with cancer. Back then, the doctors said that they could contain it, but they couldn't remove it without killing me. They did a good job, keeping me going all this time. But now it has metastasized to my lymphatic system, and once it does that, they say I'm a goner. I told them last week that I don't want to lose my hair or my sex drive, but they told me that chemo wouldn't work anyway."

"John, I never knew. You're my closest friend, and you didn't tell me a thing." He paused, considering what he would do if placed in the same situation. John Masterson was a proud man who wouldn't want well-meaning friends to begin a death watch while he had productive years left. Postlewaite pondered the revelation, realizing that he was the only person who knew outside of the team of physicians who had silently kept the senator alive for over a decade.

"Well, I always wondered if you were still boinking at your age."

They both laughed long and hard, until tears streamed down their cheeks. The relief brought on by their laughter was like a tonic, making the news easier to take. They were both talking about Adrianna.

"You were one of the few who knew how much I cared for her. I was devastated when she left us." Masterson stared out the window at a hummingbird, its wings a blur as it hovered over a coneflower.

Postlewaite hesitated for too long before asking the question outright, not wanting to step inside the senator's mind. It was an unspoken message, and Masterson anticipated that the truth needed to be told. "I loved her, Luke. I just couldn't commit to marriage, and at some point, she decided that she had waited long enough, but she stuck with me." He paused and returned to staring at the hummingbird, which apparently had alerted six other of the bug-sized birds of the bounty outside the window. They buzzed loudly, their wings flapping faster than the human eye could follow. After a minute of silence, Masterson continued.

"She was happier that evening than I had seen her. Before we took the limo to the party, I took her out in that garden, right there." He gestured toward the grand vista outside the windows. "There was a beautiful sunset. I sat her down on that bench there and got down on one knee. I asked her forgiveness for keeping her waiting all of those years, and for the second time that day, I asked her to marry me. They never found the ring. It disappeared at the same moment they took her life from me." A tear formed, and he looked away, not wanting to show his emotions. It was a feeble attempt, but the senator was unaccustomed to revealing a crack in his composure. Postlewaite took the opportunity to speak, softening the moment for his old friend.

"John, I loved her, too, you know that. I kicked myself for introducing her to you after your reelection party, and the only reason I didn't kick your ass for stealing her away from me was the way she looked at you…" Now they were both reminiscing about her. They hadn't spoken of Adrianna since her funeral six years before.

A photo of Adrianna, flanked by Masterson and Postlewaite, revealed the three in happier times. It showed them smiling and tanned in the back of a fishing boat. Adrianna had just landed a huge Marlin, which was stretched lengthwise at their feet. Even then she had her head turned toward Masterson as he stared directly into the lens. The object of her adoration was unmistakable.

"To this day, I swear that bomb was meant for me. Why would someone want to kill her? She was a beautiful soul without an enemy in the world." Masterson took a long sip of brandy. This time, he drank it straight. His standby cider sat unused in a pitcher on ice. "Sober times sometimes call for strong spirits," he remarked as the brandy had its desired effect.

He replayed the memory in his mind once again. A bomb had exploded at a black-tie party attended by most of their peers, sponsored by the Patriot Group. It was an intimate gathering, not more than fifty guests. Masterson was there with Adrianna and had excused himself to confront a party crasher he had seen standing close to her, whispering in her ear as she stood across the room. He noticed that the man looked like one of Wirtep's assistants, a man known in political circles by the name of "Darkhorse." "Can't be. He wouldn't show his face in this crowd," Masterson had thought. As he approached the dance floor, he noticed that the man who had spoken to her was moving quickly toward the main entrance, and he took off in pursuit.

As Masterson reached the outer hall, he saw the figure bounding up the escalator toward the exit door. His pursuit ended when the metal door slammed shut, and as he turned to reenter the ballroom the explosion came and the lights went out.

His next recollection had come from the hospital bed, where he had lain unconscious for more than a day. "Three dead, scores injured in Patriot Bombing" ran the banner headlines in the major newspapers. Masterson found out that Adrianna was dead through the media, who described her as "Senator John Minuteman Masterson's Beautiful Longtime Companion." No mention of her unique and wonderful spirit or her intelligence. Just that she was pleasing to the eye, and the Senator had kept her around.

Neither his doctors and nor his friends had the guts to break the news of her death. He had to see it on the Internet from the surveillance video every twenty minutes for three days. He finally filtered out the news account. He had memorized every second, but he didn't want to relive the horror of it all, as if turning it off would stop the constant replay in his mind.

Max was nineteen when she died. He was off at school when news of her death hit the airwaves, and he was on a plane within an hour. He didn't take it well. She was the first woman he had ever loved, from the moment he had been placed in her arms. She had tutored him seven days a week, and they had accompanied the senator on his many trips. Max would have a room in the hotel suite, and Adrianna slept with his father. Sometimes late at night, he could hear their lovemaking. It was natural to him, and he developed a natural outlook toward sex as a result. He had lost a mother, teacher, and friend.

They huddled at the grave in the rain for more than an hour after the other mourners had left, not speaking, just staring. Father and son felt her loss in the same way. They had lost their first love. The father had loved and lost her as a man loves a woman, and the son felt the loss of a child for a mother. Now the father was doing his best to prepare his son for another loss.

Chapter Fifteen

"I doubt if I will be around for Max's thirtieth birthday, and I know I won't be here for his thirty-sixth." He paused again, while the eyebrows joined in the middle below the scowl of his advisor's wrinkled forehead. "Luke, I know that this won't happen for another ten years, but I want to hire you to run Max's election." The scowl turned into unabashed surprise.

"Senator, I have been your man for 25 years, and you have always been able to count on me to help you run for any seat you chose to pursue, and I'm damn good at what I do."

"Yes, my friend. That's why I chose you."

"I just have one question." This time it was his turn to pause, and during the break in conversation, he looked at the senator for some sign of dementia that would explain his bizarre statement. Finding none, he proceeded. "Senator, what in Betsy's brassiere are you talking about?"

To dispel any thoughts that he had suddenly become detached from reality, Masterson launched into his plan, detailed and complete, describing his strategy for Max to attain the office of president of the United States. By the time he had concluded, Postlewaite had 23 pages of notes. Together with the information that had been meticulously compiled in anticipation of the meeting, he would leave the Masterson estate with the most innovative and optimistic plan for a campaign that he had ever imagined, even in his youthful forays into politics. He hoped that he would still be around to implement the plan when Max became old enough to run for the office.

One aspect of the plan that was glaringly evident was the lack of opportunity given for feedback on the idea. Senator Masterson had a plan, it was his plan, and he knew it was controversial. He didn't want conventional thinking to mess it up.

"Postlewaite, I have already transferred your fee into your bank account. I assume you'll take the job once you see how generous it is. I want you to begin working behind the scenes immediately."

"But senator, I can't start running a campaign ten years before the candidate qualifies to run! I have other projects I'm working on! I can't…"

"I don't want to hear that you can't. I only want to hear about how you can. I have hired you on a ten year retainer to devote all of your efforts to the campaign. Oh, and by the way, don't talk to Max about it until I have told him he's running." Anticipating the outcry, he preempted the response. "I know, I know. He knows I want him to run. He just doesn't know that I'm serious about it. You know how I get when I set my mind to things."

Postlewaite smirked and snorted loudly in response. They locked in a mutual gaze that signified that the senator had found a campaign manager. It was irrelevant that the candidate was oblivious to the fact that he would be running for president, or that the plan would not be carried out until after its architect was dead.

"How are we going to fund this thing?" Max's new campaign manager was already workingon the project he anticipated would occupy his thoughts for the next decade. It was a life-defining job, and he took his goal seriously. If the senator wanted his kid to be president, by God, he would deliver. That's the reason he had been picked for the job.

"I already funded it. The investments will mature one year before Max's thirty-sixth birthday, and when they vest, they will automatically transfer to the campaign account, and you'll be rolling."

Chapter Sixteen

When a young man has a beach house in the Florida Panhandle, and attends law school in the frigid Midwest, he immediately becomes the best friend of all his pale classmates. Max didn't complain. The thought of spending ten days in Florida after a brutal Michigan winter was an abiding dream by the time cabin fever kicked in. His childhood years in Virginia were punctuated by frequent vacations to the Florida beach house, and the annual pilgrimage to Apalachicola meant he would be accompanied by up to twenty of his classmates, male and female. Although he never pursued women, they seemed to be drawn to him like moths to a candle. His male friends wanted to be around him for that reason too, even if it meant sleeping on the floor like puppies. The girls got the beds. Max kept the master suite to himself. The door was open to anyone, unless, of course, he was busy, and he was busiest with Debbie, his default roommate for the duration of his time back in Florida. Debbie was preoccupied with keeping the other girls from visiting, and Max just enjoyed being the object of female attention.

College was a time of experimentation. Yearly pilgrimages to the senator's "District Home," the anchor of residence that qualified him to run for the Senate from Florida, were mandatory for Max. Its proximity to Tallahassee and the politicos of the state capitol made the beach house a "must attend" when Senator Masterson held his annual oyster roast fundraisers. Old guests didn't bother about invitations. They just dropped in when they knew John Masterson was down home for some fishing. This torch had been passed to Max, who wasn't running for anything. It was assumed by the locals that he would someday seek his father's seat in Washington, but Max had a standard response to the almost daily pestering, "I'm not a politician."

Regardless of his repeated denials about harboring any political aspirations, Max was treated to local celebrity status. The quiet world of the Florida Gulf Coast was made more interesting by his visits.

By the time the caravan of law students arrived in Apalachicola and made the turn onto Highway 98 to follow the coast for the ten miles to Indian Beach, they had already stopped at the ABC store to stock up on their beverages of choice. Max bought a bottle of Cabo Wabo tequila, some limes, and supplemented it all with a hot bag of boiled peanuts. He bought his from the same roadside vendor who had sat under the umbrella alongside the road for as long as Max could remember.

"Hi, Clayton. What's new and exciting down these parts?"

"You know, Mista Max. If you ain't fishin', ya'll need to hump down the road to Panama City. Go to Club 'Vela and watch them girls takin' their T-shirts off."

"Clayton, I've known you all your life so far, and I don't know that you've ever been out of Franklin County. How do you know those girls are taking their tops off?"

Clayton chuckled, his mouth opening long enough to show an irregular row of yellow stained teeth with a gap on the bottom where his incisors once grew. Max knew that the missing teeth were the result of a drunken brawl about a mile down the road at a local oyster shack. The sign out front merely advertised "Cold Beer." It was enough to keep the locals happy.

"Mista Max, are you stayin' down to the beach house again?" Clayton had a keen sense of the obvious.

"No, Clayton, I thought I'd bunk with you for a few days," smiled Max as he swung into his convertible Ferrari and plopped the bagful of groceries in Debbie's lap.

"Well now, Mista Max, I'd hafta think about that…"

The tires spun on the gray gravel as the entourage traveled the final leg to their spring break. Two miles down the road, they swung onto a white sand dual track, a path known to locals as the "maneater." Drivers unfamiliar with driving in sugar sand inevitably became stuck in the soft white dunes that lined the driveway. A local industry of four-wheel drive truckers earned beer money pulling tourists out of the sand, and each spring break was a boost to the sleepy local economy.

The cars pulled up to the two story beach house, its lights glowing in a welcome of sorts. The sun was setting over the Gulf of Mexico, an orange goodbye until the next day. Too late to visit the beach, they settled for assembling in the kitchen, the nerve center of every home get-together. After they stowed their bags, they were intent on becoming spring break inebriated. It was a test of their limits and was the foundation of a diminishing number of blurry memories that they would carry through adulthood. They had arrived.

Chapter Seventeen

Over a half century of continuous abuse from sunlight, salt spray, and occasional hurricane winds, the Masterson home, referred to by the senator as Anchor House, took on a weathered look. The yellow paint and white trim seemed to Max to look duller with each visit.

"Maybe next time, I'll put these guys to work putting a new coat on it," he thought. "Dad probably won't even notice, though. He doesn't come down here often enough to know the difference. It seems the older he gets, the more I have to pry him away from Fairlane. He hates planes, and the drive down and back takes too much out of him these days. I may have to surprise him with a private flight down just to get him into a reminiscing mood."

Max carried the two duffel bags containing a week's worth of T-shirts, shorts, and bathing suits up to the master bedroom on the second floor while the remaining members of the entourage claimed sleeping space on the first floor. Inevitably, someone would end up sleeping on the floor beneath the dining room table, but at 21, the hardness of the sleeping surface never seemed to keep anyone from getting a good night's rest. The alcohol helped to numb the discomfort.

Once they had moved in and the refrigerator was stocked with liquid refreshment, the deck was the next stop. Drinks in hand, the group sat in the abundant Adirondack chairs while Max fired up the barbeque grill. As the sun set, the idyllic orange and pink pastel clouds turned to burgundy before the sun slid low over the Gulf of Mexico. Florida legend has it that at the moment the sun touches the horizon over the Gulf, if you are focused at that very spot on a clear evening, you can see the "green hiss," a momentary flash across the horizon. Max had never seen it, but he had repeated the legend to the uninitiated at every rest stop on the trip down I-75. All eyes were focused on the horizon as he moved up behind his companions with a large squirt gun filled with ice water.

Just as the sun touched the water, Max trained the blast of the water on his classmates. In one sweep, he soaked his startled victims. "There's your hiss! Did you feel it?" The screams were his desired result and began the raucous party that lasted long into the night.

Gradually, the last stragglers turned in, and Max quietly slipped away with Debbie hand in hand, walking barefoot through the dunes. An experienced navigator from his many visits as a young boy, he was careful to steer wide of the sandspurs that lined the path. At the shore, Max held her tightly as the moon slid beneath the horizon. This was a special time, when the darkness took over and the stars seemed to hang at arm's length. He had no difficulty picking out the Southern Cross from the constellations that he had committed to memory. Max turned toward the house, lit against the night sky, then turned and kissed her slowly, their lips full and warm. "I want you."

"Max, you didn't exactly have to go out of your way to impress me."

"I know, but I just want you to know."

"What?"

"There will always be other women."

Debbie didn't need to respond. Not verbally. Her body pressed against his, and the silence took over. She knew she wouldn't be able to hold him for long, but she savored this moment and pressed her full breasts against his chest. He kissed her with the hot passion she sought so urgently. Their tongues intertwined for moments that turned into minutes, their hands roaming in increasingly bold strokes. They briefly parted, panting from the intense passion.

"You're with me now, and I have you all to myself," she said in a husky voice. She grabbed his hand tightly and led him to a solitary depression between the dunes.

Chapter Eighteen

The most dangerous aspect of spring break is not the amount of alcohol that a college student can consume in one evening nor their ability to go without sleep for long periods. The prodigious amount of youthful hormones flowing through the young blood vessels of this age group is the main cause of high risk behavior. Sure, the alcohol and sleep deprivation enhance it, but the core reason is those ever-present hormones.

After four days of nonstop partying, sunning, and beach paddleball, the law students were turning bright red, sometimes purple, a sign of the peeling skin to come on the trip home. It is mystifying to Floridians to see tourists and spring breakers spending hours on the beach until their previously healthy flesh becomes radiation damaged. To tan naturally, you are supposed to start out with a short exposure to the sun that increases over a long period of time, allowing the skin to heal. A suntan is actually dead skin on top of live skin, baked golden brown over time.

On spring break, all of the lectures about skin cancer go right out the window, and the obligatory sunburn frequently occurs after the first day on the beach. By the time the redness appears, if you haven't taken cover, your skin is on its way to a sickening purple color. This, together with the searing pain, can compel even the drunkest spring breaker to seek shelter in an air-conditioned building. These buildings are commonly known by locals as "bars."

Bored with the luxury of a free stay in a beach house, the entourage decided to pack into the SUV for the 50 mile drive along the coast to the spring break mecca of Panama City Beach, where over a million college students congregate there each year to see how close they can stand to half-naked members of the opposite sex. It is here that the inhibitions of normally studious college students can lead to sex with strangers in hotel rooms occupied by other couples who don't know or care to remember the name of their newfound friend, but most of them will go home with blurry memories of other people engaging in debauchery.

Max was hovering on the rail of the balcony of the Happy Buccaneer Hotel when he suddenly developed the urge to fly. Three days of nonstop drinking and sleep deprivation had brought him to this state of mind, and at the time, it all seemed so reasonable: just leap the twelve feet from this balcony to that one and then jump back. He had made longer jumps before, and besides, he could fly. His friends wouldn't encourage him to do anything dangerous, would they? Debbie warned him. She was just being a girl, he recalled as her stern voice echoed in his alcohol-infused brain. "Too careful. Thinks I'll hurt myself," he thought. "I just need a ten step head start until I get to escape velocity. I'm gonna do it!"

Max actually made the first leap across the gap between the balconies in Rooms 201 and 202. He landed hard and fell to his hands, turning to the loud applause of not only his friends but the hundreds of onlookers from adjoining balconies and those around the pool a mere two stories below. The words of praise were mixed a few "Asshole" and "That dude's wasted" comments that he totally ignored.

He quickly realized that even though he had made the jump, he was now standing on the empty balcony of a room that had locked sliding doors, and he had no way of getting back unless he repeated the feat of athletic prowess in reverse. This time, he would need fourteen steps to launch across the gap. "Did the balcony just get overcrowded?"

he wondered, his mind clouded with high levels of adrenaline, alcohol, and testosterone. "Max, don't do it!" yelled Debbie. "Wait for the manager to unlock the door!"

Without hesitation, Max backed up five steps and ran for the open space.

Chapter Nineteen

He might have made the jump if he had given himself a longer head start, or if the big guy from Syracuse had stepped out of his way instead of pushing into the only open spot on the balcony, but here lay Max in traction, his leg in a cast. Law school had resumed more than two weeks ago. He was forced to withdraw for the summer term, and it looked certain that he wouldn't be leaving Fairlane anytime soon.

It was precisely the opportunity that the senator and Luke Postlewaite had waited for. "You got a dose of humility, and it didn't come too soon." The paternal instinct was being revived in the elder Masterson, and he was mildly surprised that he still had it in him. He had felt it come and go over the years, but he seldom had to summon the need to protect his son from danger or direct him away from the pitfalls of life. Max was a good kid. This time, though, it was more serious than a broken leg. His son had stepped off the path to greatness, and he wasn't going to sit idly by and watch him squander his only opportunity to achieve his life's purpose. To do so would be admitting he had failed.

"I'm sort of relieved that you only broke your leg, and the way I look at it, in every misfortune there lives the seed of an equivalent or greater benefit. I know that this will be a good learning opportunity for you. To be sure you don't waste time feeling sorry for yourself, I have invited someone to help with your training."

"Senator, I'm a law student on medical leave, and I have no idea what training you are referring to." Max was still groggy from eleven hours of sleep and was frustrated by his inability to leave the bed. He never addressed his father as "Senator," unless he was desperate to have his full attention.

"I'm not talking about law," replied the senator.

"Yeah, we think you need some reinforcement of the business of politics to keep your sorry ass in tow."

Max was startled at the familiar voice coming from behind him, out of his line of sight. There was no mistaking the booming baritone of Uncle Luke. Postlewaite had been his mentor since infancy, and his visits with Max were always full of "life lessons," as he called them.

"I figured that it would take something like a broken bone to slow you down long enough for me to talk some sense to you, and now you're mine." The two elders chuckled in unison, a sinister, conspiratorial laugh.

Postlewaite continued. "In the world of politics, there are two types of elected officials. There are those with ideas, and they are rare. They have goals and foresight and think for themselves. Then there are those who never had an original thought and only look out for themselves. The difference, I think, puts too many of the nonthinkers in position to lead the people that put them there. Then, when they get voted in, instead of leading, they get busy planning for reelection. Dammit! That's not how it should be! They get their egos out and begin to think that they are experts on everything. Then, when they stand in front of the voters and make speeches, they are careful to only tiptoe around and avoid saying anything controversial."

Max listened intently, careful not to comment until Postlewaite and the senator were certain they had made a point. When the pause became an ending, he responded.

"But I'm not a politician."

"I don't want you to be a politician," commented the senator. "I do want you to run when the time is right, but I don't want you to run as a politician."

The last words were confusing, even to Max, who had been indoctrinated in the fine art of politics since infancy. "I don't see the difference."

"I want you to say what you mean and never fear the consequences of holding tight to your ideals. You should never be afraid to state your position on the issues you feel strongly about or to ask questions. You should never avoid discussion with those who don't hold your views. Nobody ever resolved a conflict by refusing to talk about it. I'm going to go into more depth, and while we have you hostage, Luke and I are going to start you on your journey into becoming a person of value."

When Max didn't respond, Postlewaite took up the silence.

"What we are trying to tell you is that you don't need to act like a politician to get elected. You need to develop a clear vision of what you intend to accomplish once you get into office, and you must be able to state your position in a way that will convince people that your way is the right way," he expounded.

"Okay, but can we do this after breakfast?"

Chapter Twenty

"How do people, most of them from humble beginnings, become president? Think about it. Most of them didn't have the pedigree." Luke Postlewaite began each of his lessons with a question that his students all wondered about, but the answer to that question would never be found in a textbook or a Google search. These were questions designed to get them to think outside the box and ponder the metaphysical. "You could make a better argument for left-handedness being a prerequisite for being president than any of the other qualifications that those elected to higher office possess, with the possible exception of being born a male," Postlewaite continued. Max laughed without knowing why.

"Lincoln literally crawled out of the wilderness. Clinton grew up in Arkansas, but ended up at Yale, and later, Cambridge, a Rhodes scholar."

"Obama. The child of a marriage between a Nigerian scholar and a hippie girl, who grew up in Indonesia, Hawaii, and Kansas. They were all portrayed as outsiders, trying to break into politics, but were they outsiders?"

Postlewaite paced while Max listened. If there had been a carpet beneath his feet, it would have been threadbare by now. When Luke talked, he walked, and the only way to silence him was to ask him to sit down.

"Our nation has always mistrusted royalty. The aristocracy has never trusted the common man. Our Founding Fathers were a talented and brilliant group of landowners and businessmen who were being taxed to death by the British. When they broke away from the monarchy and Mother England, they rejected the traditions that came with it."

Max looked more puzzled than before. "I don't get it. First you start to tell me about how the average guy can become president, and then you launch into some history lesson about England and kings and who knows what?" His words were met with an annoying glare from his teacher.

"For a kid in traction, you certainly act like you have to be somewhere else." Luke's rebuke silenced his student long enough for him to continue. "Whether you like it or not, Max, you are going to focus on what I am saying. Now, as I was saying," he smiled, and Max knew from a lifetime of experience that he was not going to succeed at convincing Luke Postlewaite to move on to another subject, even if he couldn't understand where all of this was headed.

"When the American Revolution was finished, our Founding Fathers got together and set up the infrastructure for running the country. They decided to have a president who was elected, but they didn't trust the citizens to elect him. They wanted to maintain control of who would be king, because up until then, the leader was born into the position, not elected, and the only way to get him off the throne was to hasten his death. The problem with that idea was that the king's little brother would take the job, and that's how it was done."

"Why?"

"That's the way it had always been done, that's why. So here the Founding Fathers are setting up the framework for running the country, and they don't want a monarchy, and they don't want just anyone to become president, so they create the electoral college to elect the president of the United States. After a few tries at getting the right man into office, they ran out of Founding Fathers, and we got a series of presidents who are only famous for being forgettable."

Postlewaite sat down and waited for Max to ask a question. There were several minutes of silence as he tried to remember who became president after Andrew Jackson and before Abraham Lincoln. He drew a blank. "I see what you mean. I can't recall a lot of the names, and I sure can't remember what they accomplished in office. Is this my history lesson?" Max resumed his impatience, a trait his father imparted to him when he couldn't see where a conversation or speech was headed.

"I'm not trying to get you to memorize long-dead presidents. I want you to wonder about how they became presidents." This lesson had been lost on Max. Luke had started his day with that question, and he didn't yet have the answer.

"Okay, this is your long-winded way of getting me to ask you how we get better presidents elected, right?" asked the slightly cranky student.

With that bit of encouragement, Postlewaite stood once again, and the lesson resumed. "Now you're getting it. The answer to your question is simple—The Society."

Chapter Twenty-One

"Since the early 1800s, an ultraexclusive secret organization has met privately to promote the election of qualified candidates to become the president of the United States of America," said Postlewaite, with more than a tinge of pride in his voice.

"Luke, are you telling me you're one of these people?"

"I have been a member of The Society most of my life, along with the senator, who was one of my first students."

"You mean, my dad was trained to be president like you're training me?"

"Yes, along with many famous candidates throughout history, starting with Abraham Lincoln. Oh, sometimes we win and sometimes we lose, but we have a pretty good track record of getting our people elected. The senator turned out to be too direct and honest to be our candidate, and The Society had to put Bill Clinton in his slot. We paid for his education, got him deferred from the draft, funded his campaigns, paid the pollsters and the marketers, pretty much built him from the ground up. Clinton's downfall was not that he was a bad president. It was his ego. He thought he could get away with anything without feeling the consequences. That's why we had to step in and bring his ego under control."

Max's interest had returned in spades. He would never be impatient with his teachings again. "You mean that I'm not the only one? I thought it was my father's ambition that was behind this." The teachings of Luke Postlewaite during his sixteenth summer were long over. At the time, he felt that he had learned all that his teacher had to impart to the chosen, but here was a new way of looking at politics that had never been shared with Max. This was graduate school for political hopefuls, and Max was dubious about whether he would ever want to pursue his father's calling.

"Listen, I told you to think about how those other guys got elected. Do you think for one minute that they could get themselves educated, become consummate public speakers, appear at the right events, get the press they needed to get the public's attention, do the marketing of their image…"

Max interrupted, "…and get elected?"

"Now you're starting to get the big picture. And that's just the tip of the iceberg."

Max began to understand the meaning of the lessons constantly presented by the senator and Postlewaite, each providing essential links in the chain he needed to be considered a candidate. He had been promoted by his father as a future contender, along with an unknown number of others. They were offered up at the right time after years of training by a secret group which possessed the knowledge and wherewithal to get them elected. They were on the fast track to the presidency. He had to know about his competition.

"Luke, if I'm in the running, who am I running against?"

"I know, but I can't tell you. Not yet, at least. That day will come." Postlewaite was crafty at planting the seed, but he made sure that his young study didn't have too much information for his own good. Stoke the competitive instinct, but don't let him compete. It was too early. Max needed years of training before he would be ready, and he didn't know if the senator was up to the task. That was the reason he had put the lessons on disk, in case he wasn't around to finish it.

Chapter Twenty-Two

The next fifteen years passed quickly. Max grew from a handsome, athletic and smart boy into a man possessing the same qualities, but his maturation was more complete and public. He had appeared with the senator on the Washington social circuit, and his face increasingly became famous. When the paparazzi became aware that his image would sell, Max became a social phenomenon. Everywhere he went, the cameras followed. Max continued to be a public figure, and the constant scrutiny became an annoyance.

To amuse himself, Max occupied much of his time planning escapes from the press, and he became an expert at evasion. Any opportunity to keep his photo from being taken was a private victory for him. When one disguise was discovered, he devised a new one. If an escape route was suddenly posted with paparazzi, an alternative route was available. Even so, Max was overexposed.

After a few weeks of no news, the press began its incessant commentary about the old news, and the images that they had in their possession were recycled. That is the way the press works in a 24/7 world, repeating information and misinformation in a constant loop. Once the information enters the loop, it remains there until it is removed by conscious act. With the famous and infamous, no information is discarded, regardless of accuracy, and nobody dared to take the steps necessary to get the story right. As the misinformation about Max grew, the senator resorted to the one tried and true method of getting information out; he created it.

Max had a secret publicist in Senator John "Minuteman" Masterson, and his father delighted in creating Max's public persona, complete with rehearsed sound bites, digital videos, and still shots. If the senator wanted the public to see Max playing touch football on the lawn of the White House, the image was created and disseminated to the press through the standard method, and news agencies picked up anything that had Max's name attached to it. It didn't matter that Max could never have stood on the lawn of the White House without being hauled off by Secret Service. The reality had been created and placed in the minds of the viewers.

Chapter Twenty-Three

"Dad, as long as I can remember, you have been campaigning. We go to fundraisers. We go to dinners and parties all dressed up in tuxes. We meet fancy people and hang out with them. And for what? I haven't exactly had a typical childhood, you know. I wanted to invite kids over to play, and I ended up having a fist fight with Prince Harry at Buckingham Palace. You are always running, and for what?" They walked at a fast pace along the Potomac, a route that followed the riverbank.

"Son, I'm not running for anything. The best I can do at my age is saunter."

Max looked into his eyes, once clear and bright gray, but now dull and clouded by age. He wasn't about to let the old man change the subject, which he had turned into an art form. He waited for a response that satisfied him but picked up the pace. Finally, the senator spoke, his voice loud and clear and recognizable, honed by his years in public service.

"I need to give you my inside view of politics…" The old man struggled for breath, and plunked down on a bench next to the trail. Perspiration dripped from his nose, and a bluish-white color formed around his lips.

Max doubled back and sat across from him on a small boulder, looking much like a student settling in for a lecture. "Are you alright?"

"Yes. I'll be fine in a few minutes. Now listen." He puffed between sentences, but his color was slowly returning to normal. "Washington is in my blood. I can't get rid of it. My battles began before you were born, and I have been fighting them all of my life… and they are still being fought… and I can't win the battle without your help. I have always been clear in my intentions for you." He swallowed hard.

He looked ill, but Max had been manipulated by the master before, and he wasn't going to leap headlong into one of the senator's lessons without a fight.

"…the greatest country in the history of mankind…" His face looked old.

"I want you to clean up politics as we know it.

There is so much bullshit flying around…

…Washington…

…it's a wonder we don't just decide to flush the whole town…

…politicians included…

…and start all over."

His mind began rambling, but his smile was still there. He just needed to rest a bit. He was prone to that, lately, but due to the wonders of medical science, people didn't just drop dead anymore. They lingered.

Somewhere between life and death, they existed for years until they decided to die with dignity, and they made an appointment with their maker. They could decide to do it quietly and alone, or they could be dragged from life kicking and screaming, but they could do it on their own terms. A heart and a brain were all that they needed to preserve. The rest of the ailments of old age were no longer a reason to just die, and he knew that. He just didn't feel much like carrying on unless there was a good reason, and Max was his cause for sticking around and seeing how he would turn out. Besides, he was too stubborn to just surrender.

"I'm counting on you to carry the torch. I've taught you just about everything I know about getting your way in politics. I know that you are frustrated. I had no business taking in a little boy and training him to be the savior that I can't be. I didn't realize it at the time, but I think I stole your childhood. I never thought about it…" He took a few steps and stopped. He sat down hard on a large boulder beside the trail. A tear appeared in his right eye, and soon it turned into a flood. Max had never seen him cry, and it frightened him. The man who had been his strength and security was breaking down. He put his hand on the old man's shoulder, but he chose not to speak. It was a time to share and to wait.

With his head still bowed, the senator spoke quietly. It was a voice he had never heard, a soft grumble, so soft that he had to lean forward to make out the words.

"I tried. I thought I was doing the right thing. I provided you with everything I could imagine to make you a good man. You never gave me any trouble. Even when I dragged you along to those political events, I was trying to teach you about how things get done. I spent most of my life learning that most of it is folly and ego, and you learned in a few years. You have the jump on the whole bunch of them!" He coughed.

Max began to smile. He realized that he was being manipulated, but the master manipulator had him in his mental grasp. There was no escape, and even if there was, he was enjoying the senator's orchestrated melodrama. All the same, he treasured these rare times alone with the old man. It had been a long time since they had one of their walks.

Their eyes met. The senator rose and smiled, and collapsed in his arms.

Chapter Twenty-Four

It wasn't unexpected. John Masterson was sick for longer than anyone knew. His doctor was sworn to secrecy, and his son and Postlewaite were the only witnesses to his lingering decline. When he reached a terminal stage, his doctor was there 24/7, but it didn't change a thing. There was no public announcement, no death watch, and no special reports on his declining health. The senator's quest for privacy, at least his personal privacy, had been perfected, and the press report of his demise was made public a full day after the loved ones had been notified and he was placed in the ground. That feat in and of itself would have been considered a great victory by John "Minuteman" Masterson.

PART TWO

A GUY RUNNING FOR PRESIDENT

Chapter Twenty-Five

"You can take a humble country boy from the farm in Michigan, put him in a car, and drive him inside the beltway, and he transforms into a politician. This is scary to most of us normal folks, because we sent him to Washington so he could tell Congress and the president how to run the country and what we at home want done about it, and all of a sudden he gets amnesia," rambled Leila Fox. Her hands were purple from picking blueberries from her prize blueberry patch behind the barn, and she was just about done. Her audience was her son, Andrew Fox. He was home from Michigan State. His diploma from the journalism school was proudly displayed in the dining room, where mom figured everyone could see it.

Despite the wishes of his parents, who tried to get him to learn something about running a farm to save the family business, he had majored in journalism. It was a respectable profession all right, but Leila worried about what would happen now that the auto industry was hurting in a major way. People were moving out, leaving their property to the bank sometimes, because nobody wants to buy a house in a ghost town.

"Maybe you did make the right decision, my darling boy. The politicians won't help. This time next year, your dad and I will be selling this place and moving into the condo like we planned." Leila had a habit of talking to you wherever you were. It didn't matter whether you could hear what she was saying. It did tend to make anyone within earshot into a captive audience. "I feel sorry for our neighbors," she continued. "Their whole life is tied to their farms, and they never saved a penny. But I can't worry about them and us, too." She tried to wipe a tear from her eye with her hand but only succeeded in placing a purple smear alongside her nose.

Andrew remembered the reason he was standing there and took advantage of the gap in his mother's words. "Mom, I just got a call from Chicago. The Sun Times wants to hire me as a reporter. I start Monday," he said in his best calming voice. He knew she would blow a gasket as soon as he told her, but he couldn't risk her hearing it from someone else. News travels fast in a small town. But instead of the expected eruption and the seemingly inevitable procession of circular arguments protesting his decision, she said nothing.

She stopped picking, rolled onto one knee, and raised her hand to Andrew for help up.

Once erect, she wiped her hands on a towel for long enough to remove as much of the blueberry stain as would come off without major soap and scrubbing and looked at her 23- year-old son. She looked for a long time.

"I didn't send you to college to waste your life working on a sugar beet farm, and if you think for a minute that you're going to loaf around this place without finding a good job and paying me some rent, then you are in for a big surprise, young man. Are your clothes washed? Does anything need ironing?"

He could always count on mom to bring him back to reality. He would need to pack and say his goodbyes to everyone he knew. If he didn't, they would hold a grudge for the rest of his life, and he didn't need that. He better make a list and ask mom if he left anyone out.

"I'm only 250 miles away, and you can stay at my apartment as soon as I get settled. I don't have much furniture, so it won't take me long to move in," offered Andrew.

"You may as well find an apartment on Mars for us to come visit. You know we can't leave the farm during growing season. If you want to see us, you're just going to have to come to the farm or to Florida. We'll probably try to put the farm up for sale in the spring. Pretty soon it'll be winter, and no fool would want to buy a farm when the ground is frozen. That means we're stuck here until then. Your dad's a bigger fool for waiting out this recession to see what happens…" Her voice trailed off as she entered the house. The storm door slammed behind her, and he had to scramble to open it before he missed any words. She had a complete disregard for the hearing abilities of others.

By the time he got the door back open, mom was already fully launched on another topic, and he had to shift gears. "You know, when we elected him, I thought he was a good man. I knew him since they moved here when he was six. Now his mother tells me that he hardly writes, and when he does, he tells her about how small his office is, and how he had to play the lottery to get a bigger one, or some such nonsense," her voice raised at least an octave since he heard it last.

"I read someplace about those Arabs building nuclear bombs so they can lob missiles at us, and all they can talk about is some budget. And I write the paper a letter and they say it's too long to print."

Mom had been writing letters to the Marshall Chronicle for as long as he could remember. "So I call the number on his card, and I get a recording about how I should leave a message and one of his staffers would get back with me. There was no button to push that let me speak to a live human being, and I thought that if you put a phone number on your card, I would get you on the phone. No!" She used the word for emphasis and stretched it for as long as she had wind in her lungs. He held the screen door wide, and she hauled the bucket of blueberries to the kitchen sink. "Check and see if we have any vanilla ice cream in the freezer. Your dad can't eat his blueberries without a dish of ice cream. If we're out, I'll have to send you into town for a gallon. Better bring the cooler though, or it'll melt before you get back."

Mom knew exactly how much ice cream was left, just like she knew how many chicken breasts were marinating on the counter, or where that jar of cinnamon was at the back of the spice cupboard. She had been running this family most of her life, and for her, keeping your family fed was a badge of pride that she would wear to the grave.

"Andrew, if you get over to Washington, would you tell them for me that we need those politicians to call us back?" Andrew was out the door and backing down the driveway by the time her voice began to trail off. His mind was on the new job, and the adrenaline was pumping.

Chapter Twenty-Six

Senator Masterson had chosen the steps of the Jefferson Memorial for Max to make his announcement many years before his death. It was meticulously planned for more than a decade, together with detailed instructions for working through channels to accomplish all the details. For the photo opportunity to be perfect, he planned it for 6:30 a.m. This made the press crews angry for having to arrive two hours before sunrise, lug their heavy equipment from the parking lot at the far end of the facility, and set up their mobile equipment at the base of the steps. The optimal angle was obtained for the sun to rise in the east and illuminate the side of Max's face, and the tidal basin accommodated the effect by being smooth as glass, reflecting the Washington monument and the White House from across the water.

There was no practical way for the heavy broadcasting equipment to be transported to the memorial. The Capitol Police made no exceptions. No parking on Ohio Avenue. No loitering. No stopping. No easy way to do anything, for security reasons. Heavy concrete barriers were constructed at random intervals to deflect any vehicle trying to make its way in the direction of any national monument in Washington, D.C., and once the press trucks were spotted, security vehicles swarmed the area.

Luke Postlewaite had secured the necessary permits, though, and they had official permission from the National Park Service, obtained years in advance. No previous candidate had been able to accomplish the same feat, but Luke pulled every string he could yank. After initial resistance from officials who unequivocally announced that it was impossible to accommodate his simple request, they relented. A late-night phone call to the Secretary of the Interior at his home number, and the appropriate veiled threats to disclose certain information about a certain public official who had a reputation to maintain, and Max had the venue for his press conference.

As they were erecting their powerful lights to illuminate the scene, Max appeared. "No. You can't use artificial light. I want the sun to do your work for you. It's a beautiful day, isn't it?" he announced.

They didn't agree at this hour of the morning, and it was difficult to imagine in the predawn darkness that there would be enough light to illuminate a chipmunk. The reporters chose to stay in bed while they set up for the shoot, and there were no hot microphones ready to record the encounter. They would arrive shortly before the time scheduled for the announcement, which, curiously, was 6:47 a.m. If they had consulted their Farmer's Almanac, they would have realized that this time was two minutes after sunrise, when the lights illuminating the Jefferson memorial at night turned off and the light of day cast its glow.

"I'll be back in a little while. Don't go away," said Max as he walked back toward the parking lot. The technicians, as a result of working in Washington for most of their assignments, were accustomed to politicians holding press conferences on short notice, but this one was peculiar. He seemed to be doing it all himself. There were no staff members with clipboards barking out instructions in preparation for the public appearance, just the guy in the suit.

When they had finished their preparations, they wandered as a group toward the satellite trucks, where they had coffee ready to sustain them during the inevitable wait. They huddled in the cool of the morning around their mobile command centers, waiting for the visual component of their crew to arrive and begin the primping and preening to ready themselves for their time in front of the cameras.

Max appeared. "Do you mind if I bum a cup of coffee from you? It's a long walk to the nearest Starbucks." Max's appearance startled them, but one cameraman had just finished pouring his cup and offered it to him. "If you don't mind me saying so," said one technician, "you aren't our typical political candidate. We don't usually get to hang out with you before a press conference, if you know what I mean." Max sat in a folding canvas chair and appeared to relax a bit. "Yeah, I suppose it's new to you, but think about how I feel. I've never done this before."

"I covered you back in the fall at the Kennedy Center, and I got a good shot of you walking in with some babe in a slinky black dress," recalled a slim, bushy-haired man with a Mickey Mouse watch and blue jeans. "I never pegged you as being the political type. If I was you, I'd still be in bed with the babe, but her dress would be in a pile on the floor." They all laughed a kind of nervous laugh, as if they didn't know whether Max would have a sense of humor at this time of morning.

"I know what you mean." Max laughed at the initial comment. "I don't remember which babe you're talking about, but if it was Mitzi, I don't think her dress made it back to the house." They all laughed again, looking around to make sure no women were eavesdropping on their communal male moment. Once they were satisfied that they were in the clear, each nodded knowingly, as if they had all escorted a supermodel to an event and had her naked in the passenger seat by the mere force of their male sexuality. They admired him and wanted to share in his magnetic persona, but they knew that his world was as remote from theirs as if he had been talking about vacationing on Mars.

"Those days are gone, boys. I'm a grownup now. I'm running for president."

"Why?" A slim, scruffy cameraman sat in a nylon folding chair, his equipment stowed in a black bag at his side. "You have the life every man wants, and you want to screw it up by doing a damn fool thing like that? You want to give up all that to have people gunning for you all the time, criticizing you every day, and not being able to take a piss without Secret Service telling you it's safe? You're fuckin' crazy, man." He paused, his face revealing concern that he may have said too much—and to a guy who may be the most powerful man on the planet someday.

Max was smiling at the beginning of the outburst, but his look became suddenly serious. "Thanks for your opinion, my friend. Everyone needs to have meaning in their lives. But I never said I was giving it all up." They laughed again, sharing a joke that only males could understand.

"I intend to serve my term as president with all of the dignity that the office commands," he said in a quiet tone, which produced more laughter from the mostly jaded camera crew. Much of the spicier news they had produced had ended up being discarded by producers who wanted to continue working in Washington and couldn't risk getting on the wrong side of news making politicians with secrets to hide.

A black BMW wheeled into the parking lot. Out stepped Greg Scuperman, Capitol Correspondent for News Tonight. His wet hair revealed his lack of preparation and retreating hairline. He charged past Max and the broadcast crew as if they were nothing more than yard ornaments.

"I need Lacey! Where's Lacey?" he bellowed. Lacey, his cosmetician, poked her head out of the satellite truck, and Scuperman launched his paunchy body in her direction. "We're on the air in 45 minutes, and I'm not even close to ready," he said to nobody in particular, disregarding those around him who may have cared enough to notice.

"I'll see you later," said Max as he walked toward the Jefferson Memorial, styrofoam cup in hand. At precisely 6:47 a.m., the lights illuminating the Jefferson Memorial extinguished for the day, and Max emerged at the top of the steps. He waited a moment for silence as a flock of Canadian geese flew overhead honking loudly, then looked straight into the cameras. "I'm Max Masterson, and I'm running for president of the United States."

Only the slight breeze that rustled the early leaves of spring and the sourceless drone of the city, a combination of car traffic and machines, kept the moment from being totally silent.

"I have decided to run because I believe that Americans need a leader who will restoreour country to greatness. I am not a politician, and I will not engage in 'politics as usual.' We need someone who can lead America to peace and prosperity. We need a president who has ideas for making the future better and will put Americans first. I am that candidate. Thanks for coming."

Max turned and walked away. His message was less than a minute long, and he had accomplished what he had set out to do. That didn't satisfy Scuperman and the correspondents from the five other news agencies who had staked out Max's news conference, though. They didn't have enough air time to justify getting out of bed, and the networks were left with next to nothing to occupy the daily news. In an effort to turn the occasion into an impromptu press conference, Scuperman led the entourage behind Max's retreat like a gaggle of baby chicks.

"Mr. Masterson! Would you care to comment on your chances of defeating an incumbent President? Mr. Masterson, I need a moment of your time... Please, Mr. Masterson!" Scuperman turned and glared at his camera crew as if they were to blame for the candidate's unorthodox behavior. "Turn the damn cameras off! Set up the lights with the Jefferson Memorial behind me. Dammit, where's Lacey! Someone give me a comb and a script!" As Max walked out of sight, the newsman stepped between the cameras and the Memorial and began his commentary. "I have never seen anything like it. A presidential candidate who invited us out here in the dead of morning to make a speech, only to speak for a mere minute. Surely, this is an indication of how inexperienced and insincere Max Masterson is in his pursuit of the highest office in our land. This is nothing more than a publicity stunt!" raged Scuperman, clearly exasperated that he had been taken out of his warm bed at such an early hour for copy that didn't amount to more than a sound bite.

The News Tonight ran Max's announcement in its entirety. There wasn't anything to cut and paste, except the commentary of Scuperman, which went on for thirty minutes. All Greg, all the time. Because the commentary exceeded the time allocated for the piece, Scuperman's words were reduced to two minutes. The effect was to contrast a calm Max Masterson, illuminated by the golden morning light in a patriotic, pastoral surrounding, followed by a red-faced and cranky news correspondent complaining about everything except the words Max had spoken. The brevity of Max's statement allowed it to be run repeatedly, but after the first run of Scuperman's commentary, the complaints to the network forced the editors to cut his negative portions. That left Max with a minute of air time, followed by fifteen seconds of the commentary before and after. For the second time in a week, Scuperman had been left on the cutting room floor.

Chapter Twenty-Seven

The traditional pollsters fell out of favor with politicians after the election of 2008. An analysis of their methods revealed that telephone polls had left out the huge portion of the American public who relied exclusively on cell phones, which at that time were the main means of communication by nearly every voter under the age of thirty.

By missing the opinions and voting preferences of the younger voter, the predominantly Republican households were thoroughly polled, while single, young, heterosexual and gay voters were invisible. The result was a confusing race that seesawed between poll predictions and voter tallies. Nothing matched. Polls regularly failed to predict results, and by the end of the primaries, they were mistrusted by both major parties. An important shift had occurred in which voters preferred to vote from home.

To top it off, nobody really likes a stranger asking them questions about their private lives, and the decisions made in a polling booth are about as private as they get. So, pollsters and the press began to be treated the same. The data gathered during the exit interviews was misleading and intentionally false, and the Yankee deception invalidated all of it.

Exit polls conducted after the New Hampshire primaries of 2008, when compared to actual results, showed that a substantial percentage of voters lied about who they voted for. The press concluded that there was a secret bevy of racists living in New Hampshire, who told the press and pollsters that they had just voted for a black man, but really voted for a white woman. The real reason was simple, as New Hampshire's citizens are renowned for resenting the intrusion of strangers into their private lives. So they lied and invalidated the poll results across the board, to the amusement of countless voters.

The data was worthless. It didn't predict a winner. It didn't even accurately predict a winner after the margin of error was taken into account. The enormous investment of campaign funds could have been wasted on more trivial pursuits, but in the tradition of American politics, the money went where it had gone before.

After the primary fiascoes of the 2008 elections, Congress got to work on two bills that were presented by Democrats from Michigan and Florida, who lost their delegates as punishment for moving up their primaries on the calendar. Michigan and Florida, in an effort to increase the prestige of their voting power in picking the next president, moved their primaries to January behind the Iowa caucus and the New Hampshire primary.

New Hampshire, a state that is ignored for four years between elections, went so far as to amend its constitution to make theirs the first primary in the country. Iowans, never to be outdone, continued hold their caucuses ahead of New Hampshire, to ensure that their significance in the election process would not be diluted.

The rest of the country, however, was broken into six voting regions: Northeast, Southeast, Midwest, South Central, Southwest, and Northwest. The primaries, beginning one day after the New Hampshire primary in January, began in the Northeast and two weeks later, moved to the Southeast, then to the Midwest, South Central, Southwest, and Northwest at two-week intervals.

The changes to the primary process were unique in that the states cooperated with the national parties and the federal government in a rare instance of putting the national interest ahead of individual state's rights. During the elections of 2008, an effort began in Congress to eliminate the exhausting and confusing primary process and replace it with regional primaries. It allowed the candidates to get enough sleep to speak intelligently the day after voting, and it set the stage for national debates to be held one week after the final primary.

A more difficult task for the politicians was the move to amend the Constitution to eliminate the Electoral College and bind delegates to the popular vote. The new thinking on the subject was, after nearly 250 years, to finally trust the voter to decide who they wanted to win the election. A vote to amend the Constitution requires two-thirds of both houses of Congress to pass, and debate on the subject spanned two years before it came to a vote.

A vote for change would eliminate the backroom dealing that frequently resulted in the loser of the popular vote winning the presidency, contrary to the will of the majority, and backers of the honesty in elections movement were accused of everything from promoting anarchy to aligning themselves with Socialists. They were persistent, though, and the effort was popular with the voters, who could never quite understand why they bothered to vote when someone else actually decided who was going to hold office. It all went back to the early days of the existence of the nation when most people were illiterate, naive, and easily influenced by fast-talking men who were successful at selling, persuaders who had their own fortunes to grow, and were not patriots in any sense of the word. They had their selfish interests at heart and taking the power to choose away from the public was the only way to ensure that they could control the result. In the end, change prevailed, and the Electoral College was retired by the closest vote in U.S. history.

Iowa and New Hampshire have traditionally been the states to kick off the campaign season, which coincidentally is during the same time that football playoffs and hunting season occur. In some parts of the U.S., it's a miracle that the attention of the American male can be diverted long enough to vote. Two changes in the way people vote made all the difference in the next race for president, and politics as usual failed to recognize their significance. The first was the federal law that mandated that all state primaries take place on the same Tuesday in February. The other change of great significance was the ability of voters to vote from home.

Since people from Iowa and New Hampshire are never more important than the rest of the country than when they cast the first ballots, they didn't much like the idea of voting at the same time as everyone else. As a result, they stubbornly swam against the flow and refused to hold their primaries on Super Tuesday, mandated by Federal Law to be the day after President's Day. New Hampshire had previously passed a law that made their primary the first in the nation, preceded only by the Iowa caucuses.

Aside from Iowa and New Hampshire, all of the major primaries happened on the same day, and nobody had to leave home to vote. No dangling chads, no waiting in line, no taking time off work, and no excuses. Everybody voted who was registered to vote. Democrats voted for Democrats, Republicans voted for Republicans, and Independents voted for whomever they damn well pleased. In pleasing themselves, Independents gained enormous power and so did the third-party candidates. This system put the third-party candidates on a level playing field with weaker mainstream candidates. If they didn't gather the requisite 20% of the popular vote, they didn't make it past the primaries. By the time the primary votes were in, the race was expected to come down to one incumbent, one independent, and a candidate with the support of a major party.

Max was sequestered with Andrew and Bill, strategizing before the rest of the staff came wandering in. It was 6:00 a.m., and they had spent the better part of the hours before sunrise trying to define how to reach the voters with the least cost and travel. Bill had been trying to reason with his candidate, but Max was rebelling.

"The Iowa Caucuses are attended by 100,000 registered voters. There are 1.4 million registered voters in Iowa. That leaves 1.3 million votes for me to capture, and the other guys can have the rest. They have already made up their minds, anyway. I'm not polling anyone, and I'm not flip-flopping on any of my positions just to get a few votes. I'm a package deal."

Andrew had had enough of Max's independent streak so early in the morning. Holding up the Maxims, he confronted Max with the list he had distributed, "I like the fact that you had this embossed in gold, and it's waterproof, too. Feels like paper, but when I spilled my coffee on it a few minutes ago, the stain just beaded up and rolled off. You must want these ideas to endure. Is that right, boss? You want us to follow these Maxims forever?" Andrew leaned across the table, causing Max to take his feet off of it and assume a defensive posture.

"Yes, Andrew. I want you and everyone else involved in this campaign to memorize them. Live and breathe them. To do it differently than ever before." He stood and leaned forward until their noses almost touched. "And most of all, I want you to believe that by doing so, we are going to win."

Max was intense. He and the senator had rehearsed the Maxims for years before he died, and in those years, the plan had been formulated to achieve the presidency, with each detail meticulously laid out. As a child, Max was indoctrinated into this mindset, while the senator and Luke Postlewaite worked out each step in a plan that left no room for indecision.

"Then when I follow these rules, I expect that you won't buck me on them, right?" Andrew wasn't backing down, and he wasn't backing off. He had no intention of being a potted plant in this campaign.

"Andrew, when I asked you to sign on for this assignment, I already knew that you were the only person for the job. I needed someone who tells me like it is, not how I want it to be. Besides, I've met your mom, and she would never send me another blueberry pie if I fired you for speaking your mind."

"Good. If I thought you would fire me for speaking my mind or saying something that some interest group took offense to, I'd rather go back to my long and illustrious career as a print journalist," Andrew replied. They laughed at the private joke, knowing that his career prior to joining the Masterson campaign consisted of two weeks on the road reporting about the idiosyncrasies of third-party politicians.

Bill Staffman looked on, stoic and craving his morning cigar, deep in thought about the agenda for the day. As long as Andrew and Max continued this mindless banter, he thought, he wouldn't need to go outside and speak with the ever-present media camped out across from campaign headquarters. He knew he was delaying the inevitable. Like a merchant who unlocks the doors to his shop from the inside, he knew that he was expected to do it promptly each morning. He would unlock the door, shuffle across the short expanse to the podium on the sound stage, and speak to the press. Inevitably, they left the press conference with nothing more than the topic of Max's next sound bite. No news, just the same stuff that everyone else had.

In the early days of reporting the Masterson campaign, there was a nonstop flurry of activity; the daily announcements that Max didn't make speeches, and the continuous loop of high profile commentators predicting the swift demise of Max's campaign. But in the months since, attention shifted to commentary about the message, and the networks would never report that they were becoming obsolete. The attention of the public had moved to the subjects they were interested in learning more about, and they rejected the opinions of the press in favor of formulating their own opinions on matters that were important to them.

•   •   •

TV anchormen don't start at the top. Some of them begin their professional lives as print reporters, and Andrew Fox took the position with the Chicago Tribune as an assignment that would lead him to fame and fortune in the media world. At 23, Andrew had done his obligatory stewardship on the staff of the State News while at Michigan State and worked below poverty level for a weekly in Detroit that reported exclusively about cars and the inner workings of the automotive industry. He had made his way to Chicago to hit the big time, reporting political news from Washington. Or so he thought.

Within a week of settling into his humble office at the Tribune, a full year before the presidential election, Andrew was put on assignment. Since Andrew had, so far, been able to dodge the bonds of matrimony and realizing that prolonged absences had ruined many marriages of media correspondents before him, the bureau chief determined that his new hire qualified for the job. Just the same, the bureau chief treated Andrew with the same disdain he showed other reporters of the same generation.

"They all want to be Walter Cronkite. What's wrong with print? They can't all get their faces plastered all over the big screen!" His new boss was stuck in the past, but he seldom passed up fresh news. Roger Van Harken was accustomed to growling first thing in the morning, followed by coffee, then more growling.

Andrew stood before his new boss with wide eyes. His eyebrows squinched to the point where they became a single brow separated by a wrinkle. He waited for the gravelly voice to finish devastating his long-suffering office assistant, Judy, and inevitably redirect his attention to the new guy standing at attention in front of his huge desk.

Pausing to take another swallow of the second cup of the day, Van Harken focused his steely grey eyes on Andrew. "You haven't been here long, Fox, but I'm sending you out in the field. Carver just quit to take a job doing the news in Minneapolis, of all places. I don't have anyone to handle the third-party candidates, and they're coming out of the woodwork this year. Here is a list of five candidates, their phone numbers, campaign managers, fax numbers… Hell, it's all right here. Just take this, line up interviews, and give me a bio and profile on each one."

Andrew was rapidly getting the feeling that he was sliding into deep water. "Do I go to the candidates or just talk to them by phone?"

"I don't care how you do it. Just get me something printable by Tuesday. That gives you five days. If you need to line up transportation, talk to Judy."

The meeting with the boss had concluded, and the door to his office slammed loudly behind him. Andrew realized he was standing in the hallway staring at the list; five hardy individuals with no more chance of getting elected president than he had. Pasted below the names and numbers were party affiliation and a brief biographical narrative pulled from the Internet. Each candidate had a website that promised to inform the citizenry of their views on important issues, and two of the five appeared to be single issue candidates; those who ran for office to promote their views on their sole interest were looking for one thing, a soap box. Their political lives were over after the primaries, leaving the major candidates to do battle with a heavily fortified and financed incumbent president, Warren Hudson Blythe.

Andrew took the list and began researching the third-party candidates. If he was going to be around these people, he needed more than a few paragraphs and contact numbers. He needed to know what they stood for.

He compiled most of his background information from news feeds and Internet bios. Most of the candidates stood and fell on a single issue. The United States was mired in a prolonged war of occupation in a part of the world that Americans didn't much care about. America could never master Middle Eastern names, and it seemed that every terrorist that died was reported to be the leader, only to be replaced the next day by another nameless terrorist.

The evening news was peppered with casualty statistics and bloody videos of suicide bombing victims. The voting electorate became numb to the gore on TV, and the numbness seemed to spread as the war droned on. Those who didn't vote never cared anyway, and the malaise spread until politicians were more universally disliked than in any other era in the nation's history.

Surprisingly, in spite of growing antiwar sentiment directed at the present administration, a segment of the population was pro-war. This group grew under its charismatic leader, a young tattooed Texan named Foster Gates. Gates was not political, and he never pretended to be. His public life was marred by drunken brawls and a contempt for authority that had put him in jail on a regular basis. He needed his agenda to be fronted by the only person he could find who could stand in front of a group of people and lie convincingly. His handpicked candidate needed to be able to convince the public that the only way to preserve the American way of life is to kill anyone who is not an American.

Samuel Hilton was the anti-gun control candidate, or, at least that is what his website said. His party, the Free America Party, had been affiliated with the Ku Klux Klan in the distant past but in recent years had also aligned itself with opposing the new world order. Hilton talked of returning the country to pre-1960s values, and his campaign was mainly restricted to appearances in white churches throughout the south.

Gates bankrolled the Free America Party with his inheritance from his grandfather's chain of appliance stores and gun manufacturing facilities. At the time of his death in 1978, his grandfather was a multimillionaire, and his fortune was wisely invested in a trust managed by a team of financial advisors who ran the family financial empire like a military operation.

Gates, however, never saw military service. If he had, his warmongering tough talk might have been tempered by the horrors of death caused by the weapons that had created the family fortune. Contracts with the U.S. military to produce state of the art, lightweight field arms fed the family coffers for three generations, and each military conflict spurred another round of contract bidding that always seemed to be won by Gates Arms. But as is the tradition in military service, the rich seldom enlist to serve their country. Gates had chosen Hilton to be the candidate of the Free America Party. There were no caucuses or primaries for the third party candidates. After all, they didn't plan to win the election.

The Green Party placed Tonya Jenkins on the ballot. She attended rallies organized by the main office in Stuttgart, Germany. She was known to make long speeches calling upon Americans to strike out against "the tyranny of industrialized society." The Greens attracted people who, for whatever reason, had not bothered to register to vote. Although her European counterparts had been elected to public office and held minority positions in legislatures in Germany and the Netherlands, the party was perpetually short of money and attracted no major contributions at fundraisers in the United States.

The American Way Party was headed by the Reverend Billy Brooks. Reverend Brooks had a checkered past that often returned to haunt him. Three years prior to announcing his candidacy for president, Billy was accused of spending church funds on two high-class prostitutes, both of whom thought they were the only one he was sleeping with. His wife, Janet, knew of his indiscretions but continued to appear with him in public "for the sake of the children." With her political wife hairdo and a handful of prescription mood enhancers, she attracted the gaze of Billy's supporters, who secretly bet that she would fall asleep before the end of each speech.

When Billy attempted to end his relationship with Bobbi, a stripper he had met in a Wednesday prayer group, she sold her story to the Globe for $100,000. When Janet, a widow he had "counseled" after the death of her husband, discovered the existence of Bobbi, she sold her story to the Enquirer for $200,000, and Billy went on his weekly gospel hour to beg his widespread congregation for forgiveness.

With his wife at his side, he cried and ranted about the influence of the devil, how the devil made him do those awful things, how he had asked God to forgive him, and He had, and how it would be a very Christian act to forgive him just the way God had done. The response of his viewers was to write thousands of checks to his Help the Children foundation and to pray for his redemption.

Reverend Brooks learned from his brush with moral bankruptcy by focusing his audience on the issue of abortion and hitting the talk show circuit to promote his book, The Moral Decline of America. In his metamorphosis, the good reverend made himself rich. He funded his campaign for the presidency with checks from his listeners.

The fourth candidate was a perpetual politician named Forrest Carruthers. After 24 years in the United States Senate, Carruthers retired in the face of the Republican sweep of 1994. When Clinton was reelected, Carruthers was rewarded for his many years of loyal service to his party and took the position of ambassador to Viet Nam. This time, however, Carruthers ran not as a Democrat but as the head of the Reform party. Disenchanted with the decline of Democratic power under a lame duck president and depressed to the point of suicide, Carruthers was, in effect, put out to pasture. After years on antidepressants, Carruthers was revived to the point of caring and returned to the United States as a senior statesman, where he earned a decent living working as a political commentator on any news network that would hire him.

When the executive committee approached him about running for president, Carruthers did not immediately accept. He took the news to his wife, Glenda, and they discussed the strain the campaign would place not on their marriage but on their health. Both had weathered cancer scares, but with new methods of treatment and pharmaceutical advances that were successful in shrinking most tumors, Forrest and Glenda received the reluctant approval of their primary care physician.

Forrest had days when it was hard to get out of bed, but Glenda was a fighter and had stood by her husband throughout their 34-year marriage. She had no tolerance for whining, especially from Forrest. She had even begun dragging him out for occasional evenings of ballroom dancing, an activity that she would soon have little time to enjoy. Campaigns are detours in the course of life, and she knew how grueling a presidential race could be. But if not now, when, and if not now, they might never have the chance again. His decision became hers, too.

•   •   •

The last candidate on Andrew's list had little information beneath his name. The research on Max Masterson was sparse. Age 38. Independent. Never married. Unlimited campaign funding. Does not make speeches or attend fundraisers. A 1-888 number where the party could be reached. No fax number. But Andrew knew more about Max Masterson than the bio revealed. He was a bit of a folk hero to the single men in Andrew's college fraternity. Since his early twenties, Max had been on the annual list of most eligible bachelors. He looked good in a tux, and it seemed that whenever he wore one, he ended up on the society pages with a beautiful woman on his arm. For the mostly insecure and socially inept young men of Phi Gamma Delta, the image of a poised and confident Max Masterson in the company of the women of their dreams earned their admiration.

Yet, Max was more than that. He possessed seemingly unlimited wealth and had access to the most influential business leaders of the 21st century. His intelligence level had never been tested, or if it had, that information had never been disclosed, but he displayed depth of thought and the ability to resolve complex problems. His ideas seemed to originate in his mind alone. He used his sense of humor to entertain, and it appeared that those around him enjoyed his company almost to the point of idol worship.

Max Masterson had no equal in Washington. As the sole heir of a popular former United States senator from Florida, he had access to officials at the highest levels of government. His childhood was spent in tow with his father at social events, and in his journey to adulthood he morphed seamlessly into Washington society. News of his adventures around the world was the buzz that captivated men and women alike, and when the press needed a sound bite from a prominent person on an issue of the day, Max could be counted on for an eloquent quote of thirty seconds or less.

It seemed that whenever Max spoke to the press, his eloquence clearly conveyed his message. He had the ability to simplify the issues to the point where there was only one position on that issue, and he had just come up with it. His dissenters were all being unreasonable—how could a person in his right mind even think that way?

Fox wondered what it would be like to be around Max Masterson the candidate, and he pondered why a guy who had everything would want that lousy job. "It's not for the money or the women or the attention that comes with high office," he thought. "Must be some kind of power trip." For that reason alone, Max was the first candidate Andrew Fox arranged to interview. By reading and viewing the Max bulletins from "E" and People magazine, he managed to construct a timeline of where Max would be over the next two days: both magazines reported that he was going home to relax before an important public announcement, and the only place Max would ever call home was Fairlane.

Chapter Twenty-Eight

It has become a tradition in American politics for the incumbent president to draft a letter to his successor and leave it sealed inside the desk in the Oval Office. The contents of the letter are to be preserved in confidence, not to be disclosed to anyone, despite the concerted efforts of the press to discover their message. The letter, in actuality, is a chain letter that goes back to Washington's time. Each outgoing president has added his message to the one before it on a separate page crowned by the presidential seal. Most of the letters were handwritten, and none of them bore any ill will toward the next occupier of the White House. George Washington started the tradition. The purpose of the letter, also a well kept secret, was to give practical advice to the next president to help him avoid making the same mistakes. Politics were put aside in the interest of imparting wisdom that could only be acquired by holding the highest office in the land.

The best presidents throughout the nation's history heeded the advice of their predecessors. The worst disasters were caused, at least in part, by those who ignored that advice or, worse yet, never broke the seal to read the handwritten messages inside. Thomas Jefferson was the most prolific writer in the succession of presidents. He added 23 pages to the letter and what began as a few paragraphs became a book. For the most part, though, each departing president used words economically. Bill Clinton wrote, "Don't let your vices get the best of you."

The gold-bound book looked historical with its red wax seal awaiting Blythe's curiosity. Although Blythe used the book as a paperweight on the rare occasion that there was something on his desk that required covering during photo sessions, he never cracked the seal, so he never took the advice. If he had, he would have learned the lessons of his predecessors, all copied surreptitiously by The Society at the end of each President's term and taught to the chosen few who would later seek the same office. Blythe's arrogance prevented him from accepting advice from those whom he considered his subordinates. This became problematic when the only person he did not consider to be a subordinate was Warren Hudson Blythe.

Chapter Twenty-Nine

As they walked along the Potomac, Max spoke without reservation. Talking candidly to a reporter is universally considered dangerous for a politician, but he had never been a politician before, and he actually trusted Fox.

"Maybe I shouldn't tell you this, but I'm not like those other guys. I don't give a shit." His pace picked up until Fox had to do a half trot to keep up with him. "They look at being president of the United States as their life's goal. The problem is that they have no idea what to do with the position once they get there. They care more about winning than they do about being the one person in the country who can change it for the good." Max stopped, turned abruptly, and faced Andrew with his most serious gaze. "I'm not a politician."

Andrew didn't know what say, so he just stared. "I just met this guy who's running for president, and he's talking to me like I'm his long lost childhood friend," he thought frantically. "How can I write an article on a political candidate who isn't a politician? They're paying me to report what the politicians are doing to get elected. This guy wants to talk about how he isn't one of them! I have five hours before I hop a plane to some fundraiser in Arkansas, and I'm supposed to post ten thousand words on this one before I move on to the next!"

Max interrupted the young reporter's panicky thought processes to explain. "I don't care if I win. The job sucks. The pay is too low.

Everyone is either for you or against you. Everyone knows your name, and I'm talking the whole flippin' world!" He began walking faster, gesticulating to the night.

Fox began a full trot, struggling to keep close enough to catch his words.

"I'll become the most recognized face on the planet, and I don't care. There's a lot to be said for anonymity. You can go anywhere you want without somebody trying to poke you in the face." He wasn't even breathing heavily. Fit people can talk and exercise effortlessly, and the rest suffer in envy. He stopped short, and Fox almost ran into his back. In front them a large buck, its antlers covered with the soft velvet of spring, leaped from behind a tree and looked directly at them. If they had been four feet closer, they could have touched it.

"I didn't even see him," Max whispered in an excited hiss. "He was so camouflaged that I didn't even see him!" He was as excited at 36 as he was at nine. "If my dad was here, he would have taken his picture and had it on the wall by tomorrow morning." His whispers were soft.

Fox knew enough to remain still. The deer's ears twitched once before it gracefully turned tail and loped over the river bank. The encounter had taken only seconds, but it had the effect of taking their minds off the campaign for a while, moving their conversation from politics to life.

Fox thought about asking him more questions on the list he held in his right hand, but it was getting dark and they were off the clock. It seemed more important that he just keep up and hope that Max would give him something for Sunday's article on the race.

"When I get out of the crowds and into the woods, I become a kid again. I miss those days just sitting in my tree house down here and watching the otters play. When I told my dad that I had seen otters, instead of acting like an adult and telling me that there weren't any otters in the Potomac, he asked me to show him, and I did."

He seemed contemplative, almost melancholy. Maybe it was fatigue from a day enduring the cameras, or maybe it was something more.

"Are there really otters in the Potomac river?"

"You betcha. The pictures my dad took are hanging on the wall of my bedroom. Wanna see?"

He was a kid again.

They ran up the riverbank toward the senator's gated enclosure, swiped the security card at the river entrance concealed by a thick growth of vines, and stepped inside a place few had seen.

The Masterson estate was like a scene from E.M. Forster's "The Other Side of the Hedge," an allegory that focuses on the rat race and utopia and what people aspire to in life. The most visual part of the story focuses on the description of paradise: a lake surrounded by rollingmeadows where happiness is defined by bounty and contentment. In that world, there is no poverty, no sickness, no deprivation. It is a world where beauty represents all that is good. A world where everyone wants to go. Fox was transfixed by the sight of a clear spring-fed lake with a waterfall fed by a babbling brook. Behind it were rolling hills pierced by a red brick road that led to the main house. To the north was a thick old growth forest of maples and oaks, beeches and poplars, and to the south was a flower and vegetable garden that seemed to stretch over a hill into infinity. Clearly, Minuteman Masterson had succeeded in creating his own paradise.

"This explains why Max and the senator were seldom seen in public," Fox thought. "I can report this, but who would believe me? If I don't get a quote from this guy about the campaign, I could be looking for another line of work," he worried privately.

They walked toward a low stone building to the right of the road. Soon they were seated in a small yellow solar powered electric car, which sped silently on its charged batteries past the security cameras, which turned as they moved past.

"Securing utopia must be expensive," pondered Andrew.

Just as they were crossing the stone bridge over the small stream that led from the lake to the Potomac, Max turned to Fox and gazed at him with his piercing green eyes.

"How much do they pay you at that job at the paper?"

"Not nearly enough."

"Because the work sucks or because you're feeling unappreciated?"

"It's mostly the fact that I don't know what I'm doing, and they're always pushing me for something from you that makes news. If the other papers pick it up or if the broadcast media gets hold of it, then I'm golden. If another day goes by and I don't give them something they can use for a headline, then I'll probably be fired."

Max was silent as they moved up the road toward the grand house. Fox considered asking him another political question but decided that it was time to sit and wait.

"How would you like to work for me? I could use a press secretary, and even if I don't become president, it will look good on your resume."

Fox was speechless.

"Well?"

"How much is the pay?"

"Not nearly enough."

"Then why should I take it?

"Did you ever read about a man named Napoleon Hill?"

"No. Who was he?"

"Back in the early 1900s, he was a reporter who went to visit Andrew Carnegie, who at that time was the richest man in the world. Carnegie told him that he wanted Hill to work thirty years for no pay, to develop a philosophy of wealth, and he gave young Napoleon sixty seconds to make up his mind."

"What did he do?"

"He took the job."

Max turned off the ignition and stepped out of the car, and without another word, the front door of the house opened. He walked through the open door and was gone.

Fox sat in the leather bucket seat. He made no effort to get out, and even if he had, he seriously doubted whether he would have succeeded. His hands and feet were tingling. He felt like he was going to pass out.

He had a deep sense that the decision he was about to make was going to be the momentous decision of his life. He stared at the dials on the dashboard. Behind him, the sun was beginning to set over the hill, and everything began to glow the yellow orange of dusk. The shadows lengthened until the car was completely engulfed by the shadow cast from the house. Still, he had to think. He needed to make the right decision, or face failure.

Chapter Thirty

Fox sat long enough for the mosquitoes to begin buzzing in his ears. When they started to suck blood, he finally pulled himself from the car. The sun had just set behind the hill, and the security lights lit the courtyard in response to his movement toward the house. It seemed like hours since Max had entered the house, but the door remained open. Down a long hall, he saw light in the distance.

The marble floor rang with the sound of his footsteps, echoing in a harsh tapping that was magnified by the hard surface. He entered a large anteroom, decorated with civil war frescoes of battles between blue and gray clad soldiers. It was a demonstration of art that seemed strangely familiar, like something he had seen as a kid on his first trip to the Capitol. Ahead, he heard the voices of men speaking loudly, the words unclear, and he walked slowly toward the sound.

In a large room to his right, the bass sound emanated like the soundtrack in a movie theater when the door opened. He entered a mahogany study lined with thousands of books and saw Max sitting in a large brown leather chair at the center of the room, a bowl of popcorn in his lap and a frosted bottle of beer to his side. He was staring at a large flat screen TV that was suspended from the ceiling against the far wall. The Nixon/Kennedy debate was playing in black and white, and Nixon's booming voice seemed to fill the room.

"I'm glad to see that you could make it. I ordered dinner. I hope you don't mind leftovers. I haven't been home much, and most of the staff has already left for the day," Max said, not taking his eyes from the television.

"How long was I out there?"

"Long enough to make up your mind, I hope."

He hesitated. It was time to surrender his mind to his mouth and say what he was thinking without worrying about the consequences of his actions. It was a time to be bold. He could sweep up the mess later.

"I'll take the job as long as you don't call me Napoleon."

"Good. We start in the morning."

"Wait! You haven't told me what I'll be doing."

"That's right." The candidate rose and quickly exited, leaving Andrew to witness the event that prevented Richard Nixon, the front-runner, from beating Kennedy and becoming the 35th president of the United States.

Chapter Thirty-One

"The path to greatness is not lined with roses. More like claymore mines," thought Fox.

He looked in the mirror, black circles under his eyes from stress and too much time on the road. He hadn't called to resign from his reporter's job yet. "Better to wait until I determine if he's a lunatic," he thought. He had barely finished shaving when Max burst into the room with a legal pad full of notes.

"I need you to read this," Max said enthusiastically.

Fox sat down on the bed and grabbed the pad from his tanned fingers. The problem was that Max's scribbles were illegible, and Fox hadn't seen coffee, much less had any to drink yet since it was only 6:00 a.m.

"I'll read it to you." Max took the pad from him. He hadn't bothered to put on a shirt, and his hair was wet like he had been swimming already. His body was buff from years of regular exercise, although he never bothered to adhere to a routine or weigh himself like most men his age. His fitness and sexuality appeared weightless. When he was out on the trail, women lined up for miles to be in his presence for no more than a moment in time, and he was oblivious to his effect on them. He didn't know that he was already adorning the walls of countless high school girls, and their mothers spent extra time cleaning their rooms just to peek at his pictures.

"He has the female vote locked up," thought Fox.

"I had this revelation in the middle of the night, and I'm really stoked about it."

Fox hadn't heard the use of the word "stoked" since he had interviewed a candidate from southern California who had bolted from the Schwarzenegger administration to become a winemaker, but somehow the word seemed appropriate when it came from Max's mouth.

"The Masterson campaign announced this morning that it has hired political consultant Andrew Fox to manage public relations," read Max. "Mr. Fox is a well-respected analyst who has gained recognition and expertise in third party campaigns. His experience is much-welcomed by staffers in the Masterson camp."

"Forgive me for asking, but who are these staffers? As far as I can tell, you have a couple of close friends who tell you that it's crazy to run for president, and some old guy who was a friend of your father who treats you like a son."

Max sat up straight, squared his considerable shoulders, and set his gaze two feet from Fox's face. His green eyes seemed to pierce through to his brain, and the last thing Fox would do was divert his gaze. He was hypnotized.

"The first rule I have to teach you is this. The perception of reality is always more important than reality itself."

"But aren't you deceiving people into believing that you have this huge staff of advisors who are guiding you through this campaign and that I'm a political expert with a lifetime of experience?"

"The perception of reality, young assistant. That's your reality created by my words. I never said any of those things."

"But I don't have any experience at all. You just hired me, and I don't even know what you want me to do. Now I'm being promoted as some kind of guru who is going to make you president."

"So, what are the job requirements of gurus?"

Chapter Thirty-Two

He had done it for as long as he could talk. Each night, when the tumult of the day died down, he composed a letter to his father. Although the senator passed away at the age of 86, Max still felt the need to communicate with him. To him, he wasn't really gone but lived on in the memories and the legacy of bountiful life he had left behind.

The letters were like entries in a diary, but Max wasn't communicating with a book. He felt inside that the senator could still hear him share thoughts that were important and, subliminally, his father could speak to him. In his mind, Senator John Masterson was alive. He spoke to Max in whispers that only he could hear.

Ordering the computer to attention as he walked into the house, he began to dictate. The words appeared on the screen, continuing the diary from the day before.

"Dear Dad,

I had a great day. I announced my candidacy on the steps of the Jefferson Memorial, and I kept it short. That seemed to please everyone who watched me on the news, but it really ticked off that reporter I don't like. If I knew he was going to be so upset, I would have scheduled it earlier and got him out of bed in the middle of the night." He chuckled at the memory of Scuperman driving up with wet hair, muttering, and ordering his staff around.

"I'm really nervous about this. You had a big staff who arranged all of your public appearances, but I've been making the calls myself.

I have your list of people I can trust, and I think Bill Staffman would be willing to help me out. I need to stop calling him Uncle Bill, though. He still looks at me as your orphan baby boy, and I doubt if he thinks I can beat anyone the way I intend to run. But he has been working on a list of people who might be interested in working on the campaign. Luke has been giving me a lot of advice lately, and yesterday, he and I spent about an hour going over the plan."

He ran into the kitchen to retrieve a large yellow bowl of popcorn and a beer, and continued without missing a beat when he returned. "I watched your flash on politics yesterday. I like the idea of not doing anything the way the other candidates do. You know I'm not much for sitting around listening to those blowhards rambling on and on about things. Every time you dragged me over to the Capitol to sit in those hearings and when we watched the candidates debating, I wanted to run out of the room. In fact, I remember doing just that a few times." He smiled at the memory of the senator chasing him into Senator Dole's office only to find him under a couch petting her dog, Leader. It took two legislative aides and the bribe of ice cream to extract him from under the couch, and he sat on Elizabeth Dole's lap while the ice cream was delivered to her office. She didn't seem to mind the interruption by a six-year-old boy, and it was hours before he was ready to leave for home.

He returned to the dictation. "…and I don't see much use for preaching to the choir at conventions when the voters aren't even turning out for events. I can get my message out my own way." He settled back in the plush leather recliner and reached for the yellow popcorn bowl. Chewing, he reviewed his words and directed the computer to display the news reports that mentioned his name.

"Max Masterson is for real. He has the looks and the pedigree, and he will make a credible run at the presidency. If he can just get the attention of the voters and convince them he is a legitimate candidate, we may just have the most lively race in recent history," reported ABC News.

"This whole campaign is a farce. It appears that Mr. Masterson is running for president with no staff and no funding other than the considerable fortune inherited from his father, former Senator John "Minuteman" Masterson. As we have seen in the past with other third party candidates, he is probably running on a single issue, if we could only determine what that issue is. I expect that Max Masterson will drop out of this race before the first vote is cast in the primaries when the voters fail to take him seriously. I, for one, am opposed to the idea that a candidate can run on good looks and sex appeal. What are we turning into, a nation run by image makers?" Greg Scuperman had recovered from their first encounter enough to seek the blood of his latest victim.

Max switched to Fox News and then to CNN, searching for interviews of people on the street. Fox was reporting that polls gave him an initial ranking of 23% among voters in each party, and over 70% among Independents. Based upon what he had seen in previous elections, he had no use for polls. They weren't accurate and were mostly misleading. He didn't trust them and was wary of their usefulness in gauging the effect his unorthodox strategies had on the voters. Polls could sway an electorate that believed the result had already been determined. It could discourage them from voting, and it might create a herd effect by changing the minds of voters who assumed they were voting for the eventual winner.

He moved to CNBC, where his morning announcement ran without commentary, and then to Worldview, where he could compile the information he wanted while discarding the rest.

Instructing Worldview to present only those news clips of people on the street that contained comments using "Max Masterson," he filtered out what he didn't want to hear, and obtained about 45 minutes of relevant material.

"I thought he looked good. I mean, he always looks good, but this morning, he looked really good," said a young woman in her early twenties, her voice shaking. "I liked what he had to say about hope and the future, too." She proceeded to repeat his entire sound bite almost verbatim.

The next comment was from an older woman with white hair. He could imagine that she had been strikingly beautiful in her younger days, and her gray eyes were hawk like in their intensity. As the camera zoomed in, her eyes grew larger, and as it panned back, she commented. "He spoke to me. I believe him when he says he will make things better. I'm tired of those old men telling us anything to get elected, and then they just run off to Washington and the next thing you know, they're cheating on their wives." She showed the pain of her own experience in her facial expression, as she went on. "I'd rather have a cutie like him in the White House than that old fart I voted for last time."

The camera quickly backed away to the next pedestrian, a man in his late forties. "You can't tell me that we should keep doing things the way we have always done in this country and expect a different result every time. I'm ready to try something new. That Masterson fella said he has fresh ideas. I'll take a guy with fresh ideas over one who's fresh out of ideas any time," he offered. Max made a mental note to use that one as a campaign slogan.

On the BBC World Network, the interviews were with Brits and the French, who have been known to dislike American politicians and speak their minds. Max was mildly surprised to hear that his little announcement had received worldwide attention, but he was more interested in the apparent intensity of their scrutiny. Outside of a pub in London, it was late evening when the interviewer caught up with a member of the House of Lords and his entourage, who had obviously been celebrating after a day running the Empire. "I thought he looked a lot like that bloke from Manchester United who head-butted the official in the World Cup," expounded Lord Rodney Witherington. As he spoke, his shapely young assistant approached from the rear and demurely placed her lips next to his right ear, whispering something that caused Witherington to blink hard and swallow. He continued, as if he meant to say that a candidate for president of the United States looked like a rogue soccer player.

"I saw his announcement this morning, and I must say that your young man has the full support of the Commonwealth in the furtherance of his presidential aspirations. We look forward to years of cooperation between his administration and the monarchy."

The assistant whispered again, this time in his left ear. He sagged. "When he is actually elected, of course." His two male assistants grabbed an elbow and stuffed him in the back seat of a waiting cab. As the door closed, a chorus of "God Save the Queen" trailed out of the closing window.

Max resumed his daily narrative. "Dad, you know how this is supposed to go. I agree with your thoughts that people distrust politicians. In fact, the whole time I was growing up, whenever you took me to those political events, they'd pick me up and pinch my cheek and look for the nearest camera for a photo opportunity. I can't stand the idea of having to deal with those yahoos every day of my life."

He walked to the large French doors that opened onto the walled garden behind the mansion. Stripping off his suit, he slid into the pool's grotto and activated the jets that created a vortex of bubbles in the blue water. Overhead, the stars shone brightly in the clear night sky. He reflected on his day, starting at 4:00 a.m. and continuing nonstop until he just ground to a halt. He wondered whether he could maintain the pace of a political race and pondered why he was doing it in the first place.

Chapter Thirty-Three

The Democratic and Republican parties have dominated American politics since the mid-1800s. With the exception of a few popular but disgruntled party regulars who ran on a third party ticket to make a point, the idea of a third party candidate advancing beyond the primaries bordered on delusional. But run they did, and with all of the enthusiasm of the front-runners. There is something honorable and uniquely American for those without a prayer of winning not only to try, but to be included alongside the leaders and have their voices to be heard.

Warren Blythe's party had no need to oust the previous administration from office. They accomplished that on their own, without any help. For the four years that they occupied the White House, public opinion polls sank to new lows. Inflation was high and so were interest rates. The housing market became stagnant. Nobody was buying, and in the unlikely event that a prospective purchaser had the wherewithal to come up with a down payment, the banks were crawling out of the mortgage business. The war in the Middle East was a quagmire of occupation in Iraq, Iran, Turkey, Pakistan, and Afghanistan. Terrorist activity in those nations and throughout the Middle East threatened the Saudi royal family and the Pakistani government, which the United States had vowed to protect.

Blythe ran on the promise of fixing everything that was wrong with government. He chose as vice president Arkansas Governor Justin Case, and they packaged themselves as outsiders who were going to "go in there and fix Washington from the ground up." Within days of taking office, the new administration had broken six of their major campaign promises, and Blythe began a misinformation campaign designed to convince the American people that all of those policies had already been in place, and it was up to Congress to fix them. After four years in Washington, the Blythe administration was mired in a malaise of inaction. Worse than life inside the beltway, though, was the utter paralysis felt by the rest of the country.

Chapter Thirty-Four

There will never be a pundit who can accurately predict what will happen when a powerful group of influence peddlers spends tons of money promoting their public face to promote their goals. That's really what big-time politics is all about. We spend lots of money to put our person in the highest office in the land so that our ideals are the ideals of the nation.

In this race, the pundits were convinced by the polls before the debate that the incumbent was never going to be challenged in a big way, and that the president had a secure seat for his second term. When an incumbent seeks a second term, he runs on experience, a quality which he holds uniquely. The only other legitimate claims to experience are held by former presidents, although mayors, governors, and business leaders try to hang that tag on themselves as well. But as Ronald Reagan astutely observed, the reality is that the best leaders are not found in government or private industry would lure them away.

Max sat with Luke Postlewaite in the comfort of the den, but Luke wasn't seated for long. The lesson had been going for twenty minutes, and when Luke was in professorial mode, he paced like a man possessed by demons. He raved as he paced. "You can't just run for president. There are certain prerequisites. First of all, you need to be at least 35 years old. That's the reason you can run this time around, my boy."

Postlewaite strode toward the massive bookcase that occupied every inch of one wall of the den. Although most libraries had been reduced to a small personal database that was accessible electronically from any location, the senator had chosen hardcover books to provide him with wisdom that was untraceable. Pulling a gilded copy of the United States Constitution from its confines, he flipped immediately to Article Two. "The Founding Fathers decided that once a man becomes old, he becomes wise, and back then, most people died by the time they were forty. Two hundred and fifty years ago, you were an old man."

Max chuckled and quickly became serious again as he tried to place his mind in the harsh world occupied by ancestors who were constantly confronted with predators, disease, and war.

"Read the rules, Max. They have been the same for generations. We haven't fiddled with the Constitution since the Electoral College was abolished, and the popular vote is the only reason people like you and Scarlett Conroy have any chance of getting elected president."

"Luke, what does this have to do with me becoming president? I appreciate the history lesson, but I have to get to the office to go over that sound bite that Andrew and Bill have been working on, and…"

Postlewaite glared at Max, his bushy white eyebrows narrowed over piercing grey eyes. Max knew enough to stop talking and start listening.

"Next, you must be a natural-born American." Postlewaite was trying to make a point, and his candidate was going to heed his words if he had to strap him into his chair. "Again, the Founding Fathers didn't want some foreigner coming to this country and taking over. The danger you face today, Max, is that our enemies don't have to set foot on American soil to harm us. All they need to do is tinker with our economy, make us dependent on them, and then pull the plug. We are in a state of constant war to preserve the American way of life," he declared in a shaky baritone.

Max stroked his chin, realizing that the pause in his lesson would be brief.

When Postlewaite was convinced he had covered the subject, he moved on. "The last trait of essence to become the most powerful politician in the world is the ability to persuade. This quality is the most important, and without it, a candidate can be too rich, oh so American, old enough, and still lose the election. The president of the United States must be able to stand in front of any group of voters and convince them."

Max absorbed the words and pondered their meaning. Luke instinctively knew when to talk and when to wait. If he moved on before Max signified he understood, the point of the message would be lost. Finally, Max nodded. "It is irrelevant what your political platform is or whether you actually believe the rhetoric generated by your campaign advisors. You are the spokesperson, the mouthpiece, the person who engenders trust. Americans need to believe in the image of the one they choose to lead."

Postlewaite was spry for his age. Jumping up from his chair, he strode confidently toward the senator's liquor cabinet, confident that his student was reaching the end of his studies. Extracting his favorite brandy from its reserved location, he deftly mixed himself a drink as he had done hundreds of times before. He took a long sip and continued. "There is a fifth trait that defies logic. It's petty and never discussed openly by your handlers, but in private, they obsess about it. It's 'The Look.' A presidential candidate must look like a president. Take presidential debates for example; the advance team spends weeks before the debate negotiating the height of the podium, the temperature of the room, when the candidates shake hands, what camera angles are most flattering to the candidate's image, and the color of the lights that illuminate their faces during the broadcast. Over time, that look has changed. And Max," he concluded, "you have 'The Look.'"

Chapter Thirty-Five

The view from the Oval Office was magnificent. As many times as he had seen Washington from his pillar of power, Blythe never grew complacent about what that view symbolized. From the safety of the security-enhanced Plexiglas front window, he could look across the tidal basin, past the Washington Monument, and see the distant profile of Thomas Jefferson seated in the Jefferson Memorial. Blythe had survived most of his first term intact, and despite last year's "Bimbo attacks" by his political adversaries, the President was secure… at least for the foreseeable future. The public opinion polls gave him a 41% rating, not as good as his rating before the latest blow up in the Middle East, but the best since his infidelities became the subject du jour for the press to focus on.

When the scandal became public, he took the advice of his closest aides and went on the attack, forcing his opponents to acknowledge that they, too, had secrets to hide. The Senate minority leader was sent a dossier on the sex lives of five Ways and Means Committee members, three from the Judiciary Committee, and two from Finance. Within days, his opposition dissolved. The press turned its attention to abortion, education, and health care reform. "If my marriage hasn't hit rock bottom because of the disclosures, certainly the American people will ignore them in the next election," he thought.

Sitting before the president were Presidential Advisor Ted Schoolcraft, Party Chairman Richard Partiman, and White House

Chief of Staff Waylon Cheevers. As the President blew cigar smoke against the armored glass of the oval office, Schoolcraft poured bourbon from a cut glass decanter that had occupied the oval office since Grant's administration. "I never stop thinking that Ol' U.S. poured his drinks from the same bottle. Things are more complicated now." Schoolcraft spoke to nobody in particular, and nobody responded. Regardless, he kept talking. "We need to look like it's a done deal. I don't want to spend two seconds on these guys. You just need to sit back and let them chew on each other until after the primaries, then just act presidential. You can coast through this preliminary campaign on your approval ratings, and then we'll see how you look after they get done bashing each other. We can focus on the frontrunners and get ready to attack with what we have on them after we know who we're dealing with."

Partiman took the pause as his opportunity to float his opinion. "I get nervous when we don't act proactively. We have more money in our campaign chest than anyone out there, and we need to start doing some cozy ads that get people to warm up to you, Mr. President."

Blythe ignored the advice of his party chairman and continued to gaze at the pink spring display of the cherry trees lining Pennsylvania Avenue. His mind was never really in the room, absorbed in the thought that his legacy would be intact for another four years. He turned and addressed his three advisors. "I want this thing to go off without a hitch. From what I've seen, my competition looks like they were recruited from clown college, and I want to keep it that way. Brief me."

They took his request as a call to attention, and they all stood. These men were referred to by the press as the president's spin doctors. They were his most trusted advisors and had direct access not only to the Oval Office, but to the offices of corporate heads and leaders throughout the world as well. The topic for discussion was the reelection campaign of Warren Hudson Blythe, President of the United States, and it was, in their minds, their sole purpose in life.

Partiman had just finished informing the group that the frontrunner, Representative Bob Cunningham of Massachusetts, had raised ten million dollars in contributions, making his party's presence felt months before the primaries. In his attack ads on the president, Cunningham was the first to call for debates, and his handlers were turning up the heat.

Schoolcraft was the first to express his opinion. "Mr. President, you cannot afford to stand head to head with Cunningham in a public forum. To do so at this point would validate his candidacy and make him a sure thing for his party's nomination. There are other candidates out there in his own party who can debate with him until they run out of things to say, but I think that you should stand behind the Presidential Seal and watch them duke it out." He sat down and took another sip, savoring the smoothness of the sour mash.

Blythe turned, directing his gaze over the heads of his advisors. "I can't just sit here and do nothing. That may have worked for Nixon the second time around, but look at what happened to him." Even though he wasn't quite making sense, he was the president, and nobody, especially those in the room, had the balls to correct or contradict him. "I'll be damned if I'm going to sit in the White House and let the challengers take pot shots at me."

Walsh waited for a pause in the conversation. When it came, he injected his views. "Sir, the only way you are going to get through this election and stay in office is to attack. If you don't get out there and mix it up with the opposition, every sound bite, every news clip, every editorial will be filled with their faces, their words, their voices…"

The president interrupted. "How the hell do I face off with Cunningham without strengthening his shot at the presidency? If I open my mouth too soon, he might rocket to the top in the polls, and I'll have a real battle on my hands."

Seconds turned into minutes. Schoolcraft broke the silence by rising out of his chair. As he poured yet another bourbon, he spoke quietly. "I may just be paranoid, but if you're going to debate, you may as well debate every lunatic who is running for president. Then, it'll be you against them. From what I've heard, you can make a great showing by letting them pick each other off. We can prescreen all the questions and structure the debate so that nobody gets an opportunity to address you directly. Remember Clinton, Perot and Bush 1? Clinton came out of it looking presidential, Perot got his licks in on the Republicans, and Bush tired himself out by trying too hard. We can do a series of debates after the primaries, each limited to subjects we decide to debate, and until then you can issue a statement that you will attend to the pressing issues of your administration until your opposition is defined by the voters."

"That's what we'll do. It'll look like a three ring circus, but at least I'll be able to campaign again. Who is my competition, anyway?"

Chapter Thirty-Six

"Where did Max run off to? Just when I need him to review the rules for the debate, he disappears... again!" Luke Postlewaite was back from his Washington visit and feeling the pressures of preparing Max for the biggest event of the campaign. Since his return, he had been testy with everyone, especially Max. He and Bill Staffman had been his debate coaches and close advisors for as long as he had entertained the idea of running, and they zealously guarded Max's reputation while continuously trying to monitor his state of mind.

There was a pervasive feeling among those who spent time around him that their candidate was having a minor meltdown. He was dealing with the constant pressure of keeping his best side public while concealing his private life from the microscopic scrutiny of the press. To some, he seemed oblivious. He didn't spend any time, it seemed, worrying about how people would view the sex life of a single man. His theory was that only married men had to worry about indiscretions with the opposite sex, and he could announce that he was looking for a wife but hadn't found the perfect woman. Forget reality TV. This was real life.

Max had been following his hormones, but Postlewaite saw this as something that could gain or lose his candidate millions of votes. Women who had never voted, the ones who disdained politics as the boring pursuit of the bland and forgettable, were showing a massive interest in this man. He was movie star handsome. He glowed with sex appeal. He was single, and he was running for president.

Most of his adult life, and part of his adolescent one, were spent in the solitary pursuit of thrills. He never had to worry about holding a job or serving a tour of duty in the armed forces. The senator had seen to that. Those essential activities were meant for others. It was his single-minded goal, his job, to run for president, and he couldn't be delayed or distracted from what he had been taught was his life's purpose. Max was a president in training, if the truth be told, and he was comfortable with that label. After all, he had never done anything else.

By contrast, Postlewaite and Staffman were a seething bundle of nerves. They had worked on dozens of major campaigns and stuck with the candidates who got elected, moving away from those who chose to run but failed to win. In politics, the memory of the electorate is shorter than the memory of their supporters, but not by much. One consistent thread, though, were the lists of contributors that seemed to grow by the minute. A campaign would end, the winner would take office, and the lists would survive until the next election, when they would be pulled out of hibernation and used to fill the coffers once again.

Chapter Thirty-Seven

Every Thursday night for the past six years, Bob, Phil, and Jerry met at Jesse's Tavern, a sports bar and male refuge near the interstate. Occasionally, a woman dropped in, usually by accident or at the request of an unsuitable date. None of them found reason to visit a second time. Wives avoided the place, knowing that their husbands escaped to Jesse's to get away from them and the kids for a few hours. If an emergency arose while the men were out, it would have to wait until the trio of political junkies had finished their weekly ritual. Jesse's phone number was listed on the message pad near the ancient wall phone next to the ladies' room, but the regulars could not recall it being used. Nothing ever seemed serious enough to disturb them, and the men met each week to take up where they left off the week before.

As most sports fans know, Thursday is not a typical sports viewing night. Thursday at Jesse's was reserved for politics, or as Jerry liked to call it, Current Affairs. The battles of the sports world's overpaid and over-glorified gladiators are fought on the weekend, and Bob, Phil, and Jerry watched those contests in their high definition 3-D from the comfort of their own homes. Thursday was their night away from home, and Jesse's Pub was their gathering place. Tonight, as always, they had the place all to themselves. The three men chose Thursday to tune in to WorldWeek, an interactive political program that polled the audience on issues ranging from abortion to assassination, the

environment to genetic engineering, and any topic that was reported
in the media during the prior week. These guys were as addicted to the
trivia of the week as to the latest NFL rankings. To them, a presidential
race was just another playoff, with the players wearing neckties.

Bob, Phil, and Jerry had direct access to every bit of information
that the Internet could provide. Much of what the candidates had
posted on the issues came from their websites, but they could take it all
in through Worldview. All of the information posted on the Internet
was available 24/7. The days of hunting for a candidate's position on an
issue were a part of the dust of history. All a viewer needed to do was
ask a question, and the micro-processors of the Worldview interactive
program looked for it, found it, and made it available. No typing of
words. No searching YouTube for video clips. No hunting for Web
pages or e-mail addresses. If you wanted it, it came to you, tailored to
your needs and interests.

Information was filtered and sorted according to prior viewing
habits, and the computer knew you. There was no possibility of fraud.
A scanner viewed your cornea, cross-referenced it against data on file,
monitored your vital signs, blood type and chemistry, fingerprints,
body type, and dozens of other identity verification indicators. The
audience for WorldWeek had grown exponentially. What began as a
pilot program on C-Span, telecast to a limited audience, became a
standard component as interactive TV became popular. When the
conversion to 3-D digital programming became standard technology
in households throughout the world, a true "electronic town hall"
was created.

Each week, the number of viewers grew until WorldWeek was the
number one program in its time slot, outranking programs on 500
other channels. The topic of the evening was chosen interactively by
the viewers from a list of ten topics that appeared on the screen. As the
viewers voted, the total score was listed alongside the choices. While
the choices were displayed, each viewer could change the previous vote
until the time to choose had elapsed. The votes were entered on a wrist

pad worn by most adults in America; the device was a timekeeper, computer with wireless modem, and expanded Internet system. Remote programming by the Internet provider was performed while the wrist pad's owner slept.

The device was user specific. A project begun by IBM in 2010 that transferred information from one user to the other with the shake of a hand had morphed from the replacement for the business card into a full service personal assistant with access to unlimited information. In addition, the registered voter was able to cast votes from any location, and as soon as the polls opened in November, the three political junkies intended to get their choice counted.

Like many voters, Bob, Phil, and Jerry had definite opinions about the candidates in the current race for president, but each had a specific form of amnesia about the previous one. If they could recall who they voted for, they couldn't recall the reasons why they chose one over the other. The issues that seemed so crucial four years before were lost in time, and the current occupants of the White House were viewed like tenants who had moved into the building in the middle of the night and refused to leave.

Chapter Thirty-Eight

The Masterson campaign was forced to make unexpected adjustments in staff as a result of an intensified focus by the media. The clamor for public appearances by Max Masterson came in by e-mail and phone. Fox was forced to hire staffers by the dozens just to keep up with the demand. Once the messages were received, they proceeded to the screening room, where higher level staffers, some with a full two days' experience, began to sort out high profile public appearances from run-of-the-mill, easy to avoid demands.

When Max entered the room, he was immediately besieged by his trusted assistants, all talking at once. He backed toward the corner, raised his arms, and demanded silence. As if rehearsed, everyone sat down and waited for him to speak.

"I don't do speeches."

There was silence, as if they had heard the words, but in a language they failed to understand. They silently pondered what they had heard, a politician who doesn't do speeches. Each of them began to think that their decision to work for Max was a brief lapse in judgment and began to consider all of the job possibilities that they had passed up to join the campaign.

"I could have had that job working for Senator Newman if he hadn't resigned after the men's room incident," thought Sara.

"Mom could probably use me for a while back on the farm since dad got sick," thought Andrew Fox.

"I coulda been a stand-up comedian," mused Phillip Touya, a red haired new hire from somewhere out west.

As the seconds turned into minutes, the impact of Max's words turned into shocked acceptance. When he realized that the full impact was being taken in like the first half of a joke, Max made things worse by continuing to outline his strategy, which was sounding more like his philosophy of life.

"I don't do public appearances, either."

"I don't do campaign lunches or dinners."

"I have no patience for people who talk too long and neither do the voters."

"I have prepared some rules for all of us to follow. If you don't adhere to them, you will be asked to go home," he added in his most serious tone. He passed out 5x7 cards which each staff member was to carry and memorize. Members of Max's inner circle received a gold-embossed card with additional, private themes to be reviewed only in private and never in the vicinity of the press. The press would be provided a revised set of "Maxims" when the time was right and only if their existence was somehow leaked or inadvertently revealed. He wanted to avoid the tendency of reporters to pick apart rules for inconsistency and report on any "violations," thereby creating news where none existed. The simple messages were to be followed without contradiction. The card was simple:

No speeches.
No fund-raising events.
No messages over two minutes long.
If you bore the listener, they can't hear you.
Keep each message simple.
Every statement is a sound bite.
The message is available 24/7.
It is better to say nothing than to say to say something stupid.
It is better to confess you don't know than to lie about it.
The message is more important than the image.

The image is more important than the candidate.
Don't quote a statistic unless you can back it up with facts.
Educate people before asking them to decide an issue.
American interests must prevail over world interests.
Never lie to promote the interests of the minority.
Always present an idea in a positive way.
If you can't commit to an idea, don't try to sell it.
The perception of reality is more important than reality.
It's not what you say. It's how you say it.

The thirty pairs of eyes reviewed the card then looked at Max. He sat expressionless, his eyes scanning the room for dissent. After a long silence, a small woman, fresh out of college, spoke up from the back of the room. "But I thought you were running for president."

The eyes shifted from him to her and back again. No one knew what would happen next, so they stayed silent, waiting. Max stood up so that everyone in his line of sight looked up at him. He didn't convey anger by his expression. It was more of a kind, determined look. The silence stretched much longer than was comfortable. He stared at the girl, his eyes narrowing slightly, but never betraying his thoughts. She began to back away, a frightened look spreading across her face. Then he smiled. She stopped, finding approval of her words, but not comprehending why.

The young staffers erupted in spontaneous laughter, and he knew they were on their way. It was no longer Max against the world. It was a movement.

"As you can tell, this is not your usual campaign," continued Max. "And there's one more thing. I'm not a politician. I have never held public office, and I have no intention of running for president in the usual way. If it isn't fun, we will make it fun. If the way they have always done it is not the best way or we can't find the benefit of it, we figure out a better way."

Sara interrupted again. It foretold the strength of her personality, and although most of her friends found her brilliantly lively, they also found her to be tactless and confrontational at times. "But Max, if you're not a politician, what do we tell them you are? They will ask, and we have to be ready for that."

"Tell them I'm new and different. And tell them I'm not a politician, I'm just a man who's running for president." The excitement and danger of this plan, to be different from every political campaign ever run, had them fascinated with possibilities, and that was how he wanted it. Their youth and enthusiasm was the engine that would drive his campaign.

Chapter Thirty-Nine

"Max you have got to do this for me!" Andrew Fox was apoplectic.

For days on the road, he had been drafting sound bites on every important issue in the campaign, and he was attempting to persuade Max to rehearse them. Max would read them once, shrug his shoulders as if bored, and attempt to deter Andrew from his mission. At every opportunity, Max changed the subject and drew Andrew into conversation, all to end the rehearsal. Andrew didn't realize that Max, having already written and revised each subject, had only to read the final version once and it was memorized. He was done learning.

"I don't care if you think you have it all in your head. You can't get your message out unless you tell it." Andrew was easing into the most difficult part of the encounter. He had to tell Max that he had arranged for a small test interview to be held in D.C., and he knew that Max would complain mightily about it.

"Andrew, it doesn't take a genius to stand in front of a group of strangers and tell them that you are in favor of life, you think everyone is entitled to be healthy, or that you are against crime. I want to get out there and tell them that everything's going to be better than it was, that we need to decide what is the best way to resolve problems, and that most of what politicians talk about, they have no power to change anyway," Max barked back.

"This time is probably as good as any," thought Andrew. "Max, this afternoon, a dozen members of the press are going to interview you, and I want you to use it as an opportunity to get all of these sound bites out there for people to talk about."

Max responded as predicted. He feigned a heart attack and dropped to his knees.

"My own press secretary has stopped running interference for me and has thrown me to the snarling press! I can't trust any of my minions to protect me!" He lay on his back and signaled that he had been stabbed in the chest with a sword. He lay in this pose for more than a minute as Andrew kept up the pressure.

"Listen, I'm just trying to get you to do something for once that isn't out of the ordinary. Go give them a damn interview! It won't hurt you to go out there and do something that has been done before!"

Max moaned, as if he had suddenly recovered from his life-threatening injury, and bounced to his feet. He hovered inches from his assistant's face. "Ordinary is boring! Ordinary doesn't set me apart. It's a waste of time!"

His voice was raised, and Andrew had no idea whether he would bolt from the room or show up as arranged.

Chapter Forty

He was an unknown, and even though his father was one of the most beloved and idolized politicians of the 20th century, he, the individual, was a newbie.

Max sat in the press room of the Capitol City Press Club with a small group of reporters from small town newspapers with enough money in their budgets to send a person to Washington, D.C. This was a big deal to the dozen or so who had come, and, for most, it was their first trip to see the nation's political core. Dressed in their best suits, feet blistered from walking to see the sights, they clustered in folding chairs before this new, low—profile, third party candidate. They were eager to bring home a scoop that would entertain their readers, and would give them a twenty-four hour cycle of notoriety in their hometown. The interview began as a simple list of basic questions, but it soon grew into something none of them anticipated.

"Max, why are you running?"

"Why does anyone run?" he responded.

"How do you expect to win? You have no experience in politics, and you're up against a president who is so high in the polls that he's invincible."

"Well, you can't always trust those pollsters. I figure that by the time people actually get down to voting, there won't be much to choose from," he smiled.

"How do you set yourself apart from the rest of the candidates?"

"I don't really do that. They're doing a good job at setting themselves apart from me." He smiled again.

"I tried to find some of your political speeches to view before I came here today, and I couldn't find anything…" The balding, overweight young man in the front row leaned forward and a stack of note paper with illegible scribbles cascaded onto the floor at Max's feet.

"I don't do speeches," Max replied before the young man could reassemble his notes.

"What do you mean? A politician who doesn't do speeches? I suppose you're going to tell us next that you intend to skip the primaries and stay home." He looked agitated and perplexed, gathering his pile of notes.

"Something like that. But I need to correct you on something. I'm not a politician. I'm just a man who is running for president."

They sat in silence. It seemed that those words confused them somehow, but it wouldn't be the last time they heard them.

Recovering, a young woman in a black pinstriped suit broke in. "If you become president, what are your goals for America?"

He thought for a while, until his silence made them think that he wasn't going to answer. Finally, he spoke. "I believe that our country has been wounded by 'politics as usual.' The person you choose as president should be honest with you, clearly state the position that he or she believes is right for America, and make that dream a reality."

"What is your platform?" They weren't there to debate. They were there to gather information.

"My platform is presently a stool covered with some sort of Naugahyde cushion, but I expect I'll be able to upgrade to a more comfortable platform once I get back on the plane."

The resulting laughter broke the ice.

"Well, are you a conservative or a liberal?" The balding, overweight young man wasn't about to let his victim get away without inflicting a wound. Max stared at him with an incredulous look on his face.

"Those labels don't work for me. I'm a conservative if I vote for jobs for people who don't have them. When I vote to give businesses incentives to hire new people, I suppose the conservatives would call me a liberal, when all I would be trying to do was get the jobs for Americans. I guess you'd better just call me an American." He paused and surveyed their puzzled faces.

"…and another thing. When you think about who to vote for, is it better to trust the experience of the one who is doing a poor job of serving our country or is it better to trust the only one with new ideas for making our country better?"

"Why should I vote for you?" The new question came from a new face at the back of the room, a short, middle-aged woman who worked for the St. Petersburg Times. They had to get their questions in to justify the cost of the trip.

"Stay tuned. If I do this right, you'll be answering that question yourselves before long." Max stood. "Thanks. It's been fun." He turned and walked out of the room.

Andrew was waiting in the monitoring room, where he had observed the interview on a large projection screen. He saw Max's inexperience and evasiveness as toxic. "Max, that really sucked. You spent the entire time trying to evade, when you should have been trying to charm and impress. I have seen better interviews by convicted felons."

Max looked like he had just been chastised by his fourth grade teacher for speaking out of turn.

"I know. I don't want to do that again. You know how much I love the press. They're going to comment about how I was nervous and green." He tossed his notes in the air. They floated randomly to the floor, where a sheet entitled, "Talking Points" landed on top. He hadn't touched upon any of the issues he was prepared to discuss. They were controlling him, and he felt helpless. What he had to say had nothing to do the agenda of his interviewers.

Andrew could see his consternation. "If you want to control the press, you need to do two things. First, you need to make yourself available on a limited basis on your schedule, not theirs. If they had their way, your life would be one big interview from sunup to sundown, and they would spin every word to make it fit their agenda. Second, and you're going to love this one, you get to pick and choose what you want to tell them. There isn't a question that they can make you answer, and there is no rule that says you have to answer their way. I have an idea."

As a result of the government's newly obtained ability to verify that a person was really who they were, voting took on a new dimension, too. No waiting in line to pull a lever. No dangling chad. No electronic touch screens. When a voter wanted to vote, they voted, and they could do it from wherever they were, provided they all voted on election day, the first Tuesday of November in the fourth year after the previous national election. Max and his campaign staff knew that they had only one shot at his being the top vote-getter on that particular day and attaining that goal involved setting himself apart from the rest of his competition.

"There are a lot of truths out there. Just pick the ones we want."

Chapter Forty-One

Max was in the early stages of his daily ritual, which began with a high-level meeting with his version of the incumbent's cabinet. Present at the table were political consultant Luke Postlewaite, chief of staff/press secretary Bill Staffman, media advisor Andrew Fox, and Max. At this point in his campaign, that's all there was. If it got much bigger, he thought, then the message would become diluted, and his platform needed to be simple, direct, and clear.

"Voters are bombarded by information. Politicians are the only ones who pay attention. There is so much crap floating out there that people just block it all out, and I need to find a way to get beyond that invisible wall," said Max.

"I don't see you having any problems in that area. I'm more concerned with the fact that you have never held political office. I want to run a few ads touting your father's accomplishments in Congress to throw Blythe's spin doctors off the scent," interjected Postlewaite.

"Before the next sound bite, I want to have a clear vision of America's future, and I need to get it across to them. If they are going to remember and understand what sets me apart from the rest, I need to get it into their brains now," Max declared to nobody in particular.

Fox and Staffman weren't talking. It was their time to listen. When Max was strategizing, they had learned to take notes and only contribute their ideas when he had reached the point of needing advice, and Max was far from finished.

"One thing I noticed about the debate was the look on people's faces when the speaker talked too long or went into too much detail. Hell, even the moderator's eyes began to glaze over. The time to explain is not when you introduce an idea. I'll save the explaining for after I get into the White House."

"Then why don't you tell them that? You have been thriving on unconventionality and big talking points. Just be clear and short. It's working," offered Andrew. He felt out of place in this room with two political veterans, but Max valued his ability to observe through the eyes of the regular folks, and that ability was more valuable to him than the old party political slant that his older advisors had staked their reputations upon.

"Andrew, they don't own me. They have no right to dig into my life and spread it all over the world," pleaded Max.

"I beg your pardon, but yes, they do." Andrew was awed by Max's fire and his ability to control people, but his attempts to maintain his privacy while running for the most visible job on the planet were beginning to chafe. He had to get Max to pull his head out of his ass and press the flesh with the common folk, and it was Andrew's job to promote Max's awareness.

"We're going to rehearse your sound bites, and we are going to unleash your first one at the airport. Next, we're going to Michigan, and then we'll be in Florida. You always wanted to snorkel with the manatees, and I'm going to show you a place I found during spring break a few years ago. Your bags are already packed. I have advance teams in each location, and I'm going to post your daily message at 11:00 a.m., right about the time the stock exchange posts the morning earnings reports. I want to see if we can't influence business with hopeful messages."

Max sat in silence while Fox rattled off his itinerary for the coming weeks. He saw the determination with which his young assistant was presenting his plan and realized that if he attempted to change anything, he was in for a blow up. Andrew had taken Max's Maxims to heart and constructed a plan of his own to put him in the White House. Experience be damned.

"Andrew, there are a couple of things I'd like to add, but you've come up with a good plan, and I'm going to do my best to comply. If you see me doing anything unpresidential, I want you to tell me." Max spoke quietly. He was sitting at his kitchen table, shirtless and barefoot, in pajama bottoms. He cradled a cup of coffee that he prepared in his typical way, with raw honey indigenous to the countryside where he lived. His hair winged out to the side.

Andrew looked at him in astonishment and noted that he was dressed in a dark blue suit and tie, holding a briefcase stuffed full of notes and papers, while the future president looked more like, well, everyone else at 7:10 a.m. He laughed. "Max, there isn't much that you're doing that is presidential, and I'm not the guy to be the judge of that. It would take me three life times, at least, to tell you all the things you're doing that are unpresidential. The interesting part is, I can see where you're coming from. You have managed to get the women, including the old ladies, the youth vote, guys who admire you for doing what they can't, old men who wish they were young again, and everyone who's pissed off at a politician. That's a lot of people. I'm devoted to taking this as far as we can go. It's really all up to you. I'm just along for the ride."

"Well, for a guy who's just along for the ride, you sure know where you have me riding to," he muttered. "But I'm not complaining. I have to get out there, and I need to get my message across. A couple of things, though. I want all of these sound bites to be positive messages. Can we do that? And I don't want to waste any time meeting with politicians unless they are going to support my campaign."

"Max, you're a politician."

"No I'm not. I'm a man who's running for president."

Chapter Forty-Two

Max and his political advisors wouldn't even fill a compact car, but they were enough. While the other candidates canvassed Iowa and New Hampshire and attempted to shake hands with every resident who lived there, Max rode with Bill Staffman and Andrew Fox to Reagan International Airport in Bill's ancient Ford Focus. The intention was for Bill to drop them off at the terminal, and while he had their captive attention for the 45 minute ride from staff headquarters, he was damn sure going to use the time for a staff meeting.

"I have Sara in Iowa and Jerry in New Hampshire, and they're going to town meetings and attending all the speeches they can tolerate. Once you've heard one, it's like watching reruns of the evening news, so I'm confining their agony to attending one speech for each candidate each day. The president has a speech in Washington at the Library of Congress to dedicate something, and I'll attend that one. Cunningham and his people are out at Arlington to do a press conference about the war, and they are really pushing to get a lot of press coverage. I have Richard and Janice out there taking notes," rambled Staffman.

"I don't care whether they take notes. We already know what they are going to say. I want them to sit in front and face the crowd and time how long it takes for people's eyes to glaze over and lose their attention. Then when the speech is done, I want them to poll the crowd and ask the same question of everyone," said Max in an unwavering voice.

Andrew was intrigued. "Why in the world would you want to do that? What question?"

Max waited the appropriate time to create suspense, sensing their irritation at his silent manipulation and smiled. "I just want them to ask, 'What did he just say?'"

"Why?" Bill and Andrew asked loudly, their voices tinged with confusion.

"First, I need to know how long the average person will listen to a politician before their mind wanders, because once you lose their attention, you may as well stop talking. And then I need to know whether they are getting through to these people. These crowds are mostly supporters, and they're going to vote for them anyway, so I need to focus on the rest of the voters."

"Max." Bill turned his head to his passenger and stared at him for what seemed like an eternity. They were stopped in Washington traffic, and he could divert his attention until the line of cars on the off ramp began moving again. "Max, you worry me. Why aren't we in Iowa eating corn dogs with the locals? I don't get it. You and Andrew are headed to Michigan, and I'm stuck here in D.C., and I don't know what you want me to do, for chrissakes!"

Bill was beginning to sweat with frustration, and Max knew that to campaign in the way he had devised, he needed to share his philosophy with those he trusted. "Bill, Andrew is going to post videos of me speaking on every subject we decide the voters want information about. The length of my talks will be shorter than the attention span of the viewers. I have no intention of being where all the other candidates are unless I'm debating. There will be a video assistant meeting me at each of my destinations."

Andrew had listened too long and was itching to speak.

"I get the idea of strategic sound bites, but why don't you care what the voters think about the issues?"

Max turned to address his backseat passenger just as Bill navigated the terminal entrance. He made eye contact with his young protégé, whose face was just feet from his. "I do care. I just have this abiding belief that people listen to politicians to make up their minds on issues that people disagree about, and polling is just a way of verifying that a politician is good at persuading and getting the message across. If I can get a majority of voters to pay attention to my message and agree with me on basic principles, I win. There's an old adage: When you're going to fish, go to where the fish are."

Andrew and Bill shook their heads. "It seems to me that you just beat up the bully without throwing a punch," said Bill as he pulled the road-weary Focus to the door of Airside C.

Chapter Forty-Three

Andrew and Max made it through security at Reagan International Airport without too much trouble. Stripping down to your nonmetallic essence had become a ritual of travel since 9/11. Once they got to the secure area for passengers on outgoing flights, they settled into chairs near the food court and Andrew began his briefing on issues to be addressed in the next sound bites as Max sipped on a pomegranate smoothie. "We're doing jobs and retirement on this trip," Andrew began.

Max had his feet up on a metal chair, oblivious to the crowd gathering around them. They encroached, the numbers increasing steadily. Finally, a girl, probably seventeen, walked up to Max, and said, "You're him, aren't you."

"I guess."

"No you're not."

"Then I guess I'm not." He smiled, and she screamed.

"You are him! I told my mom and dad that if they don't vote for you, I'm going to run away!" The girl was obviously part of a private school trip, with 20 companions in identical uniforms, who all screamed as well. This, in turn, brought a larger crowd of travelers until they were surrounded by a mass of humanity that was quickly becoming very close and very aggressive.

A man in a business suit pushed to the front and spoke. "I don't know about the rest of us, but I have been very interested in what you have to say, and I would appreciate your thoughts about social security."

"Who cares?" shouted a thirtyish woman, her blonde hair and low-cut business suit betraying an ample set of obviously enhanced breasts. She had bullied herself to within two feet of Max's chair by spreading her elbows and launching herself into the crowd, prompting him to stand before she finished her ground assault. "You are the most gorgeous man I have ever seen, and I want to know where you are headed. I'll go wherever you're going, sweetcakes." She gave him her best come hither look, prompting most of the members of the impromptu crowd to blush in unison.

Max had to respond. "I'm on my way to meet with some people about your future. Over the next two months, I will be bringing you messages from all over the country, and you'll see a lot of me. This man here is my most trusted advisor, Andrew Fox, and he will take your questions. We listen. Now, if you'll excuse me, I need to hit the men's room before we get on our plane."

The crowd moaned and converged on Andrew while Max slid to the back of the crowd. As he did, people touched his clothes, the woman with the ample breasts tried to grab his crotch, and he deftly sidestepped his way toward the men's room. As he looked back at the crowd, he could see Andrew's face, pleading for assistance. Getting none, he settled into information gathering as Max searched for refuge in the men's room. Stragglers followed, including the woman who had just missed sampling his private parts. He began to think about hiring security on this trip and beyond—and stifled the urge to break into a run. Reaching the men's room, he turned to his now increasing crowd of twenty and addressed them. "I don't give speeches, but I feel compelled to tell you that I have been going to the bathroom all by myself since I was a big boy, and I don't need your help in pulling up my pants." He turned and escaped into the refuge of the brightly lit stalls.

When he emerged, a small group of persistent stragglers stood at a respectful distance. The girl who first spotted him was at the front, pen and notebook in hand. "Will you give me your autograph? My friends will never believe this. Nancy! Take our picture!"

He posed for pictures for the next fifteen minutes, wondering when the damn announcement for his flight was coming to rescue him. It was a captive feeling, and he didn't like it one bit. This aspect of running for president sucked, and he resolved to travel incognito as soon as he could devise a way to do that. Maybe he should just travel by private plane and avoid public transportation altogether.

Andrew's crowd had dwindled with Max's escape, and the rest of the travelers just stared. Andrew glared at him and furiously jotted notes about people's issues of concern. Most of their comments dealt with the difficulties of living, and he didn't think that most of what he had written would be of much help. There was one common theme, though. These people were frustrated. They were ready to cast out their elected officials and start fresh, no longer trusting the promises of politicians.

"Maybe that's why they are so interested in him," he pondered. "Max doesn't promise anything except hope for the future." Andrew was, if nothing else, a watcher. He had observed Max in an unplanned, unscripted public appearance, and he had excelled at creating and maintaining interest. They needed to capitalize on that talent. Max had no trouble setting himself apart from the rest of the candidates, but they still came up short because of the perception that he had no experience.

Max knew that he had deflected the attention to his young assistant, but it seemed like the right thing to do at the time. He had no other idea how to get to the bathroom in a crowd of tourists. He knew now how rock bands feel when they are pursued by groupies and screaming fans, and he was uncomfortable in that environment.

By the time they landed at Detroit Metropolitan Airport, Max and Andrew had disguised themselves as tourists, secure in the idea that tourists actually visit Michigan in the summer. If they had landed at any other time of the year, they wouldn't have been able to pull it off. Tourists from Michigan head south for the winter, and they would have had to resort to looking like business travelers or give up disguises altogether.

What they didn't calculate was that each monitor in every public place, each personal data bracelet, could monitor their movements with such precision that crowds had already formed in the terminal as the plane landed. They knew where he was at any moment in time. By the time the doors opened, hundreds of the curious spotted his familiar face behind the sunglasses, and they surged in his direction.

Chapter Forty-Four

"I don't like politicians." Andrew's mother was sitting in the kitchen of the 150-year-old farmhouse, glaring across the table at her son and Max, cradling her morning cup of coffee. Andrew pushed his chair back, expecting the outburst of honesty that his mother was known for, ready to bolt out the back door if the fur began to fly.

"I don't like them much myself." Max leaned forward in his chair and gazed directly into her grey eyes. "In fact, there isn't much about politicians to like. They lie all the time and are so full of themselves that they think other people want to hear them talk about how great they are. They are so detached from the rest of us that they have no idea what we want and need nor do they care. I'm glad I'm not a politician."

Mom stood up and headed for the coffee pot, a confused grimace on her face. She smoothed her dress nervously, trying to absorb Max's words, unsure what to say. Andrew was silent knowing that he was witnessing a meeting that would define his life. This was a first—mom was speechless. He could tell she was gathering her thoughts as she lingered for minutes at the counter, pouring the sugar, stirring the coffee, the familiar clinking of metal against china adding to the suspense.

"I thought you were a politician." She turned suddenly, causing the coffee to slosh slightly onto the floor. In an ordinary situation, she would have pounced on the spill with a washcloth, but this time she seemed oblivious.

"No, Ma'am, I'm just a man running for president."

Mom seemed flustered. Her cheeks took on a rosy hue, and Andrew found it necessary to rescue her. "Mom, what Max is saying is that there are people who spend their lives running for something, usually rich folks who don't have much to do with the rest of us, and then there are a few who have ideas to make a change for the better. Visionaries. Max is taking his one shot at president, and if he wins, he'll change the way they do things in Washington. And I believe he will. Right, Max?" He turned to Max for a sign that what he had volunteered was copasetic with the message Max was trying to convey.

Mom wasn't about to let this new source of fascination get the last word. "Hold it right there, Mr. Masterson. If my boy believes in you, I'd say you're at risk of winning."

"I knew I picked the right guy to tell people who I am." He turned to Andrew, who had begun helping himself to her freshly baked chocolate chip cookies and compromising his ability to contribute to the rest of their conversation by stuffing three cookies in his mouth at one time.

Finally, after a sip of milk and several gasps, Andrew said, "Let's go ride horses."

Max stood so fast that the kitchen chair skidded across the linoleum. With a quick about-face, he was out the door with Andrew in close pursuit.

Chapter Forty-Five

The sound bite of the day came from Marshall, Michigan and featured Leila Fox standing in front of her 19th century farm house surrounded by flowers blooming profusely in the morning sun. Behind her stood Max, and behind the house was the most glorious sunrise ever. Their timing was perfect. The golden hue reflected off their faces, giving them the appearance of marble statues. As she spoke, the camera zoomed in on her face, and the piercing intensity of her light green eyes was emphasized by the deep wrinkles that surrounded them.

"This time around, my family is voting for Max Masterson. I know one thing, voting for the same old thing will only get you more of the same old thing. We're tired of politicians who promise everything and give nothing. We need jobs and the comfort of knowing our pensions will be there when we reach my age. And don't even get me started on how much it costs to pay to see my doctor. Max is running for president, and my friends and I like what he stands for."

The camera panned back to include a group of white-haired old ladies, then quickly zoomed back in to frame Leila standing next to Max, who was dressed in the simple clothes she had picked out for him to wear. Leila had spoken the words that her son had written for her. Now it was time to improvise, and she turned to Max and kissed him on the cheek. He blushed and smiled. The message was complete.

"Great!" Andrew ran forward and hugged her as the ladies cheered. "Mom, you're going to be famous. By this afternoon, all your friends are going to see you kissing the president," he teased.

It was her turn to blush. "Oh, Andrew, don't tell your father that I kissed another man. He's the only one except relatives that I've kissed since high school."

Andrew had concocted a campaign strategy for Max that relied on basic human values. He figured that voters couldn't reject ideas that had no opposition. Keep it clean or you will clean up after yourself. Be against crime. Educate your children so they can have a better life than yours. Americans and America come first. The best spokespeople for the American way of life, he surmised, were the moms.

Little old ladies make the most dedicated supporters of any group a candidate can hope to woo, but they are a tough audience. If they don't like you, they'll tell you so. If you can convince them to like you, their loyalty is pure. They have more energy than a person one-third their age, they awaken at a much earlier hour, and they have attained wisdom. At one time, moms and grandmas weren't very political at all. They left all of that "politicking" to their husbands, and if they didn't have one of those, they took no interest whatsoever in who was running or what they stood for. They didn't keep current on the issues and seldom voted.

The new generation of these women were_representative of an interesting phenomenon that had developed in the 20th century, which passed below the radar of the pollsters and highly compensated consultants hired by major candidates. The old ladies had become a potent political force for the first time since prohibition.

Max seemed to tap into the mother lode of this new consciousness when he decided to utilize his "match tips," old ladies with white hair, to be the backdrop for his campaign. The statistical fact that women live longer than men and control most of the wealth by default was curiously lost on the fund-raisers for most major campaigns. They spent much of their time trolling databases of past campaigns, determining where successful candidates had been most successful in their fund-raising. In the past, old ladies weren't interested and weren't going to share the wealth with an activity which held no appeal for them, and fund-raisers kept plowing the same fields. Until Max came along.

Chapter Forty-Six

"Are you freaking crazy?" Bill Staffman was sitting at the head of the table in Max's usual seat when Max dragged himself in from his latest foray into the nation. He wasn't about to relinquish his seat until Max had answered his mostly rhetorical question.

"What are you talking about?" Max hadn't had his morning cup of coffee, but aware that his chief of staff had the hairs up on the back of his neck, he knew he wasn't going to get that caffeine before he addressed the issue at hand.

"You go out in the field and enlist a bunch of white-haired old ladies to stand behind you and sing your praises, don't bother to consult with me, and send it out over the Internet without any idea what would happen," bellowed Staffman.

"Well, yeah. You got a problem with that?" Max backed up two steps, keeping the table between them, and grasped the back of one of the overstuffed leather chairs that ringed the room. "It just so happens that old ladies love me for some reason. I never had a mother… well, not an official one, and all they want to do is hug me all the time. I like that. I didn't see what harm there could be for me to include them in my dailies."

Staffman realized that he had come on too strong and hadn't explained himself well. He had never seen this side of Max, vulnerable and alone, craving what mothers provide their sons—a sense of comfort and refuge. He didn't realize how deep the loss was for a child to lack a parent, for a boy to miss the comfort of the soft bosom of his mom. He regretted his hard-ass approach.

"You don't understand what I'm trying to tell you." He paused and walked toward Max, bringing his face within inches. They locked eyes. "You may be crazy, and I know you don't pay any attention to the polls, but you just blundered into the best campaign strategy since… since… I can't remember," Staffman stammered. "I have been on the phone with the networks nonstop for the past day, and they seem to think that Luke and I concocted this whole idea. I'm taking the credit since Luke is trying to stay invisible, and I just want you to know… keep doing what you're doing."

Max looked relieved. The worry lines in his face disappeared, and he came back to the present. "You mean, they like my Match Tips?" He had been rousted from bed by the early morning conference call and was dressed only in the grey gym shorts that had become his standard sleepwear, if he wore anything to bed. His sound bite that day would come from the Florida Panhandle, and he was groggy from the late-night flight from Michigan.

"Give Andrew all the credit. He cooked it up all by himself. I personally think he wanted to make his mom famous, but he swears he concocted this plan from his extensive repertoire of campaign strategies," Max said with a smirk. Andrew had just arrived at the door, his hands full of snorkeling gear.

"Why are you guys looking at me like that? What did I do?"

"Oh, nothing," said Bill and Max in unison.

They sat in the white Adirondack chairs at the end of the dock, the clear, spring-fed waters of the Wakulla River flowing beneath the weathered boards. On the far shore, a large alligator lay motionless. Sipping their coffee, they absorbed the green of nature while looking for the large grey-white blobs beneath the surface that revealed the presence of manatees. Max and Andrew lined up their snorkeling gear for a quick entry into the water when the rare animals were spotted.

Max dove to massage a young manatee behind the flipper as it floated with the current ten feet below the surface. Andrew floated out of the field of view as the ripples settled.

The cameras focused on the river. A light gray blob was visible beneath the shimmering water, stirring the calm surface with turbulence and moving deceptively fast in the center channel. The camera plunged underneath the surface, creating the perception that the viewer had just dived into the water with eyes wide open. In the bright sunlit water, a baby manatee placidly propelled itself with a broad rear flipper, accompanied by a diver in snorkeling gear.

The next image was of Max emerging from the water, shirtless and wet, removing his mask. He stood waist deep in the river, looking fit and virile and totally successful in his quest to set himself apart.

"I'm in Florida to talk to you about our environment and why we need to keep it clean," said Max, bare from the waist up. "Here on the Wakulla River, the manatee and the otter thrive in crystal clear water that flows from an aquifer bigger than any lake in the world. But we're ruining it by not protecting it from the waste of man. If a few ruin it for everyone, we all lose. When I'm president, if you dirty it up, you'll make it cleaner than it was or pay someone else to do it."

Chapter Forty-Seven

If it wasn't already confusing to the voters, the third-party debate proved to be the circus the political pundits had predicted it would be: a mess of voices projected from dark-suited, rich men, all trying to talk over the others, trying their best to use the words that would capture the minds of the voters but failing to connect with America. This time there was no Kennedy in the race, no "Ask not what your country can do for you, ask what you can do for your country." Instead, the candidate who stood out from the rest was the young man from across the river who said next to nothing.

"Ladies and gentlemen, I'll be your moderator for this evening's debate between the third-party challengers for the office of president of the United States of America," said Roger Forrestal, respected correspondent for the now defunct CBS Evening News. When Forrestal retired, the ratings for the Evening News dropped by 40 points, and the program never recovered. Whenever a major election required a respected face and voice to deliver the message, Forrestal was pulled out of his Golden Parachute life and enlisted to serve once again. He was paid handsomely for his popularity, maintained by annual polls that confirmed that he was the most trusted person in journalism. The real reason behind his popularity as a broadcast journalist, aside from his soothing baritone, was simple: Roger Forrestal had never offended anyone.

"The rules for the debate have been reviewed and agreed upon by the candidates. Each question will be repeated to the candidate prior to their answering. Each candidate will be afforded two minutes to respond, during which time the candidate cannot be asked additional questions. At the end of the two minute response period, the moderator will pose the question to the next candidate.

"All candidates will be allowed to answer each question without interruption. The questions and topics for tonight's debate have been compiled by the League of Women Voters from questions provided by the interactive program Worldview, and narrowed down to five topics: the environment, the war in the Middle East, the economy, health care, and the qualities that are essential for the next president of the United States. We have purposely left the last topic unannounced, to ensure that we will have a candid and unrehearsed answer from all of our candidates."

Forrestal's presentation was interrupted by a commercial break sponsored by the League of Women Voters, who presented a colorful video of the history of the organization and their place in politics. Large corporations had sought commercial time, as did the United States Marine Corps and each major party, but all offers had been rejected in an effort to keep the event free from outside influence.

Forrestal reappeared and continued his explanation of the process. "There will be regional debates one week before each of the six primaries, after which the three highest vote getters will debate the incumbent president, William Blythe at Wake Forest University in Winston Salem, North Carolina."

Max looked the part. He wore a light gray suit while his opponents wore nearly identical dark suits with light-colored ties, red white and blue lapel pins. They all shifted nervously and spent much too long arranging errant hairs on their heads in the moments before the debate. He was steady as a rock. When each question was asked, he calmly shifted his gaze toward the center of the spotlight. As each candidate answered the question, he stood solid, his presidential profile drawing attention to his face. That fact was not lost on the cameraman, and the viewers saw only what the director chose to place before them. Max was a person of intense public interest, and the viewers chose where the camera focused. If they wanted split screen, they got it. If they wanted all of the candidates simultaneously, the multiple cameras were happy to oblige.

Whenever another candidate was answering the question, the viewers who chose the split screen focused on the speaker and on Max. As the answer droned on, the camera zoomed in on Max's face, solid and contemplative, his green eyes reacting. Any statement made that didn't conform with Max's view was amplified for millions of viewers by his nonverbal reaction. When Hilton was asked the gun control question, he was on his soapbox and spent the full two-minute response time presenting the canned speech he had honed into the foundation of his entire campaign. The message had been repeated in the long version so many times that searchers for news had a difficult time finding anything new to report, and the message was lost through repetition. Max practiced a bored expression, and crossed his eyes at the inevitable conclusion, when Hilton bellowed, "When guns are outlawed, only outlaws will have guns!"

When it came time for Max to respond, he looked directly into the camera in front of him while the others showed his profile. He stated his position succinctly, in a calm but direct tone. "I'm not one for telling you what you can and cannot do, and I won't be asking Congress to take your guns away. You are free to do what our laws let you do. It's only people who hurt other people with guns that should be punished. Government should leave the rest of us alone." He didn't need rebuttal. He didn't need to say anything more. His message came across without another word and in less than the two minutes allotted.

The effect of this approach was to put the camera operator in a state of perplexed anxiety. Each time he answered, there was a minute and forty seconds of silence, during which the camera would zoom in on his visage, and zoom back out to show the man in the light suit surrounded by other men in black suits, all looking in his direction. Then the camera would slowly zoom in again, as the commentator in the sound booth tried to repeat every word Max spoke.

It was not a time for commentary, but broadcasters get very nervous with "dead air," as they call it. With his response repeated and broadcast three times, the relieved moderator moved on to the next question, and the process began again. Each question was answered in exactly two minutes until the camera focused once again on Max. A short answer, followed by a long silence, with the answer repeated twice, and then it happened again.

By the fourth and final question, the story of the first debate was forged. He had set himself apart from the others in a way that carried a great deal of risk. No other candidate in the history of politics had given up a second of time on the stage of public opinion. The effect of his strategy was to cause a commotion at every level, but it was most evident in the way the public responded. Every answer to every question directed at him had been repeated three times. Everyone who heard his answer had it etched in his brain.

Moments after the first debate, polls were taken of voters who had seen the debate and those who had skipped it to watch a rerun of Wheel of Fortune, shown at the same time on a network advertising itself as "an alternative to politics." The poll results were almost identical: Every answer that Max delivered was repeated verbatim on every issue. Even the game show watchers polled in the control group could repeat what Max had said, but none of the responses of the other candidates could be remembered by anyone polled. This statistic generated a maelstrom of interest from every major network. Interviews were conducted with political science professors from major universities. Some predicted that Max's campaign would fold in three weeks and that his strategy was a disaster.

"It has never been done before, and it spells the end of Masterson's credibility. If he doesn't have enough to say about the subject, it's an indication that he's not a deep thinker. We need a deep thinker in the

White House," pontificated Lawrence Fullself, distinguished professor emeritus from Yale University.

"I have never seen or heard a less credible candidate. He doesn't have a complete grasp of the issues," opined Richard Hasselfuss of the conservative think tank, Conservatives for a Better Yesterday.

From the detractors came endorsements for the incumbent and criticism of Max, but a curious development seemed to escape their scrutiny. Max had emerged as the front-runner.

Chapter Forty-Eight

There are many examples of major elections throughout the history of the United States in which the will of the electorate has escaped the attention of those who seek higher office, and as a result, they lost to less financed unknowns. Even more numerous are those candidates who never had a snowball's chance in hell of getting elected, yet they gave it their best shot and almost pulled it off. In this instance, Max had gone in one day from a guppy in a pack of sharks to swimming as the lead fish escaping the jaws of those who were out to devour him.

The unique part of it all was that he was such a long shot that the incumbent president and his handlers failed to notice Max's arrival as a legitimate candidate. The incumbent's political machine, numbering in the thousands and occupying strategic offices in every major city, had discounted the Masterson ticket and predicted a landslide for the incumbent. Their focus was on the opposition party. After all, no third-party candidate had won an election for president, and most candidates since the Civil War who fronted third-party campaigns were spoilers at best. Blythe was feeling very comfortable about his reelection, and those who surrounded him were unanimously predicting his landslide victory in November. All except one.

Hugo Wiseman had been a trusted advisor to the president since his early campaigns for national office, beginning with the first disastrous campaign for the U.S. House of Representatives for the State of New

York at the green age of twenty-seven, when he switched home states and was elected senator from Illinois, and up to his election to the presidency. "Mr. President, did you watch the debate?" he asked.

"I don't have time to watch a bunch of losers fumble around and pick away at each other. I was in an important conference with… never mind, just do a report and have it on my desk by tomorrow morning." He had just emerged red faced from the bathroom adjacent to the Oval Office, trying to buckle his belt as he emerged.

"But Mr. President, I'm very concerned by what I saw last night. This race has come down to you and Max Masterson."

"Are you telling me that Masterson came out the winner of that debate?" sputtered Blythe. He was dressed in an old pair of jeans and had on a sweat shirt that may have once fit when he was forty pounds lighter, but he had been off his exercise regimen since his inaugural, and his diet consisted of whatever they fed him, which was usually fried and in massive helpings. Part of the problem, he surmised, was that he had inadvertently revealed to the cooks that he had a secret desire to find the perfect chicken wing, and they appeared at nearly every meal.

"No, what I'm telling you is that your previous 38% approval rating is now in the toilet, and the voters are paying attention to Max Masterson. I have never seen a bigger change in the polls. You haven't even made your first speech, and he managed to get everyone repeating his little one-liners."

"You mean sound bites."

Wiseman didn't like to be corrected. In fact, he didn't like anyone to talk down to him, and after his long career in public service, he had little patience for elected officials at all. He flushed, but considering the fact that he was addressing the most powerful man on the planet, he bit his tongue. "Worse than that. They rhyme. They make sense. You can understand them. Hell, you can memorize the whole campaign in about five minutes. I hear that school kids are repeating them at the dinner table."

"Do you mean that I'm running against Sesame Street?"

"I'm more worried that you are competing for the vote of people who grew up on Sesame Street."

Chapter Forty-Nine

"If you really want to set yourself apart from the competition, you need to be a separate story. Any time all of the candidates are in Iowa, I want you to be in Florida. When they're in New Orleans, I want you to be in Colorado. I want the contrast to be so huge that they will all be lumped together in one news report, while you get the same amount of time on your own," announced Andrew Fox. The look on his face reflected his determination.

Andrew was beginning to show his brilliance, a quality composed of his strong identification with average people, and the persistence instilled in him by his midwestern upbringing. He had taken this job with a single-minded focus on putting his employer in the White House, and he wasn't going to do it by trying to mold Max into a poor imitation of all the other politicians who had filled the position. The only way they were going to win was if America wanted someone to lead who was so different from the rest that politics would never be the same. The boy advisor was well on his way to becoming a seasoned veteran of political wars, if he could only survive until the election without violating Max's Maxims.

Max knew he wasn't paying him a tenth of what other political advisors made for a national campaign, but when this was over, Andrew could have any job he wanted at any price he chose.

Chapter Fifty

Tuesday was the second primary of the race, and Max was not in the southeast. In fact, he was nowhere to be found, if the reports from the horde of field correspondents were any indication. After the first debate, the phone bank at Masterson Headquarters lit up at the rate of 3000 calls per hour, and the Internet fundraising site was receiving contributions at the rate of one million dollars every 24 hours. It was an unprecedented contribution rate, considering that Max adopted the thousand dollar cap on political contributions at the outset.

Along with the increase in phone contributions came requests for interviews. If Max had scheduled interviews with every newspaper, TV, and Internet media correspondent, he would have had no time to eat, sleep, or go to the bathroom. He solved that problem by turning them all down.

When news came that Max had denied every request for an interview after the first one, that kernel of information became the news of the day. When no new information came from campaign headquarters in the next 24 hours, the news of the day became the news of the week, and political commentators had to have their say. White House Press secretary Wiley Talkinead provoked a laugh from the press corps at the Thursday morning briefing by answering a question raised by New York Times correspondent Annie Way, who asked, "It appears that the president is running against someone who hasn't yet figured out how to run. Is the president worried that Mr. Masterson is a threat to his reelection?

"The only thing the president is worried about regarding Mr. Masterson is whether he can find the polling booth on election day."

After two decades as a press correspondent, the White House veteran thought for a short moment, and before Wiley could move on to the next question, she delivered the second question, "Then the president considers Max Masterson to be the front-runner?"

Wiley was trapped into admitting that he was. "The President has been informed of the latest polls. He has also been informed that Masterson captured 42% of the popular vote in the New Hampshire primary, and that makes him the front-runner of the moment. I do not expect that the Masterson campaign will capture the nomination of the opposing party, because he is a third-party candidate. So, in my mind, Mr. Masterson is in a strange place. I'm certain he's accustomed to being in strange places."

Ever mindful of the Maxims, Max's staff turned away more money than was brought in. No lobbyists and no major contributors. It was essential that Max adhere to the Maxims that were the basis of his efforts to maintain freedom from outside influence. By doing so, he reasoned, the will of Americans would remain his paramount interest, and his popularity ratings had the potential of exceeding those of any president in modern times.

Chapter Fifty-One

When the press is rebuffed, it reacts by sending a film crew and team of reporters on a seek and destroy mission. Armed with cameras, lights, and microphones, the advance team stations itself in surveillance mode outside the scene of most likely contact. They dig in, setting up a satellite dish and portable sound stage with a background that describes the story. This time, they had to settle for the playground in the preschool across the street from Masterson for President Headquarters, but the routine was the same: locate the candidate outside his cordon of security; shove a microphone into the sound zone, and ask a question before other crews got the same idea; provoke a sound bite; repeat the sound bite every 20 minutes in banner headlines and run audio and visual reports as often as possible, followed by feature-length reports twice a day as justified. Continue surveillance until the subject moves, then move with him until he is no longer newsworthy.

This morning, campaign headquarters was surrounded by fourteen sound trucks, all strategically located in the playground and parking lot adjacent to the preschool. The principal and teachers had been bribed by each network for sums equivalent to three years' gross income to surrender their property to the press until further notice. Even though this development had the effect of displacing thirty preschoolers to a location on the second floor of a local warehouse, they were making the best of it, and the parents went along with the idea when informed that they had free preschool until the horde of paparazzi had moved on.

"Where is he? Why don't we have his calendar and daily itinerary?" Greg Scuperman rarely sat still for long, but today he was even more active than usual. In a state of constant aggravation, he paced back and forth in front of the monkey bars and raged into the cell phone imbedded in his right ear. With his hands in his pockets, from a distance he looked like an errant schoolboy searching for a nonexistent hall pass in his baggy pockets.

"That's not good enough, Vivien! You didn't become my research assistant by making excuses! Produce! I want to know where he is right now, and I want to know it before anyone else!" He paused, listened, and watched as the hologram image of Vivien appeared on the viewing screen projected by his sunglasses. She was awesome, seductively dressed in red, her dress complementing the increasing glow of her cheeks. It was obvious that she, too, was exasperated.

"For a guy running for president, he sure doesn't get out much. I know he likes to run along the Potomac every morning about 5:00, and he's usually inside his office by now. Nobody has laid eyes on him for about fourteen hours. You got there just after he had left for the day," she said.

"If he isn't here, where is he?"

He paused to watch an attractive young woman rolling a large computer case down the cobblestone street. She was in obvious distress, but reporters are not known for helping ladies in distress, or anyone in distress for that matter. They are there to report about people in distress. Finally, the young woman made her way to the front door of campaign headquarters and reached for the door while juggling a file in her left hand. Greg took the opportunity to get a statement and almost blew an Achilles tendon bounding across the street ahead of the cameras and microphones.

"Larry! Zoom in, and I'll get the audio off my collar mic," he hollered.

By the time Maymie Wright had the door fully opened, Greg was in voice range and launched his first question.

"Young lady, good day! I'm Greg Scuperman of News Tonight. Can you tell us where Max Masterson is this morning?"

"I have been at the dentist, but Max gets in early." She peered into the darkened lobby. "The light's on in his office. I'm sure he knows you're all out here. I'll see if he wants to talk to you." She walked in, trailing her computer case, which seemed to be stuck. With a big heave, the large bag hopped over the raised vestibule and the door slammed shut in the faces of the hastily-assembled press. There was a peculiar silence.

In an effort to fill the dead air, the cameras moved from the front door to the faces that report the news. The press holding the microphones turned collectively away from the door to begin speaking to the cameras, unsure what they should say. Just then, the door opened again, and Bill Staffman emerged, hastily adjusting his tie. He shuffled toward the portable soundstage, his large frame uncomfortably supporting an expensive Italian suit. From behind, he appeared like a large bear dressed in expensive men's clothing. Bill had never had a good clothing day or a good hair day. To compensate, he bought the most expensive attire he could fit into, but the end result was opulent frumpiness.

He slowly lumbered up the six steps and stood in front of the microphone. A teleprompter was present, but he reached forward and turned it off. "Max Masterson doesn't make speeches. He does not schedule, nor does he participate in interviews." He paused.

A collective "Huh?" was followed by a muttering sound that took on all of the qualities of a volcano about to explode.

Joe Mostatoccio of Reuters was the first to react. "We have been waiting all day for a story. Where is Max Masterson?"

"He's inside."

"How can that be? We have been here all day, and we didn't see him come in this morning."

"Max Masterson is an interesting man, who doesn't believe that the way we have been electing the president of the United States is the best way to pick the right person to lead our country. He also defies traditional politics and rejects politics as usual."

His remark compounded the derision of the press. The rumbling grew, as every voice with a microphone asked a question, more of a cacophony than a chorus. The sound was unintelligible and tinged with annoyance.

Bill raised his hands slowly, and the higher his hands rose, the quieter it got. When he had reached shoulder level, he achieved silence. "Max is an early riser, but this time, your intelligence is wrong. He has been here all night. We have been working on a press statement, which will be delivered by Max shortly."

Bill turned, walked to the back of the stage, and began to exit via the back stairs but paused and returned to the microphone. The lights came on again. "I need to tell you how this will go from now on. Every other day, you will be treated to public messages from Max, but it won't all be at press conferences. He might decide to issue a message through the Internet, a letter, or in person. He won't do the typical press conference thing."

He paused again, this time for effect. His audience seemed deep in thought.

"I won't be notifying you of coming attractions, and I won't be commenting or elaborating on what Max says. I don't tell him what to say, and he doesn't tell me what to say, but I have to live by the Maxims just like anyone else in the campaign."

"What are the Maxims?" Greg spoke to the back of Bill's head as he exited the stage.

Chapter Fifty-Two

For eight hours after Bill Staffman's impromptu appearance, the press churned and edited. Any reportable audio and video news is broadcast by satellite to the central office. After viewing by junior editors, the information is dissected and quickly forwarded to copywriters, who view each clip and write voice-overs. Any editorially relevant information is funneled through the information pipeline to the appropriate news desk, and the slant begins.

In Max's case, the lack of reportable information caused the press to use what they had, and the only bites worth reporting on the Masterson campaign had so far come from Bill. They had the promise of more tantalizing news from the candidate himself, and they weren't going anywhere until they had it in the can. Each news team stood huddled over monitors in their satellite trucks while the camera crews stood like sentries waiting for Max to emerge from the front door of his campaign headquarters. As their eyes tried to discern any movement inside the building, Max quietly took his place on the podium.

The stealth appearance of the subject of their surveillance caused several moments of controlled panic. Max stood at the podium before the microphone, dressed in his running outfit and looking composed as shouts of "There he is!", "Get the lights on!", "Where in the hell did he come from?," and "Did you leave the sound feed on?" ricocheted across the playground. He waited until they were in place, a process that seemed too long, but was really nothing more than an about-face.

"I'm Max Masterson, and I'm going to be your next president of the United States. I'll be appearing here and in other locations to present regular reports of my thoughts on issues that are important to Americans. Today, my thoughts are about war."

He paused, and then continued. "There will always be a big push for a president to go to war for the wrong reasons. The defense contractors always want war, and politicians who never went to war will be more likely to push for it. Never take advice on this subject from someone who has never been shot at. A president who goes to war, without being attacked by an enemy who isn't intent on harming the United States, commits his nation to failure. Either the voters will kick the scoundrel out or public opinion will sink him. Wars of occupation always lose.

"Our Founding Fathers would be considered revolutionaries in today's world. George Washington's army fought the battles, mostly as guerilla fighters. Thomas Jefferson wrote the messages of liberty from foreign control. Nathan Hale spoke against the occupation and was executed for the words he spoke against the occupiers. By night, Paul Revere delivered the message to resist, and by day, he was a successful businessman. These were people who were defending their homes against an occupying army. Every time we go into another country, we become the bad guys. Let's bargain with them instead. We are better bargainers than warriors any day, and sovereign countries need to maintain their independence free from occupation by foreigners."

They waited for more, accustomed to hour-long ramblings, but Max was done. He turned and vaulted off the front of the stage, then ran to the end of the street, turned toward the well-worn running path on the banks of the Potomac, and was gone before anyone had the presence of mind to turn off the cameras.

"I fooled them all this time, but I'm going to have to change my exit strategy every time. This place will be crawling with film crews in track suits within the hour," he thought. His speed had steadily increased over the mile from the stage to his car, but he estimated that he was running at a sub six-minute mile pace. The reporters were far behind, and his course through the park prevented pursuit by car. They weren't beyond pursuing him by helicopter if they had thought of it, but his unorthodox departure had prevented preparation in advance.

Max ran across the park toward a blue Jaguar parked behind a row of trees. As he crested the hill, he felt a sting at the base of his neck. "Damn wasps," he reasoned. He slapped his skin but didn't feel anything other than tingling at the bump caused by the stinger. "I'll have to put something on it as soon as I get on the plane."

Out of his line of sight, a man dressed in black disassembled a small caliber rifle, designed not to kill but to accurately place an electronic monitor under the skin of its target. The dart shot into Max's neck was so small that it resembled a black wasp, and when it hit Max's neck, it embedded an electronic surveillance device so small that after 24 hours, no evidence of its presence beneath the skin could be detected.

Max slowed when he could make out the lights lining the road at the bottom of the hill. One more turn, and his escape was assured. In the distance, the shining wax finish made the car look like a large sleek beetle. Its aerodynamic shape reminded him of his childhood. Rachel was sitting behind the wheel of the senator's XKR. As he approached the Jaguar, he smiled. "She must like this car," he thought. "I'll have to leave it to her in my will." He leaped into the passenger seat, not bothering to open the door. He had been doing that since he was 14, and old habits are hard to break. "To my chariot, Jeeves, I haven't a moment to waste," he joked in his best English accent, as Rachel slipped it into first gear and squealed away from their prearranged rendezvous point.

From behind a huge walnut tree, the man in black watched their departure through highly amplified night vision goggles. He was code-named Darkhorse, and his vocation as a mercenary allowed him to continue his passion for killing. "If they wanted me to snuff him, and the girl, too," he thought, "I'd do her for free, just like his daddy's girlfriend."

Chapter Fifty-Three

The meeting went on for hours before anyone lost focus enough to declare that they were hungry. Food was ordered, and the hours stretched into the night. Outside, the media was huddled around TV monitors watching the major news channels. It was a constant loop of Max's sound bites linked together by commentary, and the home office was getting itchy for new material.

"How long can we keep repeating a two-minute spot on illegal immigration?" bellowed Howard Rationalizer from the New York office of News Tonight. The object of his scorn was Greg Scuperman, who was glued to his cell phone, reporting nothing and getting more exasperated by the minute.

"I know he's in there, Howard. They assembled for a meeting at 10:00 a.m., and they have been going steady since then… I know that makes it seven hours straight. I don't know what to tell you. They ordered out for Chinese about three hours ago, and my people guarding his exit tunnel say that the door is locked and nobody has entered or left… I know he hasn't been seen in public… Howard, I don't have any more information than anyone else… Howard, dammit! I know how to do my job!" He hung up and auto-dialed his last hope for news.

"Greg here. Anything? You mean to tell me that nobody has left his estate? How can that be? His staff says he's here in a meeting… Are you sure? Okay, okay, I don't doubt you… Keep me posted, will you?"

In the meeting room, the image of Max showed he had changed from running clothes to a dark, three-piece suit, and he stood in the middle of the table, where his image could be rotated to the person speaking in the room automatically.

"We need to focus on a party name, and I don't have any idea who we can call to be a running mate." He directed his attention to Andrew Fox, but Bill Staffman interrupted.

"Max, you are beginning to act like you are going to win this thing, and the polls give the Democrats and the Republicans one-third of the popular vote. You managed to get all of the third-party votes and crossovers from both parties, but if it turns into a three-way race, you won't get enough votes to win. We can only hope to get enough crossover delegates to throw it over to Blythe. If you're going to really go for a win, we need to form an alliance with a running mate who has name recognition and broad appeal. It wouldn't hurt to have a little experience, either."

Staffman was still stinging from the recent news stories about the experience factor. Whenever a candidate runs for reelection, one asset they can pull out of their bag of tricks is the one that their opponent can't. Experience is only obtained by holding office, and an incumbent gains a clear advantage simply by being the incumbent. Max not only had no experience at being president... he had no experience at holding any kind of public office.

After a long meeting with Luke Postlewaite to discuss the issue, he realized that this perceived weakness had been discussed and resolved during the planning sessions that the senator held over a decade ago: inexperience can be perceived as change, but Max needed to project his candidacy as a fresh change and a separation from past policies that had failed. Not only policies, but a separation from a president who had failed the American people.

Luke and Bill had spent the previous day thoroughly analyzing their options while Max and Andrew were away recording his sound bite video in Michigan. They carefully considered the practicalities of winning, and they were still unsure whether Max wanted to win or was just trying to make history. They needed validation.

•   •   •

In a videoconference on the ride back from the airport to Fairlane, it was time to review the assignments from the previous meeting. "Max, we have done everything you asked us to do. We went to boring speeches and timed how long it took for the boredom to set in. I was as surprised as anyone to hear that nobody can keep an audience interested for longer than it takes to play a song on VH1, but it makes sense," reported Sara.

Staffman summarized. "After all of our hard work you have our total support. We believe in you, and we believe you can win. But you can't do it unless we gang up on Blythe. His people play dirty, and they're good at it. I have heard that his people are out there interviewing your old girlfriends, trying to dig up something nasty and kinky. I'm afraid that…"Max took his turn interrupting his chief of staff. He laughed, then his face turned suddenly serious. "You mean, the ladies didn't turn on me? They didn't find any illegitimate love child that I have been supporting, or a medical report showing that I got the clap on a trip to Paris, or how about that I like to be spanked?" He smirked. In the back of his mind, he knew that they would find nothing that would hurt his public persona. His father had protected his personal life since he was an infant, and the more they dug, the better he looked in the eyes of his detractors.

Andrew was the next to express his thoughts. He had served as the observer and the link to the hearts and minds of the people that politicians pandered to while seeking public office, but ignored when they had attained it—regular folks. "Max, I have been watching the reaction of people when you walk into a room." He paused to get their attention, and realized that he had it.

"The one thing you have that sets you apart is the feeling of hope that things will be better if you are in charge. It doesn't matter that you have no voting record. I don't think people care one lick that you have never been elected to anything or run for this job before. They look at you as the guy who will save them from the other politicians. But here's the thing. You need experience on your shoulder if it isn't under your belt."

"Andrew, I don't pay you enough. I also don't talk to you enough. I have been getting the same phone calls from most of the women they spoke to. I'm not worried. They called to tell me that they only said good things and pledged their affection for me. I did get one catty comment from that wild woman I dated back in 2009 who got all that money for jumping into a fountain with no underwear on under her dress. You remember. Sheila Something… Anyway, she was upset because I didn't make her press conference. I don't know why, after all this time, she's still upset with me. She made a lot of money selling her story to the tabloids," he said, looking wistful and straining to remember the details of their night on the town. He stared out the window toward the street, watching the incessant jumble of press below. They looked purposeful and productive, but so does an anthill.

He stopped reflecting and resumed planning. "Let's focus on the important issue here. I know my lack of experience is going to be problematic. I have been thinking like you do, that we need to bring in someone who can complement my assets, and we need to look like a team that people can have confidence in. I have that someone in mind, but I'm sure you and Bill have been secretly making me a list of suitables, am I right?" He sat back and waited for his two trusted advisors to scramble for their lists.

"Let's streamline this a little bit, just to save time. Do you agree on one person who is alive today and is the most qualified, whether they want it or not, who would be your first choice? Don't waste my time with anyone else." Both of them stopped their search and resumed their seats, leaning forward on their elbows with expectant looks. Bill had seniority, and he spoke first.

"Scarlett Conroy."

"Andrew?"

"Scarlett."

"Good," Max immediately replied. "That's who I picked, too. I met Scarlett when I was a kid, and she had that politician look back then. She needs to loosen up a little, but she's a perfect fit. Now we need to figure out how to convince her that she can't win without us. Oh, and her running mate may have a problem with us stealing her away."

Chapter Fifty-Four

"You really had them going, yesterday, Max. I can't stop thinking about the look on old Donald Ridgid's face when you jumped off the stage in front of him. He's got to be around a hundred years old by now, and I thought he was going to wet his pants." Andrew had watched from the second floor window of the old building housing the campaign. He knew in advance that Max had carefully exited the building through an underground tunnel built in the mid-1800s that had helped runaway slaves escape to boxcars at a railroad yard long since dismantled. The area was now occupied by upscale condos, but the tunnel still led to a nondescript building that was once adjacent to the railroad tracks. The trains that had secretly transported slaves to sympathetic northern states were now gone, but the secret escape route was still a good one.

Max had used the tunnel for weeks before the press arrived, and his lack of discovery gave him a misplaced sense of security. It wasn't that he was being careless, it was more like a feeling that all was well enough to keep him from fearing discovery. As he emerged from the old door housing the tunnel, he walked right into the bright lights of a film crew, fronted by none other than Greg Scuperman himself.

"We've been waiting for you, Mr. Masterson!"

His startled face was sure to appear on every network every fifteen minutes for the next day, at least. "Before you run off, I'd like to ask you a few questions, if I may." Scuperman was going to get his time in the limelight, and he would not be deterred by Max's quick escape. Besides, his way was effectively blocked by the satellite truck and equipment. Max resigned himself to the idea that he was trapped, but his eyes continued to look for an escape route.

"You are a very elusive man for a politician. Is this how you intend to deal with the press when you are president?" His tone was more scolding than inquiring, and Max took an immediate dislike to him.

"I am not a politician. I am a man who is running for president. When I come to live in the White House, I assure you, Mr. Scuperman, that you will not be invited to stay in the Lincoln bedroom. I think you're an asshole. Now excuse me." Max did a quick left fake, dodged right, and vaulted over the front hood of the sound truck, sliding across the hood and nimbly landing on both feet. Before the cameras could turn and refocus, he made a quick right so that the truck stood between him and the camera crew, and he was gone.

Chapter Fifty-Five

That evening, the news reports featured the short "interview," and the regulars at the Tavern began playing a constant loop of the encounter as soon as they arrived.

"I can't believe it! I never thought I would live to see the day that a politician gave what for to Scuperman. Did you see the look on his face? I can't believe it!" Phil was known for repeating himself, and every time he watched the video and sound bite, he came full circle.

"You know, I admire a guy who says what he thinks. I'm leaning toward voting for him. I voted for Blythe last time and look what he did to us! You know…" Phil stopped talking long enough for the loop to finish its latest cycle, and they all laughed, which continued through the first half of the next loop.

"I still can't believe that he called him an asshole. I always thought he was an asshole, but I never thought I'd hear anyone call him that to his face. Ya know?" Jerry reached for his third beer with his left hand and a chicken wing with his right and watched a remote camera view of Masterson and an attractive young woman boarding an ancient seaplane on the split screen. Surveillance cameras had tracked Max from his underground railroad tunnel escape to a marina, where the Beech 18 Seaplane was apparently docked. A voice-over by Scuperman droned on as the seaplane skidded across the bay and took flight.

"In his latest display of unpresidential behavior, independent candidate Max Masterson is seen fleeing our nation's capitol with an unidentified young woman…"

"I hate that asshole reporter," said Jerry, as he clicked off the reporter's tirade and transferred the split screen to a MaxTracker map. The map showed a magnified satellite image of the seaplane flying low above the treetops. "How did they know he's leaving D.C. and not know who he's with? I suppose we'll see her in a bikini on the evening report," he said as he directed his attention to Max's latest sound bite.

Chapter Fifty-Six

"Okay, take your seats!" The chief of staff had spoken. Everyone was gathered around the coffee machine, wolfing down bagels and chattering about nothing important, speaking without listening. They scrambled to their positions around the large cherry conference table, careful not to disturb the pile of papers Staffman had assembled in a semicircle before him.

To be included in the inner sanctum of the Masterson campaign was the privilege of a select few, and due to concerns that leaks might compromise their plans, no new staffers would be included for the duration. Every seat was taken, and they weren't going anywhere. To ruin that would, in their minds, be the equivalent of selling out Jesus for a few coins.

"Today, Max has asked me to exercise your minds a little. No, I take that back. We are going to exercise our minds a lot." Staffman paused and focused his gaze on every face in the room. If he detected any sign of disdain or lack of interest, he was ordered to report that person to Max for immediate dismissal and to delay the morning meeting until he or she had been removed. Max wanted total devotion, and he paid particular attention to the nonverbal cues that indicated lack of loyalty. He peered into their eyes.

Andrew Fox sat at the back, and Staffman focused his attention on his eyes the longest. If he had looked away, if his attention had been diverted for a moment, he would have been asked to leave, never to return. Fox passed the test, even though he didn't know he was being tested. From a concealed video link disguised behind a ceiling fixture in the room, Max was watching, too. The silent eye hadn't been used before, and he smiled as he focused on each face. Total devotion was what he found, and total devotion was what he required.

"He has set up a link from his home, and he will be appearing shortly," explained the chief of staff. It was obvious that Max's chair at the head of the table was unoccupied, but Staffman moved from his seat to the head of the table. He made a big production out of moving from one seat to the next, and his rotund body didn't look quite right in Max's chair, but he was determined to let everyone in the room know that he was the lead dog, and unless you're the lead dog, the view never changes. He treasured this moment for what seemed like too long, and then he announced, "Okay, Max, they all passed. They're yours!"

Max dimmed the lights remotely, and his image appeared in the middle of the table, as if a miniature Max Masterson had suddenly jumped out of the darkness. He could manipulate his holographic image so well that he could turn directly to the person he was addressing. His voice came from the image, and after a few words were spoken, the illusion that Max was in the room became their reality. Nobody dared to speak for fear that the magic would be shattered.

"Thank you, Bill. I always like it when you introduce me. It makes me feel important, even though I'm only two feet tall." The astonishment gave way to amusement. Max didn't bother to explain how he had created this fantasy or why he hadn't appeared in person. By this time, there was nothing orthodox about anything, and the campaign headquarters had become more like a building under siege than a place to get anything done. The press had discovered his secret entrance, and they stood guard over the door like ticket takers at the Super Bowl.

"Today, we are going to use our minds to change the way Americans think. I want to be more honest in my words. The problem is that the only words I have are the ones that don't describe what I'm talking about. So you and I are going to make new words."

Fred Dawson spoke first, brave enough to break the silence. "You mean, we don't have enough words?" His brow creased in a question mark. He spoke for the group, who all shared the same inquiring expression.

"No, a better description would be that our words limit our thoughts. When we use old words to describe new thoughts, we are limited to those experiences associated with the old words," explained Max's image.

"I still don't get it. We're supposed to just sit here and add new words to our vocabulary? Aren't we going to sound kind of supercalifragilistic?" Sara was no longer intimidated after her first exchange with Max, but nobody dared laugh aloud at her attempt at humor. It did provoke a room full of smiles, though, and Max smiled with her.

"That's a great question, and I want all of you to ask me whatever is on your minds. I want all of you to totally buy into this concept and understand what I'm trying, with your help and fresh minds, to accomplish. I hope you don't have any plans to go anywhere, because we're going to be doing this for a long time. I'm ordering food delivered and don't even ask to leave before we're done," explained the leprechaun.

Sara hadn't had enough time to absorb the message to fully understand it, but she wasn't going to let some Mini-Max steal her thunder. If past experience was any indication, she was going to keep asking questions until he either told her to sit down and shut up, or she became an expert on the subject. Neither of those events was looming on her horizon.

"You brought us in here to think up new words? Isn't this like Sesame Street?"

Max grinned his broadest grin, dimples deepening on his face. He knew when he brought her aboard that she had just the spark he needed to get the others moving in the right direction. She was fearless, and he knew he had her complete support. But if he couldn't win her over, he couldn't convince the others. He had to get their creative juices flowing, and flowing in the same direction.

"Now, you're starting to get it," offered Max. They all had opinions on the subject, and they were beginning to get into the idea. "You can go through this exercise and then sit for ideas and create new words. But first, you need to quit using the words that don't describe what you are talking about," Max explained.

"Max, I understand what we're doing in this exercise but you're making me feel like an idiot, and I'm getting this feeling like I get when the pastor in church makes me turn to the guy with a patch of hair growing out of his ears and say, 'Jesus loves you.' You know what I mean?" Andrew Fox was not known for expounding on issues of political importance, but this time, he hit the mother lode. Everyone in the room let out a collective sigh when he said it. Sara had been squirming for half an hour, and he knew that this touchy feely effort was going to degenerate into mass rebellion if he didn't speak up. They were feeling the same discomfort. Andrew took the response as approval, anything to get them out of this marathon sitin a circle, light candles, and sing "Kumbaya" session. He stood, and continued.

"When I was in college, I had a communications professor who got me over my shyness by whispering in my ear just before a speech." He looked around the room for some indication that his audience wasn't planning a lynching, and seeing no looks of anger, he continued. "I was scared. I was uncomfortable. I was about to stand in front of a room full of people, and I was sure that they weren't going to like what I had to say. My topic was chosen for me. I was the last person to choose from a list that the professor created." He paused, as if he was dredging his memory for details.

"I didn't like it, but I had to do a speech on canned corn. I was supposed to convince my audience that canned corn was the best thing in the world and make them want to buy it. Just before I stood at the podium, he walked up to me, and said, "Just make them laugh and pretend that they're all naked.""

They laughed, wondering how the quiet press secretary was going to tie this story into the weirdness they had been experiencing all day.

"You're probably wondering why I'm telling you about canned corn when we're supposed to be sitting here solving the world's problems and plotting how to get Max into the White House. Well, I'll tell you. Tomorrow." Andrew began packing up his papers and zipped his briefcase shut. While everyone in the room, and the elf in the middle of the table watched, he walked out without a word.

Chapter Fifty-Seven

The next morning, Andrew was purposely late. If he had done nothing else, he had the staff dangling for the next bit of information, and from the looks of things, he had their intense curiosity, too.

"Andrew, come on. You have everyone hanging. What is your point, and how does the story end?" Bill Staffman was not accustomed to dangling conclusions or upstart junior staffers who captured the attention of his subordinates.

"Don't tell this to the rest of them, okay?" Andrew was on the road to the next appearance for Max, and his satellite connection was tenuous between Montana and North Dakota. "I wanted to get their attention, and I did. My point is, you don't need to come up with a new vocabulary to get people to think your way. The reality is that I made the speech, but before I did, I cooked a pot of corn and put a bowlful in front of everyone in the room. While I spoke, they ate, and it didn't matter what I said. They had their corn."

This time, Postlewaite chimed in. "Son, I went to a pretty good college, and I did damn good in school, but I don't have a clue about what the hell you are talking about," he growled in his tidewater drawl. "Smart guy, tell me what corn has to do with what we call ourselves."

Andrew realized that he was far out in left field with these pragmatists. He needed to reel them in fast. "That's just the point. It doesn't matter what we call ourselves as long as we get their attention. It works with any issue. We decide to focus the public's attention on issues that we choose, we keep the message simple, and we let Blythe and his political machine talk about it until they lose the voter's attention. Meanwhile, Max is all over the country, beautiful outdoor settings that portray America as it is on picture postcards, he says his sound bite on any issue we choose, and we go on to the next venue. By the time Blythe can prepare a speech on our issue, we move on to the next. We avoid responding to their issues, always taking our shot and moving Max to somewhere unexpected. The plan is simple. Maintain interest, by every means possible. We will avoid repetition, and never campaign in the conventional way."

Staffman laughed. "You mean I'm not getting any corn?"

"Not until we roll through Iowa," he replied.

Chapter Fifty-Eight

The incumbent's daily itinerary was published by the White House sufficiently in advance of the president's campaign to allow for the setup of chairs, building of stages, erecting of lights and teleprompters, and transportation of the press to each speech location. The schedule was deliberately vague to give the illusion that terrorists and assassins weren't privy to the precise location of the president and his extensive entourage at any given moment, but any assassin worth his salt would be well versed in getting around those security measures. When the president was on the road, though, the best-equipped security detail in history went in advance with bomb-sniffing dogs, rooftop snipers, and the best communication available. They followed every lead, checked every bag, and only allowed a handpicked group to be in the audience.

In every crowd, though, protesters managed to infiltrate. Their carefully designed message was usually direct and brief. They would try to attract the attention of the press and get their point across in seconds, hopefully before they were whisked away by Secret Service. The force guarding the president were experts at making the campaign stops conflict-proof, but their real purpose in protecting the person at the top far exceeded the visible aspects of their presence. In any foray outside the formidable security of the White House, the president is at risk of harm. By occupying the top position in government, he becomes a target for those who desire to harm America, and for that reason, the president is never alone.

By contrast, third-party candidates and minor challengers have almost no security. They aren't targets, or if they are, it is the lunatic fringe they fear when they are out on the campaign trail. Theirs are spontaneous and unpredictable outbursts, and therefore often escape the attention of the press. The rare times that minor candidates experience a lack of privacy is when they are suddenly the focus of the press. For most minor candidates, their biggest occasions of attention come at the moment they announce their candidacy, when they commit a verbal gaffe, and when they drop out of the race.

When the Masterson campaign heated up, the major networks began assigning more correspondents to cover him, and the requests for his daily itinerary began increasing. This development left his campaign staff in a constant state of agitation since Max never informed them of his whereabouts. They were often as surprised by his entry to Masterson for President Headquarters as anyone else. On the rare morning when he did appear, the staff was usually caught chatting online and reading the news on their laptops. The chief of staff, Bill Staffman, was a traditionalist in information gathering and still relied on paper copies of newspapers from around the nation. He was usually found holed up in his office sequestered behind piles of paper.

On the Tuesday following the first debate, Max burst into the office dressed in his favorite running clothes, wet from a 5:00 a.m. five mile run along the Potomac. His abrupt entry caused Sue Follower to lean back abruptly in her chair, which then flung her onto the floor. This commotion caused a chain reaction of disarray, ending when a stack of newspapers fell off Staffman's desk onto the floor in a muffled crash.

"I see you're all coffeed up and ready to go," yelled Max, delighted that he had caught his staff in a lull. "I want everyone to be in the staff room in ten minutes for our first real meeting. I'm taking a shower."

He bounded up the stairs to the second floor apartment above the headquarters, a prerequisite in his search for a suitable location to direct his campaign. If he was going to be spending a lot of time in any location, it had to have the comforts of home. Time was wasted in transit.

In exactly ten minutes, he sat wet haired at the head of the enormous oak conference table, a remnant from the remodeling of the Maryland legislative offices in Annapolis. Because of its size, the building's facade was removed for a day while the table was installed in the "Great Room." Red, white, and blue chairs were placed around it. Already seated was the skeleton staff, which was being reinforced by stragglers who had been hastily summoned to the meeting. Several of the late arrivals were also wet haired, giving the meeting the appearance of a locker room talk in a boardroom. That suited Max just fine. He had a legendary disdain for formality and convention. He worked hard at cultivating his image as a straight talker and innovator, and rejected anything that resembled a traditional campaign outright.

"I think I did pretty well in that debate. What do you think?" He threw out the first question to nobody in general, but everyone knew that the pecking order started with the chief of staff and filtered down from there. It was startling to the staffers that the first to speak was Sara Wein, the young woman who had confronted him on the first day. She was new to the campaign business, but with the exception of Bill Staffman, so were all of the rest, including Max.

"You shocked the hell out of everyone, if that was your intention. I haven't left the office, and I spent all night monitoring the opinion pieces over the Internet. They range from total adoration to total disdain mixed with shock and awe," she said boldly.

"Yeah, but what was your take?"

"You mean, you want to know how I think you did?"

"I want to know from your mouth to my ears how you responded to my words. I had one goal last night and that was to have Americans remember what I said, agree with it, and forget what my opponents said, no matter whether they agreed or not. Did I achieve my goal?"

Sara thought for a moment, digesting the idea that the man she wanted to see in the Oval Office valued her opinion and her ability to tap the pulse of the voters. She was beginning to fall into the realm of hero worship here, but she knew that Max had no use for people who only said what he wanted to hear.

"You set yourself apart in a big way. Some of the people weren't used to it and are complaining that you didn't play by the rules, but mostly, the word on the street is that they liked it. The problem is, the only thing they have to read is from the press, and they are pretty unanimous in saying that you haven't paid your dues, you are too young to be running for president, and that your inexperience showed last night. The funny thing is, the exit polls are showing you way ahead of any of the other contenders, and the comments are mostly positive from the quotes I read."

"Sara. From your mouth to my ears. How do you feel about my performance in the debate?"

She blushed. It suddenly became apparent that she was being asked a personal question about how she felt, her gut feeling, her own response to his words. She took a deep breath and chose her words carefully. "When you spoke, I had this adrenaline rush. It seemed like you were talking only to me. In the beginning, I expected you to say more, but when they began replaying it over and over to fill your time, I began remembering every word. I have never felt that before."

"Superb!" Max stood abruptly. His chair shot back and slammed against the wall behind him as he raised his fist toward the seated faithful like a fan at a hockey game who had just watched a slap shot lift past a goalie's glove. "That's the kind of stuff I need to hear."

He sat down as quickly as he'd risen and slid his chair back to the table. Propping his arms and leaning forward, he directed his gaze at Postlewaite. "Luke, you are my ears in Washington. What are my enemies saying about last night?"

Postlewaite was nestled in the comfort of the overstuffed chair, absorbing the exchange, and waited a full minute before he spoke. In his 30 year Washington career, he had never observed a more unorthodox display of uniqueness. "Max. You're scaring the shit out of everyone except the president. They spent the evening spitting out propaganda to the press, basically dismissing you as a young upstart, but they can't deny that you got their attention."

Just then, the door burst open and in strode Fox, carrying a stack of papers in one hand and a Starbucks Mocha Grande in the other. If the dark circles under his eyes were any indication, he had not seen a bed in several days. His trademark suspenders failed to conceal the wrinkled disarray of the Oxford pinstripe shirt he'd worn the night before at the debate. It may have been the same outfit, but his red, white and green tie was long gone, there was a stain on his green pinstriped pants, and his black wingtips had been replaced by scuffed topsiders. He spoke quickly. "I have news that can't wait. There's a storm brewing out there, and it's all because of you." He turned to Max, who by this time was crunching a shiny winesap apple picked from the tree next to his home.

"I hope it's good. You're late. Where have you been all night?"

"Down at the AP newsroom, of course. I'm still a newsman, and they didn't take my press pass away just because I came to work for this group."

"What have you got?" mumbled Max through half-chewed apple and sips of green tea.

"I have never seen such a surge. The pollsters are going nuts on you. They got creative for once and began asking people to repeat what the candidates said about the issues, and, here's the kicker..." He paused for effect, as if his words were plowing new ground in journalistic soil. "They only remember you."

Chapter Fifty-Nine

The Monday morning staff meeting was composed of the hurried and stressed vestiges of the weekend. The suits were black, blue or gray, hair still wet from hurried showers, taken in the private rooms beneath the White House. If the private subway hadn't brought them in, Chief of Staff Waylon Cheevers would have been trapped in traffic thirty miles away, sipping coffee from a Styrofoam cup and using cuss words not often heard inside the beltway. Instead, he stood at the head of the huge mahogany conference table and cussed at the other twelve members of the inner circle.

"Dammit! How many of you idiots have something of substance to give me? I need dirt! Is he a homo, a druggie, or a ladies' man? I want pictures and notarized statements! You're giving me nothing but horseshit!"

"Sir, we have searched the public records. We interviewed eighteen old girlfriends. We can't find his medical records, and all the rest is locked into the Guardian privacy database. The girls all talked about him like he was a god. I've never heard such hero worship. They all want to marry him, he's a gentleman, and to hear them talk about it, he's great in the sack. Nothing kinky, and they'd do it again if he'd show any interest. The one criticism they have is that he's too busy running for president to call. We have dozens more to talk to, but they're all telling the same story," said Secretary of Intelligence Gunter Cover.

"I don't care if you have to match his DNA with an unsolved murder. I want something to take to the president before he asks!" He lingered on the word for emphasis, and it had its intended effect. The suits were squirming. "I can't face him on Air Force One again without a full dossier on Masterson. I want pictures! Videos of him in his underwear giving candy to little girls!" The veins began to pop out on his forehead. His ruddy complexion turned purple. It was 8:09 in the morning, and he was rapidly approaching a stroke. He took a long sip of cappuccino and sucked on his first cigar of the day, pausing long enough to cough. They didn't know it, but whenever he paused from his yelling, his formidable brain was recharging his mouth to spew forth another line of vitriol.

"You, Wiessel! You're worthless. I send you back to his college, and you come back with stories about how hard he studied and his good manners! The next time you leave your cubicle, I'll send you back to Flat Rock!"

Wiessel was perspiring so much that his armpits soaked through his suit jacket. "Sir, I have the utmost respect for the president. I would do anything to dig up dirt on this guy. The only thing I can find in his family history is that he's adopted, and that his father, Senator Masterson, had an ancestor who may or may not have been hanged as a witch in 17th century Connecticut!" Wiessel seemed to swell in his chair, but when he was through speaking, he deflated back to his previous cowering.

Promptly at 8:15, the double doors of the conference room swung open, and the Secret Service men parted for their corners, leaving the Ppresident silhouetted in the doorway. It was time for the staff to endure another meeting with the commander-in-chief, who had already been awake for two hours and wasn't having a good day.

Chapter Sixty

Rachel drove the converted battery-powered '66 Mustang convertible chosen from the senator's stable of classic vehicles, winding silently over the tree-lined roadway of the Beltline, and Max sat beside her, running his day through his mind. He'd sat for ideas for six hours and was kicking himself mentally for working in such an exhausting mode. No session of sitting for ideas should last more than two hours. His father had been adamant that anything longer leads to unsure and inaccurate ideas. He needed clear focus.

Each time he sat for ideas, Max ran the warm-up routine through his head:

Enter the thinking sanctuary rested and fed.
Leave all outside influences behind.
Prepare thinking points for focus.
Dictate ideas.
When detail overcomes inspiration, move on to the next thinking point.
When you begin to think about your plans for the rest of your day, the session is over.
Don't be slave to the clock. Leave all timekeepers outside of the room.
Think alone.
Review your notes for wisdom.
Share the wisdom with your advisors.

The thinking sanctuary is simple in concept but essential in the lives of those who practice the concept of sitting for ideas. The room is windowless and soundproof, comfort-controlled by an HVAC system that allows the thinker to adjust the environment of the room by voice control. The humidity, temperature, and aroma of the room can also be adjusted this way, and the computer retains data on the preferences of the user. Any scent, from spearmint to the smell of freshly cut grass, can be brought into the thinking environment.

If Max conversed with the computer, it spoke to him in the voice of his father and contained a huge database of his father's thoughts on thousands of subjects. If he chose, a holographic image of his father could be projected in front of him, making it appear as if Senator Masterson had joined him in the room.

"Dad, I think I succeeded at setting myself apart," he had mused. "I like this part of politics. If only I didn't have to do the other stuff. It's too dangerous. I never know who is going to take a shot at me or take my picture… Come to think of it, I'm not too enthused about either one of them at the moment." He had shut down the equipment and walked out, exhausted.

Chapter Sixty-One

"Our immediate problem is, what are we going to call ourselves? Let's make history!"

Bill Staffman led the Tuesday morning staff meeting like a cheerleader; the departure from his normal taciturn, New England demeanor was uncharacteristic so early in the morning, and Sara hadn't yet finished her first green tea of the day. She began to fidget in her seat, and Max detected the movement on the monitor. He was sticking to the tradition of appearing virtually from his home rather than in person. She raised her eyebrows and spoke.

"Max, we spent a lot of time coming up with choices. About midnight, we narrowed it down to two…"

Max leaned forward in his leather chair. "Sara, if I was there, I'd hug you. What have you got?"

"Well, since you have been labeled an Independent, we came up with the Independent Party, but Randy says that sucks, because Independents are candidates without a party, so we came up with the Patriot Party, because that's what we hear people calling themselves lately, and we want to get away from liberal and conservative as labels, and…"

"Did you say that people are calling themselves patriots?" Max stared intently at Sara's eyes.

"Yeah, why?"

"Don't you see? It's a symptom of voter apathy. It goes along with all of my Maxims. People are fed up with politics as usual, but they can't stop being Americans. They know the difference between right and wrong. I think we found ourselves a name."

"No, it's been done before," offered Bill Staffman, who had previously been silent as the young staffers used the free flow of their fertile minds to explore the issue at hand.

"We already have an American Patriot Party, although you probably never heard of it. The idea never caught fire. There have been Patriot Parties throughout history. I think we need to call it the New Patriot party to set ourselves apart. You have already got people talking about how you're a breath of fresh air on the political scene anyway, Max."

"Max, are you saying we go with the New Patriot Party?" Andrew felt a secure rush of excitement as he said the words. The word patriot was a word from the past that evoked a zealous American spirit, and yet it was new and fresh and exciting. Andrew could use that. "I could issue a press release that would blow their minds," he thought.

"Andrew. Draft a press release that will blow their minds." Max seemed to be tuned into his thoughts.

"I'm on it!" Andrew stood and walked toward the door.

"Before the release goes out, I want you to run it by your mom and tell me what she thinks," Max announced as Andrew reached for the door.

"Max, I don't do anything without mom's approval. I know who's boss." The door closed behind him with a hiss. He was back in five minutes. "Mom says that if you are going to be an Independent, you will have to run as an Independent, and none of that party politics she keeps hearing about," Andrew said wearily, still smarting from his mother's words.

Max responded immediately. "Andrew, I fear the wrath of Leila Fox more than Blythe himself. If mom says no, she means no. There will be no party for me in this campaign."

Chapter Sixty-Two

"She was made for it, I tell you. A natural politician, the kind of woman who will shake your hand and make you forget whether you wuz raised Democrat or Republican!" The old man pulled the night crawler out of the Styrofoam cup and baited the hook in one loop.

"I dunno. She's too purty to be a politician. I voted for her daddy, though. He come to my house one time. I offert him a beer, but he jest smiled and tole me that if he had a beer every time some constichient offert, he'd be looking for unemployment. I liked that man. I wuz sorry to hear he passed."

The other fisherman was old, too, and had spent most of his life outdoors. You couldn't tell whether his face was tanned or dyed brown. It looked like the kind of leather they make baseball mitts from, and when he talked, his wrinkles moved. He wore a weathered Caterpillar Tractor hat, faded by too many afternoons in the sun. People who live longer than their time have a wisdom that fits like a favorite pair of jeans, and their tolerance for fancy is nonexistent.

"I still think ya need ta hear what she has to say," said the first fisherman. Just then, his pole twitched, and he pulled back quickly, setting the hook. Without cranking the reel, he hauled a bass over the dock and into the open cooler. "I'm one up on ya! If you don't keep up, you get to clean 'em all, and I'll just put my feet up and watch you work!"

Outdoorsmen don't talk much when they're fishing. Come to think of it, most of them don't talk much when they're doing anything, but when they do, they don't waste words. "Ah hear what y'all er sayin'. Ah don't have much use for politicians, but Ah'll go with y'all and the Missus to that rally, provided y'all don't make me dress up."

The first fisherman turned slowly and stared directly into his old friend's grizzled face. "If I ever saw you dressed up, I'd either fall over dead or make sure you wuz lyin' in a casket yourself, cuz I can't think far enough back to remember you wearin' a suit and tie. Besides, I'm going just like I am. The wife might make me wear cologne or take a shower or both, but they can't make me do anything I don't want to do. I'm too old for that."

The next night was the rally, and for a week before, the county park was filled with the noise of pounding nails as the stage was erected by the party faithful. Some supporters offered money, others offered time, and by that night, the time and money coalesced into a well-oiled machine. As they had done for centuries before, the party had mobilized and energized, and this night was bound to be an event to be remembered...at least until the next election.

The band got the crowd moving, and then the local politicians got five minutes each at the microphone. After an hour of standing on the lawn, the old fisherman, his wife in front, began to shift back and forth on the balls of his feet. "Where is she? You told me we wuz goin' ta hear her speak, and all I heard so far is a bunch of people I never heard of." The wrinkled face seemed to sag even more if that was possible.

"Ah tole ya not to bring him!" The wife looked at her husband, his hair slicked back and still looking wet from the shower taken hours before. He'd known he'd eventually be blamed for everything out of his control.

"She'll be here. They didn't go to all this trouble for nothin'," he said to nobody in particular.

The normal rumble of the crowd changed to one of exclamation. "There she is!" a woman exclaimed, as every head in the crowd turned toward the entrance road. A white stretch limousine slowly appeared behind the stage and stopped. The crowd cheered and fell silent. It seemed a long time before anyone emerged from the limo, and the crowd whispered as dark-suited men appeared on the rooftops surrounding the outdoor amphitheater. They spoke into hidden microphones in their lapels. Security was in place.

The front door opened, and a driver emerged, dressed immaculately in a tight red chauffeur's uniform. He walked around the limo, opened the back passenger door, and stood at attention. The candidate emerged, her tanned legs sliding out first, followed by the rest. She stood smiling in a red dress, the kind that nobody wears in real life. It was the uniform of the politician.

She began waving to everyone, and the crowd smiled with her. The clapping escalated as she walked slowly toward the stage. They were hers for the taking.

Scarlett Conroy had made her political reputation the hard, traditional way. Her family was a sixth generation Charleston clan, with more cousins in high places than a tree full of monkeys. She exuded the image of stability, and she had just been elected to her second term in the Senate, representing South Carolina. Her pedigree as a politician was impeccable.

She had the pedigree to be president, but not the support in the polls. Her lack of numbers kept her in the running for vice president, but she had never been able to get that hellfire excitement her male counterparts generated. She was inspiring, though, and exciting to be around. Her demeanor engendered trust, and her running mate knew it. Scarlett was a vestige of the Old South, and Cunningham needed her to balance the ticket.

"If I had gone to war and had the stories to tell, I could be one of the Good Old Boys who sit around impressing you more every time I tell it," she told the women at the many speeches she made on the campaign trail. She knew she had their vote. Women could be counted on whenever a prominent woman sought higher office. Cunningham's pollsters had calculated her vote potential and knew she was a jewel who could bring them a win.

She approached the stage, and the fanfare grew. At a prearranged place on the stairs, she stepped to the left and pulled a gold hairbrush out of her purse, pausing for effect. The bright lights caught each stroke as she ostentatiously brushed her hair while thousands watched. When she was certain that she had their attention and each hair was in place, she deftly inserted the brush in a side pocket and completed her rise to the podium. This routine had become her trademark. It was a way of setting her apart, of defining her place as a woman in the midst of maleness. She did it well.

Scarlett had been running for office most of her adult life and felt at home in the midst of the adoration and attention. It was like comfort food to her; her life had been spent in the best private girls' schools, learning the social graces. She knew exactly what to say and when to say it, and she had a radar-like ability to be where she could obtain the maximum attention. In her speeches, she used few notes. Palming 3x5 cards trimmed to fit her delicate hands, she reduced her talking points to a few key words. With just the talking points to guide her, she could speak for hours.

"I stand before you today as your nominee for vice president of the United States, and you, dear voters, are the first to know!" For the ensuing five minutes, the cheering was too loud to hear her words. It was time to stand and smile. Eventually she raised her hand for silence and continued.

"I will be joining the party's nominee for president, Bob Cunningham, in Washington this afternoon, and we're going on to the White House in November!" An aide leaned over and spoke into a hidden microphone.

"Well, I won't be living there, and I guess the old occupants get until January to move out, but we're going to be in Washington anyway!" The crowd laughed and cheered again, as if she intended her remarks. Although she was known for her ability to speak for hours on any subject, she wasn't known for her accuracy. It didn't matter, though; this audience was hers. If she had stood up and told these folks that she was carrying Elvis's love child, they would have supported her decision.

Scarlett's speech was a well-constructed combination of worn slogans, win win statements that polls had demonstrated were safe talking points, and a rah rah patois of "hooray for our side" stories that she was comfortable repeating at every stop. From repetition, Scarlett had perfected the stump speech, and when she was tired at the end of the day, she had the ability to put her brain on repeat and give her mind a rest.

"My Female Americans…" She paused for effect.

"I'm sorry. I meant to say, 'My fellow Americans' like my opponents are fond of saying, but we aren't all fellows, are we, ladies?" She shamelessly pandered to the female vote, and as the only female running for national office, she was a member of a sorority that banned males from birth. "We have a long way to go before this men's club invites me to be a member." She paused again, and a woman in the front row hollered before she could continue. "That's okay, Scarlett, you have bigger balls than old Blythe, any day!" These words got one of the bigger cheers of the day.

In an era where the popularity of a president wanes from the first day in office to the last day in the White House, a popular challenger can enter the campaign dozens of points higher in the polls than the incumbent. After four years, Blythe's popularity was at an all-time low, and Scarlett wasn't the only one taking pot shots at him. Her running mate, Bob Cunningham, took the lead in attacking him about anything from his lack of moral character to his impotent efforts at stimulating the economy. Scarlett's job was to use the silk-gloved approach of softening the message so it wouldn't appear that the poor president was getting picked on, while Cunningham led the charge in another state. Their speeches were strategically timed to run simultaneously, so that the networks would be forced to shift all of their exclusive coverage from other candidates.

When it came to pointing out their differences, though, Scarlett was a sophisticated and devious opponent. She could pick apart her competition while smiling in that way only Southern women can muster, and her years in the Junior League had made her realize that when it comes to verbal attack, only women can swoop in without mercy, smiling, and leave their opponents dazed and confused.

Chapter Sixty-Three

"Look at those guys. They must have bought up every tie in town with red, white and blue on them," Andrew said. He and Max sat at the coffee table in the Michigan farmhouse, drinking Stroh's beer and gnawing at roast venison ribs that had been marinating in Mom's secret sauce for a week. The freezer in the utility room filled with wild game each fall, and by mid-summer, it was nearly empty. Hunting season is big business in the upper Midwest, and if they aren't hunting, they're preparing to hunt or feeding on the previous season's bounty.

On the large flat screen monitor were two conventions running simultaneously in split screen mode, the Democratic convention in blue on the left, and the Republican convention in red on the right. Each had been preserved in real time and summoned for review. Speaking at the podium, the incumbent paused frequently for the applause to subside. He had accepted his party's nomination for president 45 minutes earlier, and this was as euphoric as the attendees had been all week. He was definitely preaching to the choir.

On the other side of the screen was the challenger, a grizzled veteran of Congress who was in the process of exceeding all records for the length of an acceptance speech. He had been going at it for over an hour and a half, and his face was becoming more purple as he spoke.

"This is where old Bob Cunningham has a stroke! Watch!" Andrew held the zoom control in his right hand, and centered on Cunningham's face. As he approached the crescendo of his message, his voice rose higher than usual, and the sweat began to appear on his forehead. Then it happened— a purple streak ran up the right side of his face, and his eyes rolled back into his head. He slumped onto the podium, which was ominously draped with an American flag like the caskets that bring soldiers home from war. Two dark-suited men appeared from the side of the stage and held him up by his elbows. As they carried him hurriedly off camera to waiting paramedics, it was apparent that the party's candidate for president was gravely ill.

Chapter Sixty-Four

The nation watched the endless loops of media commentary in shock. The clip of Cunningham's public demise was disseminated almost instantaneously. By this time, Scarlett was 45 minutes into her own speech, lost in the glory of her words and creating a furor among the uninformed. Gradually, though, the back of the crowd became silent, and a murmuring rose as people looked down at their wrist monitors. Soon, an assistant spoke into Scarlett's communicator.

"He's dead. Cunningham is dead. Wrap it up."

Scarlett stopped in mid-sentence, as if she had suddenly lost her teleprompter notes. Her face turned pasty white, and it appeared for a moment that she might pass out. She looked from side to side, bewildered, waiting for a voice in her ear to tell her what to do next. Without a sound, she turned her back to her audience looking for her aides. They were waving for her to leave, but she didn't seem to notice. The audience was so preoccupied with the news that they barely noticed her exit from the stage.

"What does this mean?" Scarlett was clearly perplexed. Her trademark smile was replaced with grim concern.

"Somebody tell me what comes next." she rasped into the microphone. She scurried for the limo as staffers and security spoke in hushed tones into their communicators. An aide attempted to usher

her into the limo and put a finger to her lips. "I will not be hushed! This was all unplanned! This just can't be!" As her head was being inserted into the back seat of the limo, her fading voice could be heard to say, "Someone needs to pull a knot on this, and…" The door slammed shut as the tires sprayed gravel on the last remaining spectators.

The chief of security leaned over and buckled her into her seat, setting the environmental and security controls located in the seat back. "Miss Scarlett, I'm taking you the airport, and then we'll soon be flying to Washington to meet with the party. It looks like you won't be waiting until January to sit with the big boys."

Chapter Sixty-Five

"I'm the front-runner," said Samuel Hilton, the gun control candidate. He had never been at the top, or even received more than 4% of the national polls, but a poll of duck hunters sponsored by Foster Gates propelled him to the top when Cunningham made his untimely exit from the race.

"I'm the front-runner," announced the Reverend Billy Brooks, who had just been named the front-runner by the American Way Party, as the result of a poll of 1,000 Baptists in New Jersey, together with a poll of viewers of the popular anachronistic TV show, "Our Family Home," set in the idyllic fictional Ohio town of Millville, which reached 12 million viewers nationwide. "I stand before you today in a state of sorrow," he stated with utmost sincerity, his head held high in the posture of a Baptist preacher. "America is at a crossroads. We need to restore family values and avoid the excesses that led to Mr. Cunningham's premature death. We need to keep the family intact, refrain from society's vices, and return to the days when people didn't have to worry about locking their doors when they went out. We will not lose our values to those who seek to change our way of life."

Forrest Carruthers was in Arkansas, where his power base had established its national office in the small town of Quincy, where the only two-story building was the church, which he had prominently placed in the background. Its famous three-story cross was visible

behind him as he spoke. "I may be an old dog, but I learned to fetch
long ago. I'm going for the position that Mr. Cunningham so aptly
filled, God rest his soul." His wife hustled him off the stage.

Two days later, it was announced that the Carruthers campaign
was folding its tent and going home, as the campaign coffers had been
depleted. The real reason was that Carruthers had lapsed into the early
stages of Alzheimer's, and the microphones had recorded his statement
about how he was going to kick Dick Nixon's ass in the general election.

At the airport, Scarlett was mobbed by the press and took the
opportunity to make a short statement from the steps of the plane as
her staff stood behind her. "I am the party's candidate for president
now, and we will take this campaign across this great country. I want
every American to know that I appreciate your support in this time of
great sorrow." Scarlett's speechwriters, who saw her present status as
presidential candidate by default as their best opportunity to boost her
standing in the polls, had wasted no time in preparing her speech.

Her running mate's death bounced her up to third place in the AP
and Reuters polls, and she was sure to maximize her press exposure in
the ensuing days. On stage and in front of cameras on an exhausting
schedule, her face was everywhere. In the rush to prepare her for the
appropriate words to say in the nation's time of grief, however, her
handlers forgot to prepare words of substance for her.

"Scarlett, can you tell us, upon your running mate's demise, what is
the future of your run for president," asked Rita Orbot, an independent
news gatherer for YouTube.

"I can't worry about that now. It's not important. We need to
attend to Bob's funeral, which will be tomorrow at 11:30 a.m. A
horse-drawn carriage will take his body for internment in Arlington
National Cemetery. It's a closed service, and afterward, there will be
refreshments at party headquarters. Invitations have been e-mailed to
3,000 selected friends of the family." Instead of her trademark red suit,
Scarlett chose a proper black ensemble but wore a white pearl necklace
so as not to look too depressed.

"As the front-runner, do you have any comment on the issues of the day, particularly the issue of illegal immigration, which has come back into the news due to the recent measures by our present administration to support amnesty for the 20 million people who are here illegally?" Rita had been trained well. A reporter never gives up the opportunity to ask another question when the microphone is in use.

"I don't care about that now. If it was up to me, I'd put them all on a bus and send them back to where they came from!" Scarlett stepped into a black stretch limo and was off. Rita stood there for a moment before realizing that she had just recorded the best sound bite of her career.

Max issued a statement on his website. "I'm sorry he's dead. I'm thinking about his family, as I'm sure you are. He left behind a wife and two young children, and I'm calling upon all Americans, young and old, to give a dollar to his family, to be matched dollar for dollar by his party. His campaign owes it to him. It's the right thing to do."

Within 24 hours, direct deposits by contributors to the Cunningham Widow and Orphan Fund had topped all previous single day contributions to Cunningham's presidential campaign fund. It seemed that America cared more about his family than his run for the White House.

Chapter Sixty-Six

"That son of a bitch! If we put up matching funds, we'll drain our campaign fund down to nothing, while Masterson propels his sorry ass into the lead, and there's nothing we can do about it!" National Party Chairman Victor Miniver pounded his diminutive hand on the rolltop desk in the party conference room, while Scarlett, fifteen consultants, and a number of hastily assembled state party chairmen looked on in silence. They didn't know what to say, and it probably would be masochistic to interrupt Victor mid-tirade.

"I assembled the dream team of Cunningham and Conroy to steal the presidency, and Dammit!" He began choking, perspiration coating his red face like he had just stepped off a treadmill. He reached for the glass of ice water that Scarlett had just poured for herself, and without asking for permission, downed the contents in six gulps. With water dripping off his chin, he continued. "We got more money contributed to his wife and kids than we did to the campaign, and all of those ads we bought and paid for before that… that… son of a bitch dropped dead is all in the toilet! Hell, we may as well run them anyway. We can pick up a few sympathy votes for whomever we choose to take his place."

They were each silently wondering whether Miniver was blaming Cunningham or Max for the unexpected woes of the campaign, but it was not the time to ask questions. "And Masterson drained the rest of our funds by pulling this stunt! How would it look if we showed our disrespect by refusing to pay? We may as well get caught lighting puppies on fire. This campaign is dead."

Scarlett took advantage of the pause to stand and face Miniver. She'd had about enough of Miniver's histrionics. She had come to this meeting to get the blessing of the party leadership and discuss who would be her running mate. "Victor, it appears that the idea of the vice president stepping into the role of president has been lost on you…"

Miniver charged in Scarlett's direction, picking a newspaper up from his desk. "Read this to everyone. I'm not the only one who feels this way. Our polls back them up. You were brought on board to balance the ticket and get us the female votes. I'm in the business of getting people elected. I don't give a damn about what you do once you get there."

Miniver turned his back on the room as Scarlett read the lead editorial of the Manchester Union Leader: "When New Hampshire partisans are asked to defend the nation's first primary, we talk about our ability to see the candidates up close, ask tough questions and see through the baloney. If a candidate is a phony, we assure ourselves and the rest of the world that we'll know it. Scarlett Conroy is such a candidate. New Hampshire residents and independents must vote no. Bill Cunningham was our choice. We now endorse Max Masterson for President of the United States."

"They can't do that… can they?" raged Scarlett at nobody in particular.

"Actually, they can, and they did, and we're not going to do anything about it." He was a political boss. A small man, diminutive by all accounts, but if a person's qualities were tattooed on his forehead, "Shrewd" would be the word displayed on the head of Victor Miniver. "I want you to know that you are not my choice for president. You were the decided choice of the committee, and I voted against you. The party has no faith in your ability to attain the presidency."

Scarlett was intimidated by the sheer meanness of the man, but she wasn't about to let him belittle her in the presence of the party heads with whom she had so faithfully networked throughout her political career. "But the vice president succeeds the president," she muttered, looking for support on the faces of the twelve males who surrounded the conference table. None of them made eye contact with her, and she knew that they had discussed and decided her future before she got off the plane.

Miniver wasn't through intimidating, and he sneered at her words. "You aren't the vice president, he wasn't the president, and at the rate of your erosion in the polls since Cunningham dropped dead, you won't even come in a distant third."

He was ruthless. She could tell by the slight affirmative nodding of heads that her chances of convincing them otherwise were somewhere between "not a chance" and "hell, no."

"We have the New Hampshire primary in three days, followed next Tuesday by the Northeast primary. If it wasn't for the fact that you and Cunningham were the consensus picks, we wouldn't be having this conversation. I predict you'll go down in flames."

It was Scarlett's turn to show her rage, but her lack of practical experience in screaming at people forced her to delay her saying anything until she could pull her persona back together. She sat silently, her hands tingling. Although the temperature of the room was too cold for her comfort, she felt her cheeks flush. She was too much of a lady to cuss, and even though she felt the same urge to strangle Miniver that had passed through the minds of many candidates before her, she maintained her dignity. After all, her proper childhood of cotillions and Junior League socials would forbid any kind of angry response.

She chose to deal with this in her own way. Standing without a word, she gathered her purse and coat, then turned toward Miniver. She couldn't bear to look him directly in the eye for fear of losing her composure and focused her glare on his forehead. Her campaign was dead in the water. Her reputation was not as a hard-charging leader, but as a popular public figure with a knack for getting her face in the news without getting arrested. She knew that, and the despair produced by Miniver's harsh appraisal of her chances passed through her like a wave of ice water.

"I trust that you haven't had time to find another man to take Cunningham's place in this election, so I will tell you now. You will be looking for two candidates to run against Blythe. I hereby withdraw my name as the party's candidate for the vice presidency, and I will be asking the party's delegates to support me in my campaign for the presidency as an independent."

Scarlett's face and hair took on a similar hue. "Mr. Miniver, you haven't seen the last of me, and by the time the sun sets, every registered voter in every state, every woman, man, and child, will know what you have done here today. I wish you and your henchmen all the success that you deserve, and no more. Good day, Sir!"

Before Miniver could respond, she pulled open the heavy conference doors and made her escape. As the doors closed, she heard Miniver squeak angrily, "You won't get my delegates, and you won't get more than 20% of the popular…"

Chapter Sixty-Seven

Cunningham died so close to the New Hampshire primary that it was too late for the ballots to be changed. The voters cast their ballots the old-fashioned way, following the Yankee tradition of going to the polls in the many small towns across the state. Although all of the regional primaries had gone to electronic voting from the security and comfort of the Internet, New Hampshire chose to remain a rebellious vestige of the past. The state constitution mandates that New Hampshire hold the first primary in each presidential election, and they weren't about to change a thing.

It didn't appear to be important to New Hampshire voters that they were casting their vote for a dead man and a running mate who had just resigned from the party. In fact, they took perverse pleasure in overwhelmingly voting for Cunningham and Conroy. Voters who would have otherwise voted for Blythe and Case crossed over to ensure a substantial victory for the Cunningham and Conroy ticket, a vocal symbolic protest that signified the degree of angst the voters felt toward party politics, and more significantly, toward politicians themselves.

Max was a close second, followed by the incumbent, a distant third. Blythe watched the returns broadcast on a virtual screen. Ted Schoolcraft, his advisor, sat in a plush chair in the corner, careful not to be in the president's line of sight when the eruption occurred, which he was certain would happen shortly after the polls closed and the results were broadcast. He could have excused himself and gone into hiding at that moment, but it was his job to be there, and he was prepared for the wrath of Blythe.

Blythe was furious that he had been beaten by an independent. "Ted, what I'm seeing here is a new trend, and it's got me worried." Blythe was unusually subdued, but Schoolcraft knew from experience about the low rumbling preceding most large explosions, and from the look on his face, he knew it was coming—and soon. Blythe stood suddenly, knocking a tray full of chicken wings onto the carpet, oblivious to the mess. He addressed the screen directly, as if talking to the many political commentators, self-appointed advisors, and consultants hired by the networks to cast their spin on the election.

"How in the name of Geronimo did I finish third place to a dead guy and an independent?

Who am I running against, anyway? I didn't even get my own party to vote for me!" He paused, noticed a particularly plump chicken wing that remained stuck to the tray, and snatched it off the floor. He didn't bother to use a napkin, wiping the grease from his face with the sleeve of his sweatshirt. As he stared at the numbers on the screen, he hopped from foot to foot and pondered his next move.

"This young guy, Masterson, I met him when he was a kid, I think. His dad was a real character. A senator, you know. Adopted that kid from a car wreck. Raised him as his own. Never married, but he sure could pick his women. Looks like the son took after daddy. Good looking kid, but not ready to be president. Not yet," he said, still chewing. "I want more intelligence on this guy. He could cost me the election from what I'm seeing here. I'm sure there are some hot stories to come out of the babes he's been hanging with. Maybe some pictures, too. Get on it."

Cover stood silent. All of his previous efforts had been obviously ignored, and he had no idea what the president had bothered to retain in his memory. He resolved to repackage the same information, but this time, he would paste a picture on the front.

Chapter Sixty-Eight

Back at the White House, Secretary of Intelligence Gunter Cover waited patiently for the president's helicopter to arrive from his weekend at Camp David. Security was tight, as it typically is, but in recent days, terrorist activity had been increasing beyond the comfort zone. The terrorist surveillance system was massive. A gargantuan computer monitored all activity of interest, defined by the algorithms and protocols designed to detect threats against the United States. As of 3:00 a.m., Internet communications signaled that an "event" was imminent.

After he took this appointment to head the Department of Intelligence, he spent months of sleepless nights in his cavernous office in Langley, Virginia, worrying that monitoring wasn't good enough. It seemed as if the main job of his agency had become guarding nuclear material throughout the world, keeping it from falling into the hands of terrorists. That was compounded by the insurmountable task of keeping that same nuclear material from crossing the borders to be used as a nuclear "dirty" bomb. Constructing the bomb inside the U.S. had long been considered a standard aspect of Al Qaeda training, and it was a priority surveillance issue for the agents who reported from remote areas in Pakistan.

Within the previous two weeks, there had been four security breaches at nuclear facilities in Pakistan, Afghanistan, and Russia. There was an unverified report that nuclear material had been removed from a facility in Kazakhstan, and with the shoddy record keeping in that facility, nothing could be verified. Reports indicated that an undetermined amount of fissionable material had been delivered by an underpaid shift worker into the waiting hands of a man with middle-eastern features for payment in American dollars.

As he processed this recent information for presentation to the president upon his arrival, the sound of an elevator got his attention. Suddenly, four Secret Service agents entered the room, did a quick scan, and took their positions in concealed booths adjacent to the Oval Office. In walked the president with his trusty golden retriever, Buddy, at his side. Buddy sniffed each object in the room and resumed his position next to Blythe.

"Mr. Cover, what can I do for you?" The president had obviously been visiting the wet bar on Air Force Two, and his breath lent an aroma of gin and tonic to the antiques in the room.

"Mr. President, I came here to…"

"Mr. Cover, how is our little surveillance going?"

"Sir, which surveillance?"

"You know."

He leaned back in his chair and put both feet, caked with mud, on his desk.

"Mr. President, we are presently engaged in active surveillance of terrorists in Pakistan and Kazakhstan who have gained access to nuclear material, and we are…"

"Mr. Cover."

"Yes, sir."

"I want to know, and I want to know now, how our little surveillance of Max Masterson is going, and I want to hear all of the sordid details."

"Mr. President, we have assigned a team of agents to Mr. Masterson, and he seems to be traveling the country by plane filming political advertisements. He has his girlfriend with him, and she flies the plane when he isn't waiting in line at commercial airports making a spectacle of himself. I don't know what else to tell you at this point."

Blythe rose and rocked on his heels behind the desk, his red eyes and red face betraying his state of intoxication and anger. "I told you weeks ago that I wanted dirt!" His hand rose and a pen flew across the room in the Intelligence Secretary's direction. The veteran martial arts expert and former Navy Seal snapped it out of the air when it propelled within arm's reach and discreetly slid it inside his sport coat without making a scene.

"I'm giving you, the FBI, and the Secret Service a deadline. I want a complete report. I want to know if he has warts on his testicles, and I want to know by this time tomorrow!" The president slumped into his chair, and Cover took the opportunity to extract himself from hostile territory.

"Yes, Sir, you will have a report in the morning," he said as he backed out of the Oval Office.

Chapter Sixty-Nine

The seaplane had two occupants. Rachel was the pilot, and Max was copilot, but she flew the plane as she had done for him on many occasions. The Beech 18 was originally designed to carry ten passengers, but Max had converted the passenger area into a flying Winnebago, complete with queen-sized bed, kitchen, and entertainment center. The twin engines were capable of carrying a 2,550 pound load, and although a jet was much quieter and faster, the sense of adventure they felt when escaping D.C. from the water was unmatched by more modern transportation. They could land where they wanted, and by flying at low altitudes, their coming and going was seldom noticed. There were no air traffic controllers and no runway delays to slow their flights.

As the seaplane slowly lifted off over the large expanse of water, Max reflected on the ways his life had become complicated since his announcement. He never had the same level of anonymity, but one never misses what one never had, so that didn't affect him much. It was the constant pushing that intruded. The paparazzi had always been a sporadic interruption for him, but now they were everywhere 24/7, and he couldn't devise enough ways to elude them. It seemed like they had some kind of radar that knew where he was at any given moment, and it was making him wonder if he was becoming paranoid. When he was a private citizen, he could go for a walk without worrying about some photographer shooting a picture of him before he had showered that day, but now…

As Rachel piloted the plane southward, she thought of their first meeting. It was her idea. In the 14 years since their first encounter on a dive boat in Belize, Max Masterson had maintained the same nonchalance, even during the three days they were together offshore. Every diver needs a dive buddy. Solo divers get paired up with other solos, and the dive guide gleefully matched Max and Rachel for the entire three-day excursion on the world's second-largest great barrier reef.

For the first two days on the boat, Rachel managed to resist Max's piercing eyes and charming smile, but when he talked, her resistance gradually eroded. They were with each other continuously from sunrise until sunset and a little beyond. Max didn't engage in small talk or the flirtations that countless young men before him had tried on her without success. He fascinated her with the story of being there as an escape from Washington society and the shallow social climbers who jumped at the chance to have their photo taken on his arm.

He told her that his father had trained him to run for president and about the lifetime of wisdom he had inherited. When he spoke, she believed he would accomplish his goal. Rachel, on the other hand, had come to Belize for a more personal goal—to lose her virginity. By the time they disembarked at the end of the third day, she had accomplished her goal, and Max had accomplished his—he had found his perfect match.

For appearance's sake, Max had purposely kept Rachel away from the lights of the cameras, choosing to keep her to himself as his father had instructed him to do. To place her in the public light was equivalent to surrendering her personal diary to strangers, and he zealously protected her from the dark side of public life. She was always close, though. Her passions for flying and driving classic sports cars were fulfilled by her chauffeuring and piloting duties, which took them on frequent adventures. She was not one to hold back from enjoying those aspects of life that keep a person from growing old, and Max supplied Rachel with the means to experience passion to its fullest.

As they made their way south across Virginia, Max turned to Rachel, who was intent on navigating their course. Her focus was a major reason he had never sought his pilot's license. His mind was the type that could focus on one thing at a time, and he could absorb himself in that effort to the point where nothing could distract him. A pilot, on the other hand, had to absorb multiple stimuli and coordinate them to maximum effect. Neglect fuel consumption, and you run out of fuel. Headwinds and tailwinds could send you miles off course.

There were too many things to know and know well. She did it so well that, in that environment, he was hers. It was best that he left the navigating to Rachel and concentrated on the myriad of ever-changing factors that his latest effort entailed. He had embarked on a most imprecise course.

In the afternoon glow reflecting off the water, he could see every crease in her face, but in his mind, she was flawless. She was his girl, his lover, his chauffeur, and his confidante, and in the years that he had known her since their chance meeting in Belize, they'd had adventures that others only dream about. He liked her spirit, her determination, and her love of the high-risk activities that they shared when he could get away. She conformed to no conventional image of a woman that he knew of, and the more time they spent in each other's company, the more complete their connection became.

She steered the plane toward a small island in the middle of a lake in North Georgia, where they would spend the night. The sun was setting, and the seaplane was not equipped with the night navigation devices that modern navigators relied upon. It was better suited for short hops from island to island than across long stretches of the country. As the orange glow of the sun began to move behind the cypress trees that lined the lake, she carefully and expertly landed the plane on the smooth water. Max dropped anchor as the plane gingerly bumped up against the small island, and they jumped out to explore before the darkness lured them back into the comfortable living room of the sleeping quarters.

When they returned to the plane, a satellite communicator blinked red in the dim interior of the cabin. Max picked up the device and pushed a button that immediately broadcast the image of Luke Postlewaite.

"I've been trying to reach you. Where the hell are you, in the middle of a swamp or something? It irritates me that you don't think enough of your chief of staff to confide…"

"What is it, Luke?" he interrupted.

"Your latest jog has people talking. Scuperman is running around trying to gather support for the idea that you aren't fit to be president, and everyone he talks to is calling him an asshole. That just makes him madder. You should have seen him at the Press Club. He looked like a Bantam rooster, strutting around and cussing you out for embarrassing him. The only footage he had of you was you calling him an asshole, so the network ran it," Bill confided.

"Well, what did he expect? He got in my face, and was being his arrogant self, and I just said what first came to mind. Besides, he is an asshole," Max replied.

"Max, you know I'm your biggest supporter, and I love you and Rachel to death, but be careful out there. Somehow, they know where you are and where you're headed, and I'm worried that the crazies will be hunting for you."

"Listen, don't worry about me. I have the cutest pilot in the world right here, and she doubles as my bodyguard." Rachel had discarded her clothes and was buried beneath a mink comforter he had brought to cover the bed. She giggled as he stroked the arch of her foot with a snowy egret feather he'd found on the walk around the shore of the island. Her toes curled.

"Luke, I have to go. I'll see you and Andrew Friday at the beach house. I'll get the seafood, but bring me four Taco Bell beef burritos so I can do some bartering in Eastpoint. Last time I went, that was good for two pounds of grouper and as many bulldozers as I could eat." Max tapped a button on the console, and it went dark.

Chapter Seventy

"When I gave up being reverent, it was the turning point in my life. It defined me, somehow."

Rachel laughed. "What do you mean?"

"I don't think anyone is better than me, and I don't think they're any worse. When I meet a billionaire, I think, 'How did he or she get to the pinnacle? I can learn from this person.' But they're no better than me. They're different, and maybe a little lucky, but that can just be a matter of being in the right place and the right time. The difference between us is that they were there at that exact moment, and I wasn't. Not yet, anyway, but soon." He got a faraway look, his face reflecting the last shimmer of the turquoise water as the sun dove slowly behind the palm trees on the shore. On the sand at the edge of the lagoon, a light danced to the far side. Soon, the shoreline began to resemble a black cutout in front of a pastel colored painting, and he turned to face her. He was still nude, and she was equally bare.

"I'll say you're no worse. Maybe even a little better in most respects." She grinned impishly. Her eyes were transfixed between his legs. He definitely needed more attention. She motioned for him to lay with her.

He was still restless. It happened whenever his brain was on overdrive. When he was like this, sex was the only the distraction that, if you could call it a distraction, was capable of rescuing him from that turgid state. He ran his finger up the outside of her leg, and she turned to him. They melted together, their tanned bodies still slick from tanning lotion and a day in the sun.

Hours later, he awoke, still inside her, feeling the wetness and warmth of that familiar place. The slow swelling became an urgent hardness once again, and he took up where he had left off. She awoke, feeling the pressure, the slick friction of his insistent member pressing against her. Wave after wave pulsed through her. Feeling her response, he quickened his strokes, and she arched her back, her hands clawing his muscular back.

"That's it! Ohmigod! Yes! Yes!" They spoke in unison, each saying the same words as each nerve fired in languid ecstasy. As their heart rates slowly returned to normal, they spooned together, the heat of their intercourse melting each curve of their bodies into one. Rachel snuggled in his arms, and Max's mind began to move on to business and obligation.

They had traveled by seaplane to Florida to escape the paparazzi and the press, and they basked in the illusion that they were alone for the moment, secure in the beach hideaway on the coast of the Florida Panhandle. He planned to meet with Bill and Andrew later in the day to deal with the serious issues of running for president, but for now, the feeling of being away from the turmoil and attention was refreshing. He stepped from the bed and unlatched the Key West style shutter that covered the windows of the bedroom and threw them open. As he leaned forward on the window sill, still nude, he inhaled the salt air and took in the tropical landscape of the yard.

Two dunes covered with sea oats stood between the house and the Gulf of Mexico. Deep in the cover of a thicket of Palmetto palms adjacent to the walkway to the beach, a lone figure lay camouflaged in the mottled shadows of the thicket. He focused his sights upon his target, who was unaware that his solitary foray onto the veranda was exposing more than his nudity to the morning sun. From this vantage point, which he had maintained since shortly after midnight, he had a perfect shot.

Sensing movement in the yard, Max turned toward the end of the veranda. Before he could withdraw into the semidarkness of the room, he heard the continuous clicking sounds of a digital camera, followed by, "Thanks, Mr. Masterson. Thanks for my kids, too. See you in the funny papers." The photographer emerged from the palmetto and hurdled over the coleus plants lining the fence. As Max watched helplessly, he sprinted around the dunes and was gone.

Chapter Seventy-One

When she had something to report, Lucy "Butch" Gable was accustomed to sending an e-mail to her superior at Langley, posting a red flag. When it arrived at the desk of Gunter Cover, Intelligence Secretary, the only indicator of the importance of the voice message was that red flag, and when he saw it, Cover immediately accessed the secrets contained within. Upon Cover's return from the White House, he accessed the database in a desperate search for some information about Masterson that would placate the president.

He was still fuming about the dressing down he had received from Blythe, but his sense of duty and impending unemployment motivated him to gather all of the information the agency had compiled, however trivial, to present the next morning. His briefcase was still filled with the documents and photographs that established the nuclear proliferation crisis in the Middle East, and he replaced the red "High Security" folders with a plain brown folder that looked pitiful in comparison to the crisis that had him worried that a terrorist attack was imminent.

He hadn't been able to get the president to focus on Pakistan, or anything else, for the past crucial week, and he obsessed about how he could spur the administration to action privately, quickly, and decisively. "Maybe," he thought, "I'll be able to bring it up at tomorrow's meeting. If only I knew a way to get him off this Masterson issue." He scoured the folder for fresh dirt. Finding none, he scanned his e-mail until he found the message from Butch. "Good timing," he thought. "I might have to buy her a drink if this pans out. She may like girls more than she does me, but I can't stop thinking about how it would be if she didn't."

Clicking the attachment, a full color photograph of Max Masterson scrolled up the screen. Full frontal nudity, even if the good parts were obscured by the rail. They didn't leave much for the imagination. "He doesn't look much like presidential material with his clothes on the bedroom floor," he sneered, then shifted his attention to the woman in the background of the image, wondering if he could get the boys in the lab to digitally enhance her face and body for a better look. He debated the issue in his mind for a few minutes but decided that this situation called for discretion. It could turn bad very quickly if it became common knowledge that the Secretary had leaked the pictures to the press. "Besides," he reasoned, "I can get the press to do it better, and I can read about it in tomorrow's news." Cover saw the photograph of Max in flagrante delicto as his opportunity to contribute to the president's reelection campaign and had sent the image to three friendly news agencies in one keystroke.

The 8:00 a.m. meeting at the White House started promptly, and Blythe had ordered that the Cabinet members be delayed until the completion of his briefing by his Intelligence Secretary. This caused considerable huffing and muttering from the Secretary of Defense and Secretary of State, who earnestly believed that they should be privy to all matters of national security, but after all, he was the president and could do as he pleased. They reviewed their confidential folders in the anteroom as aides hovered over them with coffee pots and plates of fresh bagels while the president dealt with concerns more pressing than affairs of state.

"Mr. President, we have been conducting intensive surveillance on your opponent since your directive two weeks ago. Our background searches and interviews have only revealed the usual data, and I'm disappointed to report that we have been unable to obtain his medical records for anything other than a broken leg when he was in law school. He was apparently treated by a personal physician all of his life, and the doctor's records were destroyed after his death three years ago. His legal dossier is squeaky clean. He hasn't even had a speeding ticket! If there was dirt on Mr. Masterson, we would have found it. But the senator, you know, was a man who enjoyed his privacy, and he protected his son in every way he could. I do have something for you, though." He pulled an unmarked manila folder from his satchel and handed it to the president with a look of undisguised glee. "As you know, we have been working with members of the press who are in our employ to, how should I say it, perform certain intelligence activities for us in exchange for news which we selectively leak to them. On a slow day, we create the news."

He paused for effect but Blythe sat passively. Receiving no response, he continued. "We have been monitoring Masterson's movements by satellite and leaking that information over a continuous live feed. He can't scratch his ass without us knowing about it. The news networks are getting a lot of viewers by running a 24/7 "Where's Max?" program. As you know, he doesn't seem to want to play by the rules and show up where the other candidates tend to congregate."

Blythe held the folder and waited for the prologue to reach a crescendo before he examined the contents. When Cover had paused long enough for him to conclude that he had finished, he slid the color photograph from its covering to see Max Masterson standing naked behind a deck rail. The rail concealed his private parts, but it was obvious that he had just emerged from the bedroom. Behind him, through the veranda doors, an equally nude woman reclined on the bed. The room was dark, her facial features were indistinct, but her shapely profile looked very enticing.

"I took the liberty of leaking it to the press about an hour ago," Cover volunteered.

"What authority do you have to anything? I make those decisions! You answer to me and me alone! Do you understand what you have done? This looks like a cologne ad! You have injected sex appeal into this race! Trust me, Cover. Nobody will be talking about my economic reform plan tomorrow or next week or ever!" He raised his voice enough for the entire West Wing to hear, and his tone could not be misconstrued. The president was pissed.

Though they never spoke the words, everyone within earshot privately felt relief that it was the Intelligence Secretary, rather than any of them, who was within striking distance of Blythe. His penchant for throwing objects during his temper tantrums was the direct cause of several nearly impossible reconstruction efforts underway to restore artifacts that had previously survived over 150 years of White House activity. He had a special love of destroying priceless crystal, but assiduously avoided the mementoes of his numerous personal encounters with famous, powerful, and rich figures that adorned the White House walls.

"Mr. President. You wanted me to come up with a way of discrediting Masterson, and I thought…"

"Dammit! I don't want you to do my thinking for me, either! I have an entire Cabinet waiting in the next room who do that for me!" He was whirling out of control now. His arm knocked a ceramic figurine of Martha Washington onto the floor, sparing George for the moment. "I don't want you to breathe a word to anyone about this! If the voters find out where this beefcake picture came from, I will personally peel your hide off your body with a toothpick! Better yet, I'll let them do it. Now get out!"

"But Mr. President, you haven't heard the rest. Masterson is being followed by our people, the press is doing what they can to follow him, but there is someone else out there, too."

Blythe paused in his tirade, absorbing what he had heard. "What do you mean?" Red-faced and sweating profusely, he plopped into his overstuffed leather chair.

"We don't know the details yet, but a hit squad has been shadowing him for the past three days. We suspect that it's a radical terrorist group who call themselves the 'Infidel Extermination Squad.' They're more of a shadowy group of mercenaries who go after anyone someone is willing to pay good money to eliminate. He suspects he's being followed, but he has no idea that they want to kill him or why."

"Do you know why?"

"My sources say that their employers think he can beat you."

Chapter Seventy-Two

Rachel and Max flew back from Apalachicola according to the flight plan filed before they left the hangar on the Potomac. His intended meeting with senior staff at the Anchor house was hastily cancelled after the nude encounter with the photographer, and Staffman had ordered him back to campaign headquarters to help with damage control.

Flight plans were not required for small planes that were not occupying airspace near Washington D.C., and were not utilizing areas near airports, but Rachel was a meticulously careful pilot. The plan called for mthe to travel the length of the Apalachicola River until it joined the Flint River, and on up the Chattahoochee, which they would follow to Atlanta. They would spend the night in Atlanta before heading home. GPS positioning was available to navigate at night, but the old Beech was not designed for night flying.

Rachel trusted the plane during the day, and Max trusted Rachel to fly them home by the best route that she could devise. With the flat water of the river below them, Max felt certain that if they encountered rough flying weather, Rachel could set down in one of the many coves that stretched below them.

Still, Max was running the encounter with the photographer through his head. He couldn't understand how his whereabouts were made public in real time. He continued to reject the idea that he was being watched continuously, but the danger of the situation had begun to creep into his awareness. "Rachel, I think we are about to be exposing a whole lot more skin in the tabloids than we ever have," he announced as they passed over into Georgia. Ahead of them lay vast acres of pine forest, which stretched on either side of the strip of water like a green buffer.

Rachel was intent in thoughts of her own, realizing that her long run of anonymity was about to end. She laughed nervously, but no amount of laughter could assuage the sick feeling in her gut. "Me? What about you, standing naked on the deck? I'll just be another woman in your entourage, but you will become the poster boy for college girls everywhere… if you aren't already…"

Concealed beneath the dense forest, Darkhorse watched the approaching plane through a digital scope. The scope was attached to an 80 millimeter cannon specifically designed to shoot dum-dum bullets. The cannon had no peacetime purpose. It was designed by the Gates Arms Factory to knock airplanes out of the sky without an explosive charge. The large caliber bullets could rip an airplane in half, and the wreckage would yield no evidence of the cause of the crash. The irregular hole produced by the dum-dum bullets would be indistinguishable from the torn wreckage of the downed plane. At a range of five miles, the bullet would pass though the plane without exploding and would be buried in heavy forest far from the crash site. By the time his target had crashed, the assassin would be riding away from the scene of the crime in his pickup truck with the cannon concealed in the cargo area. One shot was all it would take to eliminate Max Masterson from the race, and the cause of the crash would never be determined.

"I have been waiting for this day for a long time," he thought. "It was nice of his girlfriend to come along and put him out here in the middle of nowhere where I can do my work without taking out a lot of eyewitnesses. I would have done it a lot sooner if he didn't have people around him all the time." Taking aim at the seaplane's fuselage, Darkhorse squeezed the trigger.

The report of the cannon was loud, but anyone within the sparsely populated national forest who heard the sound would reasonably conclude that it was a sonic boom from one of the military jets that frequently used the area for war games. He waited until the gaping hole in the seaplane's fuselage appeared in his scope's sights and calmly watched as it lurched and passed below the treetops. When the plane was out of sight, he drove away in the opposite direction, the off-road tires producing a pink tinged cloud of dust. The red clay road was devoid of traffic, and he smiled. This time, he was confident that his employer would reward him for a job well done.

Chapter Seventy-Three

Max turned at the ripping sound as the dum-dum bullet passed through the aluminum sheath of the fuselage. Miraculously, the damage was limited to a jagged, gaping hole three feet behind the passenger seat, the bullet narrowly missing the cables that controlled the aileron and rudder. If they had been severed, Rachel's ability to keep the plane in the air would have been compromised to the point where no pilot could have leveled or steered, and a crash would have been inevitable. At the time of impact, their altitude was only 50 feet above the treetops, allowing them to avoid the sudden decompression that would spell near certain death in more modern planes, which flew at altitudes this old plane would never attain.

After a disorienting minute of struggling to regain control, Rachel brought the seaplane to a wobbly landing on the river. From land, it looked like a wounded duck as it struggled to stay aloft, but her skill as a pilot prevented disaster. They splashed down and glided to a stop next to a fishing shack on a small island.

"What just happened?" Max shouted. The hole in the fuselage had ripped larger, allowing him to look out the back of the aircraft, its aluminum ribs the only structure holding the tail onto the body. If he wanted, he could have dived through the hole into the clear waters.

Rachel recovered quickly from the rush of adrenaline and began inspecting the damage as the current brought the plane against the shore. "I've never seen anything like this before. It's like a boulder just ripped my plane in half." She poked her head through the hole, and looked directly into the barrel of an antique shotgun. The holder of the weapon was an elderly black man, and behind him, a woman and a teenage girl, who held onto each other, obviously fascinated by the sight of the damaged plane floating at the end of the dock.

The man spoke first. "I'm Elias Petrie. I don't know much, but I do know that you ain't from these parts. If you's here ta hurt me, I will hurt you back. If you'n here ta hurt me family, Ah'll hurt ya plenty, an then we'll see who all's standin'."

Max swung the door of the seaplane open with great care, and the man turned the shotgun in his direction. Max spoke in measured tones. "We're not here to hurt anyone, sir. As you can see, we had a little trouble with the plane. I'm sorry if our landing hurt your fishin'."

The girl spoke excitedly. "Grampa, it's him!"

The old man was quickly becoming overwhelmed. "Who, girl?"

"That man who's running for president," she replied.

The woman, who had stood in stoic silence, spoke softly through the gap in her teeth. "Daddy, Maizey's right. Put that gun down and invite these folks in fer some catfish an greens."

Rachel stepped through the hole in the fuselage onto the dock and turned to Max. "See? I told you that you're famous. Just don't start shaking hands and kissing babies, or I'll conclude you're a politician."

Max ignored the bait. "Mr. Petrie, how's the fishing?"

"Fishin's fine. Catchin' ain't so good," he replied, smiling.

Chapter Seventy-Four

After a filling lunch of fresh catfish and collard greens, washed down with a large amount of sweet tea, Elias Petrie rowed the pair to shore and drove them the 27 miles to town. Max and Rachel sat in the front seat of the ancient Ford pickup. The noise of the engine made it impossible to talk, and the truck lacked air conditioning that would have allowed them to roll up the windows. The dust from the dirt road covered the windshield like a thin layer of red paint and billowed through the open windows, coating their skin. At every rare opportunity where the thick woods gave way to a clearing, Mr. Petrie pulled off the road to clean the windshield, and they briefly disembarked.

Standing in the opening in the thick cypress forest, Max pulled out the satellite phone he had removed from the plane. Although he suspected that their movements could be tracked from its signal, he had no other way of communicating with Andrew. The plan for them to meet in Florida had been aborted, and Andrew waited in D.C. with the rest of the staff for further instructions from Max.

"Max, why are you in the middle of nowhere, when you're supposed to be on your way to Colorado?" Andrew's voice betrayed his annoyance. "And what the hell has gotten into you? Your naked butt is all over the tabloids…"

"I know, Andrew, but I'm giving everything to this campaign," he quipped.

"Very funny. Just get back here so old Staffman doesn't take credit for this stunt. Your naked romp has you up 20 points in the polls."

Rachel couldn't restrain her delight. "I told you so," she giggled.

"And I'm not in the middle of nowhere, I'm in the middle of somewhere," replied Max in the most insolent tone he could muster.

"Max, I've known you long enough to know that I never know what you'll do next, but could you tell me here you are headed?"

"Chattahoochee. In a Ford truck with my friend, Elias. Say hello, Elias." Max held the phone in front of Elias's face.

"Hello," said Elias.

Andrew knew that he had better wait for an explanation instead of trying to extract one from his candidate. Max finally became serious. "Andrew, there has been a little accident. Something tore through our seaplane and almost ripped it in half. Rachel put us down on the river, and now we're making our way to Chattahoochee. It's a small town at the headwaters of the Apalachicola River. It's the only civilization between here and there. They have a nice mental hospital there, and I'm sure we'll be able to find a way to get back from Chattahoochee without too much trouble."

"While you're there, why don't you check yourself in for a little R&R," said Andrew sarcastically. "I'm getting worried. Planes don't just fall apart, and your movements are being monitored. We need to get you to safety."

Max sighed as Rachel cleaned the dust from her sunglasses and swatted at the cloud of mosquitoes that were intent on sucking the blood from her neck, her ankles, and the back of her knees. "Andrew, we need to get back on the road, but why don't you guys head out to Aspen and we'll meet you there in a few days. I'm going to chuck the phone and be out of contact for awhile." Before Andrew could protest, Max cut off the signal and tossed the phone into the black water of the cypress stand, where it landed with a plunk.

"Great, now we have no way of calling my mom," exclaimed Rachel.

"Don't worry, I'll let you call from a pay phone when we get to Chattahoochee," Max replied.

"Now I'm getting worried whether we'll ever get back to civilization," she said with a smile. "Come on, they're eating me alive."

Chapter Seventy-Five

After the first debate and the New Hampshire vote, it was down to Max and Scarlett Conroy, both Independents, and the incumbent. After Cunningham's death, his party had attempted to revive the campaign, but Conroy had stolen the votes of the party regulars, and Masterson had depleted their campaign fund. In a desperate move to recover from his misogynous attack on Scarlett, Miniver recanted and apologized, but she was determined to proceed without the support of the party, and Miniver was promptly discharged from his position in the campaign. For the first time in modern history, a major political party had no candidate in the general election. The party politics that had been so essential to success at the national level appeared to be gasping its last breath.

Postlewaite and Staffman saw no utility in putting Max back in a room with the other candidates riding on his coattails. Max was making better progress as the challenger and by addressing issues of his choosing in the format of his choice. He had learned that one bad debate can destroy an election, and the remaining debates, absent Max, Scarlett, and Blythe, were watched by the smallest audience since the networks began broadcasting them in the 1960s. The only debate of substance was the single debate that Blythe would agree to, and Max was able to focus on that event.

"You can't win this election. We control the result, began Walsh." Luke Postlewaite sat with Presidential advisor Ted Schoolcraft and White House Chief of Staff Roscoe Walsh in a conference room.

"What do you mean?"

"We control the mechanics of this debate. Your boy hit a home run with the third-party candidates, but he can't play that silence game with the president. People want to hear, in detail, what he has to say about the issues, and we decide what issues to talk about," bellowed Schoolcraft. "I don't think he has the balls to try that with an incumbent street fighter like Blythe. He's going to look like a school boy fighting a gladiator with a toothpick."

Postlewaite knew Schoolcraft and Walsh from his early days on the Hill when the senator was defending his efforts to preserve privacy for Americans. He didn't like anything about them; their imperious attitude, their no-compromise, scorched-earth approach to conflict, and most of all, their shifty little eyes. He couldn't trust them to do anything that they said they would do, even though their Ivy League, aristocratic tough guy approach would scare the bejesus out of lesser political advisors. He felt certain about Max's chances of bumping off Blythe. The polls were amazingly supportive of this new figure on the political scene, and he was privately surprised by his confidence in an untested newcomer.

"You didn't invite me here to try to intimidate me. You read the same polls as I do, and you're running scared," he replied.

"Don't be naïve."

Postlewaite paused, feeling the flush of anger. Nobody, especially these prima donnas, called him naïve. He realized that his face must be crimson and that he didn't need to speak to convey his feelings. He waited until he stopped sweating and composed himself as he had done countless times on the Hill. They were taunting him to provoke a reaction, and he knew that whenever a person reacts in anger, their mind shuts off. He could wait until they began to question their words, and then he would counterattack from a position he could more easily defend.

Walsh was the first to budge.

"I have worked with you on several campaigns, Luke, and I thought you were smarter than this. Your boy has no experience. How does he expect to pull this one off? He has the pedigree, but no history…"

"Why am I here? For you to talk to me in rap lyrics? What are you going to tell me next, 'If the office don't fit, you must quit'?" He hunched his shoulders and moved from side to side to enhance the folly of their words. "I was in your seat thirty years ago. Don't try to tell me how to run a campaign. I've never done it this way before, but Max is kicking your incumbent's ass, and Blythe hasn't taken his head out of it for so long that it must feel like he's being kicked in the teeth."

The attempt at intimidation was not going to influence Postlewaite to do anything. This meeting was over. Besides, thought Schoolcraft, Old Luke was right. A gambler holding all the cards never bets against himself. With no more words to say, Luke Postlewaite picked up his iPad and stood facing the president's men for the last time. With a quick sweep of his arm, he knocked his opponent's coffees into their laps and ambled slowly out of the room.

Chapter Seventy-Six

Blythe stood facing his opponent, foil in hand. A mask covered his face, and not much else covered the rest of him except burgundy striped boxer shorts and white ankle socks. His opponent was similarly attired, her blonde hair jutting out behind her mask like a lion's mane, flowing down to her shoulders, below which her abundant breasts were restrained by a pink Victoria's Secret bra and matching panties. She wore ankle socks, too, but no man she had ever encountered could recollect anything she wore below her curvy hips. On their chests was an electronic device that glowed and beeped loudly if the foil reached its mark. Clothes, both his and hers, were scattered around the perimeter of the room.

Schoolcraft burst into the room to report the results of his meeting with Postlewaite, but he wasn't prepared for the sight that met his eyes. He'd made no effort to enter quietly, but the president was so absorbed in attempting to score with his young fencing opponent that he failed to notice. "Mercedes, if I score two more times, you'll be naked, and I win. Three times, and I get anything I want, those are the rules," he announced as he parried to the right.

"Mr. President, you always get whatever you want," she replied. As she spoke, she thrust the foil to the center of his chest and scored again. She squealed with delight. "Now what do I get?"

Schoolcraft took this opportunity to clear his throat and announce his presence.

"Schoolcraft, what have you got for me?" He removed his fencing mask and walked toward his assistant, ignoring his compromising state of undress. Mercedes began to assemble her clothing and covered her breasts, to the disappointed scowl of the president.

"Sir, I have just left our meeting with your opponent's people, and you told me to report immediately," he said, uncertain if his political career would be over by the time he left the room. Droplets of sweat appeared on his forehead, not caused by the temperature of the room.

"Well, dammit, report, and then get the hell out of here!" The mighty Blythe had spoken.

"Sir, Postlewaite won't budge. He has seen the polls, and he was bold enough to predict that Masterson will be the next president. I recommend that we implement Plan B."

"Then do it! I have to get back to my workout. I'll expect a full report of the meeting on my desk by the time I'm done with my break."

"Yes, Sir." He backed out of the room as Blythe returned his attention to his shapely fencing partner, who had unclasped her bra and was stepping into a sauna in the corner of the room.

Chapter Seventy-Seven

The dirt road opened onto County Road 270, and the ride became smoother. Elias had been taciturn during the bumpy ride from the river, but when he could speak without yelling, he opened up like the floodgates of the dam that appeared in the distance. "Ever since the guv'mint took mah pension from me, mah family been livin' hand to mouth. That's why Ah fish. We sho' could use some sto' bought goods, an' Ah'll need ta top mah tank," he began. Without waiting for a response from his two passengers, he launched into the story of his life, how he was born downriver from Chattahoochee and spent his days working on the dredges and barges that kept the river channel open for the Army Corps of Engineers. He went on and on about how Atlanta, "the big city upriver," had sucked all of the water from the river, leaving his livelihood high and dry.

Rachel sat between the two men, and held her breath when he leaned close. His aroma of sweat and fish was overwhelming at times, and she was silently thankful that the open windows of the truck allowed the man's smell to escape her confinement.

"We need to get to the Quincy Municipal Airport," she finally said, interrupting his continuous monologue. "I'm a pilot," she continued. "I need to file a report with the FAA. My plane crashed. I don't want to lose my license. They need to do an investigation and find out what happened to us up there." She turned to Max, who had spent most of the ride in deep thought.

"Elias," Max responded, "Quincy it is. But when we get there, we'll stop at the Winn Dixie and get you some groceries, and I'll leave you with some gas money. You have been good to us, and I take care of my friends."

"Thank ya, Mistuh President," responded Elias Petrie, smiling ear to ear. "Ah'll be votin' fer ya in the Fall."

Chapter Seventy-Eight

At Quincy Municipal Airport, Rachel met with local FAA official Buddy Gudolby, a local legend in rural North Florida for his ability to down more beer and shucked oysters at one sitting than any living person in the long and colorful history of the Panhandle Seafood Festival. Although Buddy was famous in his own right, he was positively overwhelmed by the sudden appearance of the popular presidential candidate and his girlfriend.

While Rachel filled out the crash report to fulfill her duty to the FAA, Buddy occupied his time by closing his office door and calling every news agency in a 50 mile radius to announce the arrival of his famous guests.

"Ah hope ya'll don't mind," Buddy announced upon emerging from his cluttered office, "but one of mah duties as airport manager and the regional FAA official is to report all plane mishaps. The local news is sending a crew over to do an interview with you and the little lady here, and I told them that they could use mah office to conduct the interview. I imagine there will be a contingent of politicians from Tallahassee right behind them wanting to get their picture taken with ya'll, considerin' it's an election year. They sounded real excited about it, considerin' that you are runnin' fer president and all."

Max turned to Rachel, wrinkles of concern furrowing his forehead. "What do we do now? We have to get out of here."

Rachel gave Buddy her best annoyed look and began scanning the airport for possible escape vehicles. At the end of the runway was a Beechcraft Premier III, the most advanced single pilot business jet in the world, its sleek outline looking very odd in its present setting. She was already envious of the pilot, who could be seen going through his preflight checklist. From the look of things, he appeared to be flying without passengers, although it could hold four passengers. "Come on!" exclaimed Rachel, grabbing Max by the hand and propelling him with a lurch toward the door.

Max turned to see Buddy mouthing words with a surprised look. The sound of the idling jet drowned out his voice, but he was certain that he was using colorful language to express his disappointment at the lost opportunity to be the center of attention in his quiet corner of the universe. Max wondered how Buddy would explain their departure when the press and politicians converged on him, but sprinted behind Rachel toward possible escape.

Rachel arrived first and could be seen talking to a large man adorned with three thick gold chain necklaces, a Dale Earnhart ball cap, and a tank top that prominently advertised "Lou, the King of Barbecue" across his chest. Beneath the slogan was a cartoon pig wearing a chef's hat and apron, holding a spatula. The man inside the costume was Lou, himself. Lou Sossman was nationally known among aficionados of good barbeque as the entrepreneur who franchised a chain of barbeque stands throughout America. His success came from catering to the customer's choice of the best from Texas, Kansas, and two recipes from North Carolina, depending on whether the customer preferred East Carolina or West Carolina barbeque. His trip to North Florida came as the result of a rumored new recipe that he planned to test market in his popular Quincy location.

As Max came to a stop next to Rachel, he and Lou simultaneously exclaimed, "You're him!" Max recognized Lou from his many TV commercials and billboards that seemed to sprout spontaneously from lonely hillsides, and Lou expressed his obvious surprise at running into a presidential candidate on a rural airstrip with tufts of grass sprouting from cracks in the runway.

Rachel had already explained their predicament to Lou, and he was sizing them up with great amusement. "Turn around," said Lou with a high-pitched chuckle. Max and Rachel spun in unison to see a caravan of press vans and official-looking black cars roaring into the chain-link fenced parking lot. A considerable cloud of dust rolled in behind them. "Get in," hollered Lou. "I could use the company, and I can fly you to Kansas City faster than anyone in this pretty baby."

As they taxied down the runway, the radio crackled with Buddy's perplexed voice, "Now Lou, I ain't cleared you ta take off yet, dammit!"

"Sorry, Buddy, I'll leave you some free coupons the next time I'm in town," Lou replied, and with a "Yeehaw," Lou's plane achieved escape velocity and banked north toward freedom.

By the time the Beechcraft touched down at Kansas City International Airport, Max and Rachel had eaten their fill of barbecue and learned more about the difference between Lou's trademarked recipes than anyone has a right to know. Lou had been touring his franchises solo for too long, and his constant bravado made Rachel privately weigh the benefits of flying against bumping silently along in an old truck on a country road. She admired Max's ability to fall asleep at any opportunity, even in the presence of a commanding personality like Lou, but she was finally able to fly in one of the most technologically advanced flying machines on the public market, and the tradeoff was, in her mind, a good one. Max could extract himself from the conversation, and she could learn to fly a jet most pilots have never seen outside of a glossy magazine.

Chapter Seventy-Nine

"Where is he? You assured me two days ago that he would be here on time and ready to go, and the only way I have to track his whereabouts is to look at that map!" Staffman had been berating Andrew for the past two hours, and the abuse was taking on the tone of a street fight.

"He'll be here. He won't fly commercial, won't spend the money on a private flight, and when he called from Kansas City, he said he and Rachel were going to get here the American way, whatever that is. Judging from the speed at which he's traveling, he must be driving across the plains. He seems to be stopping in small towns along the way, but they aren't campaign appearances that we set up. I haven't seen any news reports since he left Kansas City." Andrew was getting nervous, but Max made everyone nervous. He did everything on his own time and in his own way.

While other candidates were attending political appearances and making speeches, Max did whatever he chose, much to the consternation of the people who worked for him. This time, though, his habit of falling off the radar screen was giving them fits. Andrew had been trying to contact him on his communicator, but it had been turned off since the press had obtained his private number. They had tried to change it time after time, but a day would pass and the information was mysteriously back in their possession. The last call from the press had prompted Max to toss the device into a cypress swamp, and although it was waterproof, it was no longer attached to its owner. Andrew had no way to speak with him until he showed, if he showed at all. "I thought that Max was being tracked by satellite by his communicator, but since he cut me off, I don't know how they are tracking him now. That map on the grid is current, and it shows that he will be here in about an hour. Then we'll hike up to the staging area, he can say his piece, and then it's off to the Oregon coast for another visual backdrop for his next sound bite."

Bill looked weary. He hadn't slept well for days. He longed for his memory foam mattress and his own bedroom. "I meant that Max and the video crew will do that while I sit here at 8,000 feet. Did you know that you can get pleasantly drunk on one beer at this altitude? I plan to test that theory with this here bottle of brandy," he drawled while waving the amber spirits in front of the video cam. "I've got to tell you, Andrew, this campaign is wearing me out. I need to be back in Washington polling delegates, not here in the middle of nowhere wondering if he's going to show." Staffman was ready to return to the familiar cocoon of his office. He feared the unknown and the unpredictable, and Max, by design and behavior, set off all of the anxiety he could handle. Andrew had youth and optimism to get him through his day. Staffman needed his coffee served in his cup, the way he had come to expect it, everything as it had been for the past forty years. Predictable.

Chapter Eighty

He had been on assignment for two days now, ordered to set up his covert op station at the curve in the road where the highway to Aspen passes between two fissured granite bluffs. He answered to his superiors in Washington and had been in deep cover for so long that he had almost forgotten his true purpose for being there. He had been trained as a sniper in advance of his first mission to Kuwait, parachuting in from high altitudes at night when the moon was at its ebb and the Iraqis were celebrating the recent conquest of their fellow nation. He was in and out before sunrise, his prey dispatched silently in a pink spray of blood. Since then, his training was narrowed toward one objective—to kill without a trace, his victim dying without a forensic roadmap back to the cause of death. He considered himself a professional, but he was only a lackey doing what they wanted, whenever it was requested, wherever he had to be.

Max and Rachel sat in the back seat of Lou's limo, unsure where they were headed. They needed to traverse the 800 mile expanse of prairie and mountain terrain in two days, and they weren't going to make it on foot or risk their safety by using public transportation. Max's campaign stops were becoming more dangerous each day. They had managed to make it this far by providence, but for the moment, they lacked the link to their destination and were waiting, strategizing about the next step. Max continued to stare out the window deep in thought, willing a solution to their predicament. He had promised to be there, and he kept his promises, not only to the people he met but to the people he chose to represent.

"What do we do now, smart guy?" Rachel was snuggling close to him, pressing her breast against his arm and resting her head on his shoulder. She was weary from the trip, while Max seemed refreshed from his nap.

Lou had directed the driver to take them to his Kansas City franchise. When they arrived at the restaurant, a group of adoring fans of Lou the King of Barbeque stood cheering at the limo's arrival. When they pulled up to the curb, Max leaped out. "I know you're disappointed to see a guy running for president standing here instead of my good friend Lou, but can anyone tell me how I can get to Aspen by the day after tomorrow?"

The crowd was silent, stunned by the unexpected appearance of Max and Rachel. Lou stayed inside the limo behind mirrored glass, not wanting to interrupt the impromptu exchange and delighted that he was about to get all the free publicity a presidential candidate can generate. "I do believe that Max just made me another million in sales," he pondered.

A biker wearing an American flag do-rag stepped forward and removed his sunglasses. "Max, er... Mr. President, er... Dammit, you just stepped into Harley Davidson country, and my friends and I would be proud to lend you a couple of my favorite bikes to make the trip. Hell, we'll do the ride with ya. Whaddaya say, Max?"

Chapter Eighty-One

Max and his newfound friends left Kansas City Harley Davidson in a loud and colorful rally. The Harley's unmistakable roar was multiplied by 30, and then by 100 as word of Max's arrival reverberated through the close-knit biker community. The 800 mile trip across prairieland to the Rockies would take two full days, but the riders planned to stop for the night before the mountain phase of the ride. Rachel rode in wing formation while Max took the lead. Their bikes were fresh off the assembly line at the Kansas City Harley Davidson plant, and in exchange for some video footage, Max and Rachel got another free ride.

The route across the prairie was windy but warm, and it was exhilarating to get out of the crowds and into the wide open. As the sun began to set on the distant mountain range, the colors lit up the sky with orange and yellow hues, then purple and pink as the last vestiges of the day settled behind the horizon. They set up camp outside of the small town of Seibert, the only source of food and fuel for many miles. While dinner cooked over an open fire, Max and Rachel slipped away and lay on a blanket in the tall grass.

"Why have you been so quiet today? I know when you get in these moods that something is up," she whispered, as the sunset gave way to a sky full of stars, bright enough to illuminate everything around them.

"I have been thinking about why I'm doing this."

"You mean, riding a Harley, a jet, a pickup truck, and a seaplane just to get to Aspen, when you could have just booked a flight?"

Max's face took on a puzzled look. His mode of transportation hadn't occupied one moment of his thoughts. "No, this gets me out with the real people, and it keeps them focused on me. Everywhere we go, they recognize me. I mean, it's not like they didn't know what I look like before I ran, but they look at me now with hope. I'm beginning to take this whole thing more seriously. I don't have any answers, and I don't have a lifetime in politics, but they come to me with their fears and their dreams, all wanting me to make the fears go away and their dreams come true somehow."

Max's appearance on the political scene had struck a chord with conservatives and liberals alike, but mostly, he had the unwavering support of average people struggling to make a living and raise a family. This segment of the American public was a vastly diverse group who looked at politics in the same way they viewed the task of buying a used car or treating warts. They didn't like it, had no patience for it, and most of all, they avoided it every opportunity. They wouldn't attend a political fundraiser unless the organizers were serving free beer, and if they did, they wouldn't part with any of their hard-earned cash. Max was different. His campaign was mostly self-funded, but the bulk of his political contributions came in small increments from average people: families who felt that they had to do something, and who desperately craved having someone to believe in.

He lay next to Rachel, looking at the stars. It seemed reverent to gaze in silence. They held hands, and the evening chill made them pull the blanket closer. In the morning, they hadn't moved from their seclusion, spooning tightly.

Chapter Eighty-Two

After a predawn breakfast of bacon and eggs washed down with coffee strong enough to take the paint off a park bench, they set out in the early mist of morning. Riding into the mountains earlier would have been unwise, as the passes remain treacherous until the sun has evaporated the dew. The sun was just coming across the prairie as they entered the mountain stage of the trip. Near Glenwood Canyon, the road began winding through the reddish rock walls along the Colorado River, and their pace slowed. The riders slowed to adapt to the slick, winding road, but after a long ride through the featureless landscape of the vast prairie, it was also a chance to absorb the oasis-like beauty of the place.

He had remained hidden in the craggy rocks for two days, listening to his receiver for updates on the progress of the Masterson riders. His trail bike was concealed under a craggy overhang, and he pulled his camouflage jacket tight around his neck to hold in his body heat. There was no tent, no campfire. His escape would leave no clues that he had been there, and his route had been meticulously planned. He was to shoot once. His target was the front tire of Max Masterson's Harley, shredding the tire to force the crash at the top of the long downhill stretch leaving the canyon. At that point in the road, the rider would be pummeled by the pavement before being propelled into a hundred foot deep ravine. There would be no luck this time. He would not miss.

His sniper rifle with its silencer would rip through the tire from a mile away, and he would ride off in the opposite direction before Masterson hit the pavement.

Through his high-powered binoculars, the assassin saw the first of the riders as they approached. Masterson rode in front, his features clearly recognizable even at over a mile away. Taking aim, he fired and waited for the tuft of smoke as the bullet found its mark. Then he turned and strapped the powerful rifle to his back, mounted his bike, and rode down the mountain trail.

Max felt the sudden drop as the tire deflated. His body began to launch him over the handlebars, and he reared back while laying the bike down, sparks shooting menacingly as the chrome pipes scraped the pavement. He managed to kneel on the upper part of the bike, the hot pipes burning through his leather pants, but avoided being trapped under the heavy machine, would have spelled certain death. Rachel screamed in terror as he hurtled toward the edge of the chasm beside the road and went over the edge.

The entourage came to a screeching halt.. With a loud boom, the motorcycle came to a sudden stop on the boulders next to the river below. A burly tattooed biker with enormous arms was the first to reach the precipice, and peered over the edge. He suddenly smiled. Perched precariously on a small ledge was Max, looking roughed up but intact.

The biker extended one arm and grasped Max by the shoulder. With one strong pull, he hauled Max back to the edge of the road to the amazed cheers of the entourage. As he panted on his hands and knees, Rachel rushed to him, tears of relief streaking the dust on her face. "Come on," she exclaimed, "we have an election to win."

Chapter Eighty-Three

The sound of a Harley Davidson motorcycle is unmistakable. When it is joined by a dozen other Harleys, the growl of the engines takes on a life of its own. Before they emerged from the shelter of the forest, it was obvious that the Masterson campaign was about to be visited by a motorcycle gang, and from the sound, there were a lot of them.

Andrew's attention was drawn to the sound that was amplified by the rock walls surrounding the clearing. The distant rumble took on the low vibration of the multiple engines, and it was hard to do anything but await the arrival of their visitors. Black specks moving in the distance gained color as they approached, and he could make out detailsof the 20 or more riders, all perched low on chrome chariots. The affection they had for their bikes was reflected in the loving attention paid to painting and detailing their rides.

In front, the leader wore black leather pants and a leather vest, no shirt or jacket. His rippling muscles revealed a high level of fitness, no paunch acquired by physical inactivity. On his head was a do-rag in red, white and blue with stars along the rim. As they approached the makeshift command center, Andrew could make out the leader's features, and he smiled broadly. A familiar face smiled back.

Max roared to a stop inches from Andrew's feet. Rachel pulled up next to him, dressed in identical road gear with the exception of a tank top that displayed Max's image, beneath which was the slogan, "Max.

A man running for president." She displayed it well, her full breasts pushing Max's image to prominence above the slogan. His entourage held back, stopping at the perimeter in obvious deference to their leader and his companion. He removed his reflective sunglasses and looked at his young assistant from head to toe.

"Did you miss me?"

"Max, you have been on the missing list for three days! We had no idea where you disappeared to or how you were going to get here."

Bill Staffman appeared, holding a very thick roast beef sandwich in his right hand and a cold beer in his left. Max grabbed the beer and downed it in one large draw to the applause of the other riders. They took that as an invitation to share the bounty and dismounted in unison.

The advance team had set up a large tent and, to avoid making the 40 mile trip into town, had brought a generator, gas grill, and refrigerator to banish the thought that they were roughing it in the Rockies. Inside the tent was another cooler that held the cold beers, and they helped themselves.

Staffman greeted Max with a snarl. "You could have let us know what was happening. The only notice I had of your arrival was that damn monitor that the network has posted for everyone to see. I still don't understand how, but they know where you are at any given moment," he said before tearing into the sandwich.

As Bill chewed, Max addressed Andrew. "I ran into a bit of trouble on the road," he said, ignoring the tone of authority from his senior advisor. "I blew a tire and had to lay the bike down outside of Aspen and hitch a ride on Rachel's granny seat to get here. She wouldn't let me drive." He looked over at Rachel, who smiled and blushed slightly, her tanned features darkening.

"Are you hurt?" Andrew looked at the scuffed and torn leather of Max's right pants leg and was alarmed to see dried blood along the edge.

He recalled the momentary terror of the incident—the bullet ripping through the tire, laying the bike down, riding the bike on its side and skidding. He had prayed that it wouldn't begin the flip that would pin him to the road and carve the skin off of the side that met the pavement. He'd managed to stay on top of the spinning metal until just before it left the road and came to a stop at the bottom of the ravine. If he hadn't been pulled off the bike at the last second, the Masterson campaign would be planning his funeral.

Max ignored the request for a damage report, and continued. "Just bad luck, with a little help from whoever wants me out of the race. I saw a bullet hit my front tire."

As his staff looked at him in horror, the bikers cheered loudly. They had witnessed a clear act of bravery by one of their own and shoved their hero to the front of the group. Woody Fixton was a weekend warrior who owned the local Harley Davidson dealership and had spent his life repairing and riding between stints as a rebel from society. He was an avid Max Masterson fan and spent much of his leisure time sizing up his hero over the Internet. He had been at the right place to save Max from certain death, and he would carry that pride to his dying breath. The crowd clapped as Woody smilingly accepted a beer poured over his bald head.

Max shook Woody's hand gratefully and continued. "I flatted at Glenwood Canyon and I had to lay the bike down. It was a total loss, but these folks were kind enough to supply me with this mighty ride." Max stood to the side so that they could admire the Harley Davidson, a classic 1972 Shovelhead, stripped down and tricked out. The blue paint job blended into white and red, with the the defiant visage of a bald eagle on the side of the gas tank.

Staffman recovered from the shocking news first. "I told you someone was trying to kill you. It's now a verified fact. I'll prepare a press release and make a public statement."

"The hell you will."

"But I'm your campaign spokesman. That's what I'm supposed to do." Bill looked like a little boy who had just been told he couldn't have a cookie before dinner.

"Think about it, Bill. Andrew, you too. If I am in the crosshairs of some assassin's gun, whoever wants me dead only took one shot. They wanted it to look like an accident. They saw my bike go down on a mountain highway in the middle of nowhere, and they think I'm dead. Nobody has heard from me in days, so they assume that they accomplished what they set out to do. My bet is that they will show their hand by announcing my demise before you do. The longer we remain silent, the better chance we have of finding out who is behind all of this."

"But Max," replied Andrew, "Postlewaite has been calling me from Washington demanding to know what's happening, and until this very moment, we had no idea that an assassination attempt had been made…"

Max cut him off in mid-sentence. "Don't use that word. Assassination. I hate that word. To me, it means that someone shot his ass down in front of the nation. That word is banned from our vocabulary. It should only be used for dead presidents, and the rumor of my untimely demise is highly exaggerated," Max said, paraphrasing Mark Twain. Max's words met with applause from the bikers, who enjoyed his bravado and were observing the exchange from the shade of the tent canopy. Max grinned in an attempt to disarm the profound concern displayed on the faces of his staffers.

"Will you quit worrying? I'm fine. Nobody is going to mess with us while my friends are here to protect us." All heads turned at the sound of multiple bullets being cocked into their chambers. The entourage was armed to the teeth, and they took almost as much pride in their weapons as they did in their Harleys.

"As your representative of the Max for President Chapter of Boulder, Colorado, I'm pleased to announce that your future head honcho is better protected than that idiot who will soon be leaving the White House!" The speech came from a potbellied man with a gray ponytail sprouting from the back of his mostly bald head. They cheered and held their beers in one hand and weapons in the other high above their heads for all to see.

"I rejected the Secret Service because they cramped my style. I didn't want to be surrounded by black suits and sunglasses 24/7. Without you guys to save me, Rachel would still be trying to retrieve my corpse from the bottom of that ravine. Thank you for all of your help. You saved my life."

Chapter Eighty-Four

The Secret Service has one primary purpose. From the time of McKinley's assassination, they had been entrusted to protect the president and those around him. After the shooting of Bobby Kennedy in the 1968 presidential race, those duties were expanded to protect candidates as well, and a team of Secret Service protection was assigned to each of the major vote-getters in the race. After the primaries, Max was offered Secret Service protection, but declined, wary that the Secret Service was under the jurisdiction of his father's long-time nemesis, Adam Wirtep, Director of Homeland Security. Wirtep had a much-publicized disdain for anyone remotely connected with the Masterson campaign, but extended the offer of protection out of obligation.

Max reasoned that by accepting their help, he was attracting attention that made him more of a target, and he would be treated like a prisoner. Wirtep would have been pleased if he got his ass shot off after rejecting his half-hearted offer, but still, he couldn't let that influence him. His life would be changed from that of a free soul without a firm agenda to a series of planned public appearances with advance teams to sweep for bombs at the next stop. He disliked the idea that he would never be alone again, followed and surrounded by a faceless sea of dark-suited and sunglassed bodyguards who talked into their lapels.

Then came the apoplectic call from Postlewaite. "Max, you are trying my patience," he bellowed. "I am an old man. It's not nice to abuse the elderly." Postlewaite's flair for understatement barely contained the fury in his voice. "I have the FBI, the Secret Service, and the CIA here in my office, and they're telling me that someone has been taking shots at you, and I'm the last to know! I've seen photos of your wrecked motorcycle and hear stories that you're out west somewhere. I can even go online and track your movements on a virtual map, which can zoom in on you from a satellite, but I haven't had a call from you."

Luke Postlewaite sat in the study at Fairlane with Gunter Cover, Intelligence Secretary, Homeland Security Director Adam Wirtep, and FBI Director Betty Mizt. The video conference was planned for 10:00 a.m. Pacific Time, and Andrew had placed the call faithfully at the appointed time, excited to witness a behind-the-scenes event open to only a select few.

Max and his staff sat in the tent in the mountain park, still dressed in biker clothes. The entourage looked more like participants at a bike rally than members of a political campaign.

All of the representatives of the intelligence community wore black, which matched their grim expressions. Max remained calm, but immediately fixated on the steely eyes of Wirtep, whose face was contorted into a permanent scowl. "Living proof that the older you get, the more your wrinkles reflect what your thoughts are," thought Max.

"Mr. Masterson, you are in grave danger." Wirtep took the lead, owing to his substantial seniority over his companions. Even though they rode to the Masterson estate in the same motorcade, they rode in separate limousines, reflecting the unspoken competition between their government agencies.

Max chose not to respond to Wirtep, waiting for someone else to volunteer more information. There was a long silence as they waited for him to speak.

Postlewaite took the cue to step in. "Max, I know how you feel about crowds, and I especially appreciate your zealous regard for your privacy…" He looked at Wirtep, who suddenly began examining the artwork in the room. "But we need to talk this out. I made a promise to the senator to get you through this campaign, but I can't do that if you are lying on a slab in a morgue someplace. All your potential gone…" His eyes became distant as he slipped into the past.

Betty Mizt had been uncharacteristically silent for longer than she could endure. Not known for her diplomatic skills or social refinement, she stood up as she spoke. She often explained that she couldn't think when sitting down. When testifying before Congress, she was known for demanding the right to stand, and her detractors had unsuccessfully tried to make her sit while she talked. "Look kid, you think that you can do things in private without me and my agency knowing about it, but I can tell you this. I can get pictures of you screwing or taking a shit if I ask for them, so don't get all noble on me about protecting your privacy. You don't have any and neither does anyone I choose to pay attention to. Just the idea that you can run for president and think you can get away from my prying eyes makes me question your intelligence. Now they tell me that I have to save your pretty butt," she snapped in her Boston accent. Her glare shifted to Wirtep, who smirked behind his right hand. "And someone is trying to kill you. I had a hell of a time getting my people out there on such short notice."

Max furrowed his eyebrows. "What do you mean, Betty? I'm out here in the middle of nowhere surrounded by friends…"

Two muscular bikers stood behind Max's chair within arm's reach. "Max Masterson, meet Gary and Mike. Gary, would you tell Max who you are and show him what you have hidden underneath your leather jacket?" Betty's face had acquired a certain confidence.

"Max, sir, my partner, Mike, and I are Navy Seals assigned to protect you. I am here to keep you alive. I answer to you and the director and my little friend here." He pulled back his jacket to show a holstered handgun and machine pistol, while Mike revealed a disassembled sniper rifle and scope, as well as a small black electronic device. "Pleased to make your acquaintance," Mike boomed in a soft baritone.

"Mr. Masterson, have you wondered why people always know where you are and what you are doing?" Betty continued. "We think that your security has been compromised."

Mike stood and pressed a button on the black device, which emitted an electronic voice.

"Object detected," it spoke in a clear female voice.

He moved toward Max, and the box flashed from blue and green to orange and red. "Subdermal GPS with audio surveillance capabilities," said the voice.

Mike placed the device against Max's neck. "Hold still. I'll get it." Making a small puncture slightly above Max's jugular vein, the device beeped twice. Max felt a slight suction and pressure, and the lights went from red to green. A small window on the side of the device showed what looked like a black, pointed stinger.

An attractive biker chick who bore a close resemblance to Rachel walked to the center of the room and removed her wig and sunglasses. With a dramatic flair, she plucked the device intact from Mike's cradling hands. "I'm going to insert this baby into a guy who looks a lot like you, and we're going to take a long trip until the election. I'm going along as Rachel's double, and we get to have fun while you're out doing whatever you politicians do."

"I'm not a politician. I…"

"I know, you're just a guy running for president," she chuckled. She looked down at her tank top, which ran his slogan across her unrestrained breasts. Without another word, she walked out of the tent. Her Harley came to life and she rumbled toward the road.

Max wasn't looking in her direction. He was studying the face of Gunter Cover. The CIA Director hadn't even said hello.

Chapter Eighty-Five

Max was humbled by all of the attention the government was suddenly paying to his survival, but he would not be deterred from the mission that had brought him to the Rocky Mountains. He was out snowboarding with some of his hard-core constituents, who considered him an icon. Max Masterson was the political equivalent of some of the cool older dudes that they hung with, according to Ricky and Sage Frangipani, Hawaiian surfers who were brother and sister. They had come to the Rockies because snowboarding on Mount Kilauea was getting "too mundane." They would be back on Maui by spring when the waves were totally awesome, but now they were standing at the bottom of the lift line, waiting for their next ride to the top.

"Don't let them tell you what to do, bro," said Sage. Ricky nodded in the background, not sure who she was talking to, but from the attention of all of those Haolies around him, he must be a movie star or something.

"I'll bet you won't be voting for me in November," replied Max.

"Why? I'm tellin' all my friends to."

"Because you don't know squat about politics, and you probably don't vote, anyway."

Max was tired of talking and saying nothing, and he was tired of answering questions about how it was going to be if he was in charge. He wanted to say, "I don't know, and I'd be lying if I spouted the bullshit my opponents are telling you, because they don't know what will happen next, either." He'd traveled for 12 hours by motorcycle to get here, and he was cranky. As soon as he got off the bike, it started again. "People want the president to be the Great Poobah of Everything, an all-seeing, all-knowing leader who will solve all of their problems and look good, besides," he announced to nobody in particular.

He waited for the cameras to be adjusted, fidgeting in his red, white, and blue ski outfit. Andrew had bought it for him at a local ski outfitter, and he felt like it made him look too much like Captain America. Secretly, that was the image that Andrew and the staff wanted to convey, but they didn't tell Max that they also had the ski outfit tailored to show off his physique.

"I'm here today to talk to you about terrorism. We seem to be far away from the world's problems when we are away from the big cities of America. But just last week, terrorists were captured not far from this spot crossing the border from Canada. They were headed to the Sky Needle in Seattle, where they intended to explode a dirty bomb. They would have succeeded in killing thousands of people if good Americans like Rory and Phyllis Trueblood hadn't spotted them and called Homeland Security."

The camera panned back, and two figures dressed in identical Captain America ski clothes were slaloming down the hill. They performed two flawless stem christie turns and stopped on either side of Max in a spray of spring powder. They removed their hoods in unison, revealing a middle-aged man and woman. The man exclaimed, "We're watching out for our neighbors, and we're voting for Max, right, Phyllis?"

Phyllis Trueblood looked straight into the camera. "Right, Rory," she said matter-of-factly as she turned quickly and kissed Max on the cheek, to the appreciative roar of skiers who had passed up their chairlift to witness history in the making.

The film crew had hiked miles to the top before they found snow, and the weather was nice to them. The ambient temperature at the top was 65 degrees, but the snow lingered, replenished at night by the flurries that managed to keep the top white with fresh snow year-round. The finished message that was broadcast over the Internet was classic Masterson, short, direct, and visual. Words scrolled up the screen and the mountain panorama faded to black:

Max Masterson
For America
The Time is Now.

Chapter Eighty-Six

The League of Women Voters was once a perennial sponsor of the presidential debates, but in keeping with their mission statement, they withdrew their sponsorship when it became apparent that the candidates were attempting to dictate every aspect of the debates. They could no longer remain nonpartisan if the candidates controlled not only the questions that were to be asked, but even the height of the podium and the placement of lighting to flatter their profiles.

In 1988, the League of Women Voters issued a statement: "The League of Women Voters is withdrawing sponsorship of the presidential debates, because the demands of the two campaign organizations would perpetrate a fraud on the American voter. It has become clear to us that the candidates' organizations aim to add debates to their list of campaign-trail charades devoid of substance, spontaneity, and answers to tough questions. The League has no intention of becoming an accessory to the hoodwinking of the American public."

Over the next three decades, the League of Women Voters stayed out of the debate business. In the meantime, the major political parties took over the debates under the guise of the Commission on Presidential Debates. The parties took control of a process that voters had previously used to assess a candidate's electability, and America lost a valuable tool. The debates became stale, repetitive, and rehearsed, and the viewership steadily declined to next to nothing. The backlash started when television merged with the Internet, and the public regained control over what they watched and when they watched it. Along with this shift came the ability of individual voters to design debates that answered their particular questions about the person they wanted to lead their nation.

The League got their debate back, but before they agreed to assume this responsibility, they had to do two things; first, they had to return to their basic precepts on which the League was founded, and issued a mission statement that assured that they would remain non-partisan:

"The League of Women Voters, a nonpartisan political organization, encourages informed and active participation in government, works to increase understanding of major public policy issues, and influences public policy through education and advocacy."

At the annual meeting held in Washington D.C., the local chapters of the LWV reaffirmed their goals and regained the prominence that they lost in 1988, provided, however, the participants in the debates relinquished control to the League. The parties were required to sign an agreement that they would not attempt to control the format of the debate. They agreed to comply with whatever rules the League established. No longer would the parties design the questions in advance, and the candidates could only prepare for the big day by trying to predict the questions that would be asked. The League zealously guarded the process. The voters submitted questions that were screened for interest level, and a list of questions was generated minutes before the actual event. Nobody knew what would happen until the live event, and excitement returned to the debate process.

The incumbent's team of advisors prepared him for answers to possible questions for a week prior to the debate. In the last campaign, they wrote the questions that were submitted a week prior to the debate and had avoided any subject that would reveal the weak or unpopular positions held by the parties. This time, though, Blythe was debating under enormous pressure and would be forced to defend the failures of his administration.

"Mr. President, we met with Masterson's senior advisor, a Mr. Postlewaite, with whom you are familiar. I am told that you have been butting heads since he worked on the John Anderson campaign in 1980." Presidential advisor Ted Schoolcraft paced as he talked, silently hoping to avoid the wrath of Blythe, who was showing sure signs of cracking. His indiscretions and recent fencing incident were being whispered about by his staff, and it would take only one well-placed call to the press to sink all hope of his second term. Party chairman Richard Partiman and White House Chief of Staff Roscoe Walsh stood silently in the background as Schoolcraft waged his preemptive attack.

"We warned Postlewaite that Masterson's little performance in his first debate wasn't going to be tolerated by the American people, but now the League of Women Voters has imposed rules that will allow him to do just that."

"You mean to tell me that he can stand up before an international audience of billions of people and recite his little nursery rhyme policies, and I can't do a thing about it?" Blythe's neck began to turn red. He was about to blow.

"I think Masterson will abandon that tactic. It worked when it was a surprise, but it can't possibly do him any good now that he is playing with the big boys," drawled Waylon Cheevers in his booming Texas voice. He held his eternal glass of bourbon on ice, which tinkled as he moved to sit in his customary chair. "I bet he'll come out swinging at the failures he will promise to fix, and that's what you need to prepare for."

Partiman demurred. "I agree. You need to go on the attack from the time you open your mouth. The questions don't have anything to do with the message you are trying to get across. To hell with the issues. Go after his lack of experience. Call him names that people don't like. Attack, attack, attack!" The party chairman was known for his imposing and abrasive personality, but he quickly sat down in silence. As a strategist, he was better suited to fund-raisers than debate strategy, and he decided to leave the details to be discussed after he was safely out of the Oval Office and away from the president.

Blythe shifted uneasily, contemplating the words of his advisors. He would debate dirty in the hope he would come out of the mess with more votes. He only wished he had more dirt.

Chapter Eighty-Seven

Scuperman had had just about enough of being kept in the dark. After his much-publicized humiliations at the hands of Max Masterson and the early encounters where Max had further destroyed his reputation in front of millions of people, he had been reassigned. He no longer covered the leaders in this presidential race. Instead, he sat, day after day, reading news feeds and calling his legion of sources for tips. His official beat was covering the lone straggler in the campaign, Scarlett Conroy, who was reeling from the untimely death of her running mate. His obsession, though, was bringing Max Masterson to his knees.

"Bultosky, I haven't heard from you in days. Where is he?" Scuperman had the kind of voice that bore into you and created fear. He could be heard over the crowd noise at political conventions, and his early assignments had been mostly crowded rooms and hurricanes.

"His GPS is still pinging, but I have him in Hartford, Connecticut and I just saw him on TV talking to the President of Brazil, you know, about the rainforests? And… and they said…"

"Yeah, I know. He was in Brazil. You're worthless!" He slammed the phone shut, wishing that he had a big, corded receiver to slam down for effect like in the good old days. He realized that the only way to follow Max Masterson was to really follow him, and he began the process of scheduling flights to any public appearance that he could find. That would be child's play for any other candidate, but Max didn't play by anyone else's rules.

His phone rang again, and after the last call, he dreaded that this one would be another link in a chain of bad news. He decided to let it go to voicemail, preoccupied with combing his hair over his bald spot and spraying lacquer to keep it in place. When the phone beeped, he retrieved the message. "Greg, Masterson is sitting in the back row of the League of Women Voters speech. Where the hell are you?" The frantic voice of his assistant, Judy, screeched from the speaker as Scuperman grabbed his coat and tie and scrambled out the door.

Chapter Eighty-Eight

Scarlett wasted no time in informing the public of her decision to run as an independent. She had scheduled a speech before the League of Women Voters on her limo ride from the airport before the meeting with Miniver, and her surprise appearance successfully bumped both national party chairmen from the agenda. The League organizers were only too happy to substitute her speech for what was already shaping up to be a dry primer on procedure in the wake of Cunningham's death, and Scarlett was determined that her message become the news of the day before Miniver had an opportunity to put his own spin on it.

On her way to the Washington Hilton where the luncheon speech was to be held, she ordered the driver to put up the privacy screen so that she could change from her black mourning clothes to her favorite red dress with blue and white lapels. With her red pumps and matching purse, she was almost ready to go by the time the black limo pulled up the circular driveway. Waiting inside were her staffers, makeup girl, and speechwriter, none of whom had a clue that she was no longer the party's candidate for vice president. She kept that information to herself. They all chattered in seemingly oblivious abandon, none of them listening or caring if their words were heard. They were excited to see her and equally excited that she would soon be announcing her candidacy for president.

Scarlett took her speechwriter aside and spoke to her in a quiet whisper. Her assistant began gesticulating in protest, raising her voice. Suddenly, she dashed toward the stage to perform last-minute changes to the teleprompter's computer controls as Scarlett settled into the chair to groom in preparation. "I like being the woman in charge," she said to nobody in particular.

Max's information-gathering staff had received a quick phone call from an unidentified attendee of the Miniver/Conroy flare-up, who was only too pleased to report to Bill Staffman that Scarlett was no longer running as the party's choice for vice president and that she and Miniver almost came to blows over her misplaced assumption that she would succeed Cunningham as the party's presidential candidate. As the informant went into great detail about the fiery exchange minutes before, Staffman was furiously passing the information to Max by e-mail. Before the message was complete, Max was sliding into the driver's seat of his Jaguar and winding down the driveway toward the Capitol, driving the senator's favorite car himself for the first time since his father's death. By the time Scarlett had changed her clothes, put on her makeup, and choreographed her entrance, Max was securely situated in the back row of the conference room.

Under normal circumstances, the attention of the audience would have been focused on the front of the room, where two large screens displayed photographs of the speaker and promoted upcoming events. This day, they turned their chairs to face Max, who was failing miserably at remaining anonymous. They didn't directly engage him in conversation, but they stared openly and spoke to each other in low voices while Max smiled and tried to remain nonchalant. The mystery of his presence was compounded by the fact that he was apparently alone, with no staff and no security. If there were Secret Service agents assigned to the event, they were obviously focused on Scarlett's security, not Max's. The vacant chairs in the room were around Max, in curious violation of the time-honored tradition of surrounding political candidates with a cushion of adoring humanity at every public appearance.

The audience had one thought about his presence, "Why is he here?"

Scarlett was patiently reviewing her 3x5 card when her staffers burst into the room. "He's here!" they announced in chorus.

"Who's here? What are you talking about, why are you so excited? Miniver didn't follow me here, did he?" she worried.

"No! Max Masterson! He's sitting in the back row!" sputtered Trixie Francis, her youngest event planner. Trixie had assumed the duty of crowd control and was charged with making sure that signs prominently displaying Scarlett's name in red were in the hands of anyone who agreed to hold them up whenever the cameras were pointed in their direction. She hadn't noticed Max's discreet entrance until the rumbling of the audience began, but when she saw the cause of the commotion, she wasted no time battling her way backstage to announce the surprising news.

"Well, I don't suppose you asked him why he is here," responded Scarlett to nobody in particular.

"Uh… no ma'am."

"Well go out there right this instant and ask him, then get right back to me. I don't want to be the last to know, ladies, and I expect you to give me a complete report before I walk out on that stage. I will not be upstaged by a political opponent at my own event." Scarlett's tone was stern, and her normally gentle demeanor had been affected by the events of the day. "Did you misunderstand me?"

"No ma'am," they chirped in unison as they trailed backwards out the door.

When they reached the main room, Trixie took control. "She means for me to do it. We can't walk up to him like a pack of high school girls. You two stay back, and if you see me signal, come and rescue me. How do I look?" Trixie's subordinates looked glum and wouldn't answer. She was only a messenger, but they both silently wished that they could spend a moment alone with the handsome man, even if he was the competition.

Trixie made her way across the room, weaving deftly between the tables of local dignitaries. As she approached, Max watched with interest as she tripped headlong over a purse that blocked her way, recovered by grabbing the back of a large woman whose hat blocked the view of most of the audience behind her, and regained her dignity as she skidded to a stop directly in front of her target. She timidly held her hand to the side of her head and whispered into his ear.

"Mr. Masterson, I'm Trixie Francis. I'm from Miss Conroy's staff. She… She asked me to come over here and ask you what you are doing here… No, that didn't sound right. She wants to know why you came to hear her speak… You are here to listen to her speech, aren't you? Really, you have everyone curious."

"Trixie, it's a pleasure to meet someone so graceful in maneuvering through that minefield," he remarked, still appreciating her approach. "Tell Scarlett that Max Masterson would like ten minutes of her time," he whispered back.

Chapter Eighty-Nine

"This is unprecedented. It wasn't planned. I can't just change my speech to suit Mr. Masterson. What is he trying to do, rattle me? I fully intend to take that stage and make my planned presentation and then I'll deal with Max Masterson. How do I look?" Scarlett's agenda had been scuttled from the moment Cunningham dropped dead, and she was uncomfortable dealing with constant change. That morning, she was the apparent candidate in her party's quest to unseat an incumbent president, now she was swimming alone in shark-filled waters.

"Miss Conroy," whined the staffers in unison. "Are you going to talk to him?"

Scarlett averted her gaze from the mirror for a moment, her annoyance apparent in her expression. "Please ask the moderator to make my introduction. I am going to make this speech. Now." She stood, and made her way toward the door as her three assistants scrambled to make the last-second preparations.

Already on stage, Martha Worthington, the chapter president, was warming up the crowd with a rousing introduction of their featured speaker. News of Max's presence had been relayed to her, and the audience was buzzing about it. She was uncertain whether to announce his presence, along with that of the local dignitaries who had graciously taken time to attend. Part of her believed it would be rude to have another presidential candidate in attendance and fail to acknowledge him, nonetheless she couldn't help wondering why he was here. Candidates didn't customarily crash their opponent's speeches, Martha didn't know what to do, and she was further confused by Scarlett's premature appearance on stage. It all seemed so rushed and impromptu. Scarlett was walking to her prearranged position on the stage, forcing Martha to hurry her introduction, abandoning the notes that she had spent the entire morning drafting and refining. "Ladies and Gentlemen, I present to you Scarlett Conroy, candidate for president of the United States of America!"

The applause began, and Scarlett moved into the stage lights, pausing to pull her silver brush from her purse as she had so many times in her political career. As she began combing her red hair, the spotlight swung to the audience microphone, where questions were asked during the give and take session following prepared remarks. Max stood at the microphone. Scarlett's expression betrayed her annoyance at being upstaged by her opponent.

Realizing that the microphone was dead, Max stepped back and, in a loud voice, announced, "Ladies, would you mind if I took ten minutes of Miss Conroy's time? We'll be right back." Max walked up the steps toward Scarlett, who shook her head. The audience, knowing that they were being treated to an event that would end up on every news feed in the world by day's end, murmured their consent if only to be part of the unplanned excitement. He took Scarlett's arm as she protested and escorted his opponent to a private anteroom.

The press assigned to cover the event quickly delivered the news by cell phone. Video coverage of the event was provided by the lone camera of the League, and anything newsworthy would be edited from the group feed, which would not be ready for broadcast until after the event. The delay launched them into panic mode, and they rushed to get the news to the newsroom.

"Max Masterson just showed up at a Conroy speech and dragged her offstage!"

"What is he doing there?"

"I don't know. He said he would be back in ten minutes."

"Where are they now?"

"In another room. Alone."

"Get in there and find out what's happening."

"I don't think we can. They asked to be alone."

"They're presidential candidates, for chrissakes. They don't have any right to be alone."

Greg Scuperman, Capitol correspondent for News Tonight, would have none of this. Masterson had thwarted him at every opportunity, and he would not sit still for another report that parroted the rest of the press corps. He was the lead dog, the one who got the news before his competition. He was in charge, and no third-rate politician was going to upstage him in front of his audience again. He made his way through the crowd toward the room, film technician in tow.

An elderly woman returning from a trip to the ladies' room was slowly making her way back to her seat. Not moving fast enough to avoid Scuperman, she was unceremoniously steered her into the lap of a large black woman, who loudly proclaimed her annoyance to everyone in the room. "Who does that white man think he is? I don't deserve to be treated like this! Now look what you've done! My dessert is ruined!"

The elderly woman looked apologetic as she pulled her hand from the strawberry shortcake and stood up.

Scuperman continued barging forward, intent on getting into that room. As he made his way to the stage and hurried across the lighted expanse toward the door, two secret service agents tackled him from behind, taking him out at the knees.

The applause was deafening.

Chapter Ninety

It took two minutes for Scarlett to stop protesting in her most authoritative and presidential voice that Max Masterson would never work in Washington again after this stunt, until she realized that her opponent had never worked in Washington before and that he was smiling.

"What are you smiling about? I hate you!"

"No you don't. You love me."

"I do not! I'm leaving this room right this second!"

"Before you leave, I need to ask you a question."

"Max, you exasperate me. What could possibly be so important that you have to drag me off the stage just before a speech?" Her complexion was quickly reddening to match her hair, and her normal composure was degenerating into a state of uncontrolled anger. Max paused, waiting for her to stop talking and calm down. He knew he had little time left before they broke the door down and rescued her from his grasp. He sat down, releasing his grip, realizing that Scarlett wouldn't bolt out of the room until she satisfied her curiosity. She collected herself, and he marveled at her ability to recover from the unexpected in so short a time. Finally she sat down, waiting.

"Will you be my running mate?"

Scarlett's mouth fell open, and for the first time in her political career, she was at a loss for words.

Max continued. "Scarlett, I have known you since we were little. My father had a great deal of respect for your daddy, and whether you realize it or not, we have both been raised to…"

"Reared."

"What?"

"You rear children. You raise livestock."

"Okay, reared then, dammit. Are you going to correct my diction, or are you going to let me finish before they break the door down and haul me off?" The sound of muffled voices was accompanied by an authoritative knock. Scarlett was oblivious.

"Why on earth would you want me?'

Max tried to continue, but the knocking became pounding. He got to the point.

"Scarlett, ever since we were kids, you have been good at all of the stuff I'm not good at, and I was better at the rest. I can't think of anyone who would be better at balancing the ticket for the benefit of the American people. Now, if you are so inclined, would you be so kind as to inform the Secret Service that you are not being molested, and that we require a few more minutes alone?" Scarlett jumped up and hurried to the door, pulling it open so fast that a Secret Service agent lost his balance and stumbled into the room, followed by a surge composed of Scarlett's staff, several reporters, and the collected leadership of the D.C. Chapter of the League of Women Voters. They all looked crazed. Max sat with his hands folded in his lap, smiling at the throng.

"I am in a private meeting, and I require several more minutes to discuss a matter of great importance with Mr. Masterson, and I do not want to be disturbed again. Now, everyone out!"

The surge reversed, and she slammed the door loudly.

"She'll make a good VP, if I can get her to take the job," thought Max, as she settled back into her chair.

"Now, Max, before I give you my response, I'd like to hear more about what you have in mind."

"Scarlett, as I was saying before your adoring supporters interrupted me, is that we have both been reared since we could talk for one goal. Now that we are both pursuing that same goal at the same time, it is beginning to look like neither of us can succeed without the other. So… Be my running mate. I know about your meeting with Miniver and his henchmen. My people had a similar meeting with Blythe's henchmen a few days ago, and they said basically the same thing. I am at the top of the polls, as much as I loathe them, because people are fed up with politicians and the usual way of electing a president, and you have succeeded because you are better at playing the game than anyone in politics. Together, we can't lose. Apart, we both lose. So what's it going to be?" Max began to count off the seconds in his head. If she didn't respond within one minute, the offer would expire and he'd walk out of the room.

Scarlett didn't wait. Her response took less than ten seconds. Without a word to Max, she stood up and walked out of the room, greeted by the cheers of 3,000 curious supporters and made her planned speech.

Chapter Ninety-One

Intelligence Secretary Gunter Cover took his directives from the president, and he took them seriously. After serving four previous administrations, he had made friends and avoided enemies. There was one enemy who was unavoidable if he was to do his job, and Cover dreaded him more than words could express. "The pompous asshole has been around longer than I have, and homeland security is the farthest thing from his mind. Adam Wirtep collects secrets and uses them against anyone who stands up to him," he thought as the limo wound through the streets of Washington. His meeting with the Homeland Security director had been hastily arranged after his run-in with the president, and he resented the time he was diverting from the terrorist threat to deal with the president's insecurities about Max Masterson. If anyone had any dirt to throw at Max, Wirtep would be holding the shovel.

He could have taken the secure underground route to the Homeland Security headquarters in the Eisenhower Office Building, but he wanted to be as conspicuous as possible in the event that Wirtep tried to deny that he had met with the Intelligence Secretary. He wanted his whereabouts to be documented if Wirtep decided to add him to his enemies list, which was becoming longer than the roster of serving members of Congress. If his suspicions were correct, he would confirm that the director of Homeland Security was at the center of a conspiracy that had simmered for a generation, and he had no doubt that things would get ugly. Wirtep had a long reputation for taking names and destroying his opposition in sinister ways. Max's father had been the first of a long line of politicians who had stood up to Wirtep and had suffered for it in profound ways.

A long-hidden report on the bombing of the Patriot Society meeting many years before had never become public. Anyone who had any intelligence experience would immediately conclude that a domestic conspiracy was directly connected to Wirtep, but Wirtep would never see justice. He was too slick to leave a trail that would stand up in court, and his enemies in the political world had too much to hide. Adrianna McVeigh's death and the near-demise of John "Minuteman" Masterson had Wirtep's modus operandi all over it, and he could see it happening again.

It had been long known in the intelligence community that Homeland Security had direct contact with mercenaries who were actively carrying out Wirtep's orders, purportedly in the interest of eliminating terrorist threats within America's borders. As the years went by, their assignments extended throughout the world, and their purpose grayed into any area that the Homeland Security director chose to define. It was his prerogative, and the mercenaries hired to carry out his orders never questioned his intentions.

Cover entered the plush office and marveled at the cost of furnishing the immense suite. Dark mahogany paneling with ornate baroque trim was accented by burgundy curtains that hung heavily to the sides of arched windows, whose thick panes extended from floor to ceiling. He surmised that the windows and walls were reinforced to withstand a bomb blast, and if the building took a direct hit, Homeland Security would likely survive intact after the rest of the area burned to ashes.

Cover was scanned for weapons by devices concealed in the doorway. If the scan revealed metal or any chemical residue, a silent alarm would trigger an immediate intercept by security personnel who prided themselves on a response time of less than five seconds. He was ushered into Wirtep's office, across a huge expanse of thick gold carpet was a single chair in front of an immense desk that made a visitor feel like he had been transported back to the high school principal's office for a well-deserved scolding.

The Homeland Security director was unaccustomed to visitors languishing in his office and got directly to the point. "Cover, what is this cryptic message I received from your assistant that you needed to speak with me about a matter of timely and crucial importance?" Wirtep glared over antique reading glasses that revealed a reverence for the past and a disdain for modern science, which had all but eliminated the need for eyeglasses of any kind. He didn't bother to rise and shake the hand of his contemporary, and he had long-since dispensed with the formalities of social discourse.

Their previous meeting had taken place shortly after the attempt on Max Masterson's life two weeks earlier, and Cover's internal radar had immediately sounded alarms at the discovery that Homeland Security had been briefed on the details of the shooting before his agency was alerted to the attempt on the life of a presidential candidate. After all, his responsibilities extended to the Secret Service, which was assigned to protect those running for the highest office in politics. He held a disdain for Wirtep and his imperious ways. Even his body language revealed complicity.

"I won't take much of your time. I need to know what you know about Max Masterson. Anything that might weaken his candidacy. And I want to know how you knew that someone took a shot at him before I was briefed."

Wirtep shifted in his chair, his face showing that he was pondering how much to reveal. "It is my duty to report to the president anything that could compromise national security. My sources report directly to me. Your sources report directly to you."

Cover knew that the only way Wirtep could know more than the CIA and its web of operatives would be for him to be involved in the conspiracy itself, and he was involved up to his eyeballs. If he reported directly to the president, Blythe's complicity was confirmed by the feigned surprise he had displayed when Cover disclosed that Max was being targeted by mercenaries. He was sitting as across from the ringleader. He struggled to remain expressionless.

"Cover, you and I go back a long way. You know how the game is played at this level. Anyone who gets in the way of our shared ideals is to be eliminated. That's what the president wants, and you aren't going to stand in my way. Don't you think that if I had any dirt on that young rabble-rouser it would be splattered all over for the world to see? It's that damned privacy cloak that his daddy set up. We can't penetrate it. If we could, we would have planted enough false propaganda to sink him for good." He sat back and took a long draw on a cigar that smoldered in a crystal ashtray, the only adornment on his massive desk.

"Clean desks can say a lot," Cover surmised.

"Mr. Director, I also report to the president, but I take it he has already been briefed on this. I anticipate that he will know of my visit by the time I leave the building."

"He already does."

Chapter Ninety-Two

Cover wasted no time in seeking out the president. If his position as Intelligence Secretary couldn't get him into the Oval Office unannounced, then nobody could get there, and if a door opens in Washington, the opportunist takes it. It was of no consideration to him that the final debate was two days away. To save his own ass, he was going to take the initiative. The limo ride to the White House was brief but gave him enough time to gather his thoughts and make two phone calls from his secure connection. The first was to Luke Postlewaite. The second was directly to Max Masterson.

By the time the limo was two blocks from the White House, Cover had passed security, another perk of his being the symbolic head of the world's largest intelligence agency. Once inside the building, he was ushered directly into the Oval Office and sat waiting for Blythe to appear.

The president came in red-faced and sweating, his jogging suit sticking to the lumps of adipose tissue it concealed. "Cover, this better be good. You forced me to pull out of an important meeting. Don't you know that I am preparing for a debate?" Blythe was acutely aware that his Intelligence Secretary was not buying any of his window dressing, but he was equally unconcerned that his activities would become public.

Cover had no intention of engaging in social niceties. He would speak his mind for once, and get out. "Mr. President, I resign."

"What the hell are you talking about, resign? You resign when I tell you to resign. I own you!" His face took on a deeper shade of red.

Cover calmly pulled an envelope from his suit pocket and slid it across the Kennedy desk.

"In my resignation letter, you will find my reasons. You and Adam Wirtep have been implicated in a long-standing conspiracy to commit treason against the United States of America, and I have disseminated a full report, together with a recording of Wirtep's admission, that I obtained an hour ago during a visit to his office. But you already knew of my visit when you walked into this room, didn't you, Mr. President?"

"Do you actually believe that the American public will believe you over me? You dirty…" Blythe slumped in his chair and pressed a concealed button. He was used to the immediate response of the Secret Service and was rewarded with the appearance of two black-suited men who stood silently on either side of Cover's chair.

Cover was not easily intimidated. "I have also gathered convincing evidence that you authorized an attempt on your opponent's life on the eve of the election. As I speak, this information is being broadcast on all major networks."

Blythe growled in a tone normally reserved for professional wrestlers. "Before I order my men to take you away, I have a question. What do you expect me to do with this information?"

Cover paused, knowing that the words he spoke would be the last the president of the United States would hear from his mouth.

"If I were you, I'd be looking for a new job."

"Cover, surely my own intelligence guy would know that I have nothing to do with Mr. Masterson's recent string of mishaps. I am the most monitored man in history. If I allowed it to happen, every word I speak in the White House would be recorded."

Cover watched the sweat form on Blythe's forehead and imagined that he was interrupting another basement fencing match. The First Lady hadn't been seen in public with her husband for a year, but she had his sympathy.

The president went on. "I said no to that idea. Didn't think I should share everything with the voters. They might not like the real Warren Hudson Blythe as much as the suit they see on TV." He took a long swallow of imported beer from the can that he had pulled from a mini refrigerator disguised as a wooden filing cabinet and leaned far back in his chair, placing his stocking feet on the smooth walnut surface of the desk and sighing. On the day he took possession of the Oval Office, Blythe had ordered the refrigerator made to match the decor. "You have got to understand, my man." He took a longer drag on the can, draining it, and crumpled it loudly. "I will expect you to report the truth about me to the American people. I am innocent."

Cover took a moment to absorb all the strangeness, then fired back. "Mr. President. If my job was to tell the truth, the whole truth, and nothing but the truth, I would have been gone a long time ago. There isn't a politician alive who can stand the truth."

Blythe smiled and wiped his forehead. "Then we have an understanding, Mr. Cover?"

"No, you misunderstood," he said, weighing his words. He fought the urge to speak the thoughts that were screaming inside of his mind, begging to get out. If he said those words, he wouldn't be counting the days to retirement. He would be counting the seconds. "If there is one thing that I have learned in my 37 years in the espionage business, it's the basic fact that the truth doesn't matter. It doesn't matter whether you plotted with terrorists to kill off your strongest political opponent. You wanted it to happen. It doesn't matter whether, years from now, you are vindicated, and the bastards who took you down are all dead along with you. It only matters what the people are thinking at the moment. You're going to go down because the people believe you were involved, and all of them are pointing at you."

Cover turned to leave and was startled to see two Secret Service agents standing at arm's length on either side of him. They were poised to immobilize him and restrain any movement he foolishly chose to make. These were his employees at the moment, but they answered to the man popping a beer behind his desk. Cover quietly left the room with his escorts at each arm.

With his Intelligence Secretary secured away from the world for the time being, Blythe ordered the door to the Oval Office closed. Using the voice-activated intercom, he notified his secretary that he was not to be disturbed, leaving his Cabinet members waiting in the conference room.

Chapter Ninety-Three

"Our Intelligence Secretary has betrayed the American people and has brought my administration into disrepute," said President Blythe in a hastily assembled press conference. He addressed the world from the Oval Office and spoke in measured tones, his heavily made-up face and hair resembling a caricature of his previously manicured features. Years of prescription drug abuse and alcohol had bloated him, and he no longer carried the swagger of a confident young politician. He was succumbing to years of stress and physical abuse, and no amount of makeup could restore the past.

"He has been taken into custody and charged with treason, the highest crime an American can commit against his country," he continued. "My message will be short, as you know that in two days, I will be debating Masterson and Conroy in North Carolina. After that, I will be spending the final two weeks before the election attending to the business of running this great country, as I intend to spend the next four years of my presidency."

The camera and lights were turned off. "Are we through?" asked Blythe.

"Yes, Mr. President," replied the cameraman.

"Good, now get the hell out of my office," Blythe bellowed.

The assembled crew scrambled to comply with the demands of the most powerful person in the country and were gone in minutes.

Chapter Ninety-Four

There was no valid reason for the president of the United States to enter into the most contentious debate of his career unprepared, but Blythe's rapid decline was of his own creation. Inside the isolation of the White House, the only witnesses to the deterioration of his mind were the very same people who were there to promote his image. By design, Party Chairman Partiman and Vice President Case spent no time in the presence of the president to witness it, but Presidential Advisor Ted Schoolcraft and Chief of Staff Waylon Cheevers occupied the outer offices of the White House and saw it manifested in the ever-growing wall he was building around himself.

The president of the United States, the most public official in the political world, was under a self-imposed siege. Aside from brief public appearances to make recorded stump speeches before audiences handpicked by his campaign staff, Blythe was isolated from America.

As they sat in the White House conference room awaiting the 10:30 a.m. meeting that would never happen, Schoolcraft and Cheevers assessed the situation.

"I'm getting that mushroom feeling again," offered Schoolcraft, a personal joke that the two had shared since their first days of service to Blythe in the early days of his senate race twelve years before.

"Keeping you in the dark and feeding you shit again? Yeah, me too," replied Cheevers. *He's lost it. I don't just mean the presidency.*

I mean, he's getting as cuckoo as he's ever been, and if it doesn't come out in that debate, I'll personally get him an Academy Award. Better yet, a Pulitzer." They chuckled quietly, but there was no humor, just a shared nervousness.

"I can't get him to focus on this debate, he cancels a good portion of his campaign appearances, and all the press seems to be interested in is who Masterson will pick as his running mate. He needs to be out there pressing the flesh and looking presidential." Shaking his head, he lowered his voice to a whisper. "He has this idea that an Independent can't get elected. The polls are beginning to say otherwise."

Schoolcraft cradled his coffee and clutched a meticulously organized notebook. He had reduced all of the paper to his iPad, but he chose to have something more substantial to occupy his hands when he was dealing with Blythe. The president was mistrustful of electronic information and had demonstrated a fondness for throwing iPads against the wall to see if they would break. "Whether he pulls this out of his ass and wins a second term or not, I'm leaving this nutcase and going into the private sector right after the election. You should, too. Maybe we can both get a lobbying job and make some real money for once," he whispered.

After half an hour of waiting, Blythe had not emerged, and they returned to their offices in the East Wing. Another day wasted, and no time left to prepare for the inevitable.

Chapter Ninety-Five

Had his handlers known that he was abusing drugs and alcohol to mask his depression and paranoia, Blythe would have been micromanaged. But he carried his own pill container, which he used to supplement the medication presented to him as prescribed. Only his personal physician knew the full extent of the problem, but Dr. Quaxley was almost as isolated from the president as the rest. A personal checkup was obligatory to convince the public that he was in good health, but two checkups per year were all that he allowed, and the details of his condition were barred from public scrutiny by the same laws that protected everyone else. Secretly, the president was getting stoned, and since his showdown with his Intelligence Secretary, his need to douse his anxiety had grown to new proportions.

Blythe's campaign abandoned any hope of disgracing Max and Scarlett. As the two remaining candidates receiving more than 20% of the primary vote, they would be at the podium with the incumbent, and the focus of the press was on the final three. Max was far ahead of Scarlett in the polls, but she hung on doggedly, continuing to make stump speeches throughout the country. She had succeeded in eliminating her party from the campaign from the start, and for the first time in her life, she assumed the role of independent. For a traditional politician, going bare without the resources of the political machine was scary at best, and at worst, it was uncomfortably lonely.

Scarlett needed to remain viable as a candidate. Excerpts of her speeches were continuously broadcast to provide contrast to the highly polished rhetoric that was put out by Blythe's reelection staff. In the last days of the election, her talking points had been repeated so often that one speech was basically the same as the one before it, and she had nothing more to contribute to convince the undecided to give her their vote.

Max made no effort to match or contrast either campaign's message. His campaign was so unorthodox that there was no way to accurately predict the effect his message would have on the voters. He had made no speeches and had managed to shift attention to his campaign while obscuring his opponents in too many of their own words. There were only Max's sound bites, accompanied by the intense attention given to Max himself, and a new disdain by the public for the usual process of electing the next president. It was a battle of the new challengers against the old. For the first time in modern history, an incumbent was being challenged by two independents, and the incumbent was stumbling badly.

"I need my notes. Where are my notes? Where are the questions? How the hell am I going to know the answers if I don't know the questions?" Blythe sat in a barber chair, dressed in the same sweatshirt and sweatpants that he had worn for two days. He'd showered, but the old, sweaty clothes were not replaced with clean ones, and his body odor was offensive to everyone in the room. He was vibrating with agitation.

"Mr. President, stop fidgeting. You stink like a dumpster, and I'm supposed to make you look and smell like a president. Go change your clothes." Yawanna Hawley was the makeup artist for the White House, and she had been there for three presidents before Blythe. Her official job description was "image consultant," a title bestowed upon her by Hillary Clinton, and the title stuck. She didn't have a political bone in her body and had no fear of being fired for her insolence. Greater men than Blythe had confided in her over the years, and she provided her own unadulterated version of public opinion. His predecessors had valued her opinion, but this one didn't have a clue. Clucking with disapproval, she rattled on. "The Bushes had good hair, but don't get me started about Romney. And I can't wait to get my hands on Scarlett Conroy's hair. I can always tell how well a politician will do by their hair, you know?"

He ignored her, but changed into the standard dark blue suit and white shirt upon which the image of the president is built. When he had changed, he settled back into the chair and resumed barking orders. "Someone bring me an ice water," he bellowed.

Two aides scrambled to comply, while Walsh and Schoolcraft continued to brief him on answers to possible questions. They had the mutual angst that they were bailing out a sinking ship with a thimble, and they dreaded the inevitable shredding of the Blythe administration during the debate. They had no major accomplishments to tout and were only able to weakly defend a presidency that was mired in a malaise of endless wars and economic stagnation. There had been no promises kept, and Blythe's belligerent approach to international issues had created many enemies.

While the president popped two small pills from his pocket, Yawanna went to work on his face. She carefully blended the red of his Rosacea with the sparse natural flesh tones of the rest of his face, all the while fighting the feeling that she was dressing a corpse. He had spent the morning drinking whatever scotch he could find, and he radiated the heat and sweat that his body produced to expel the toxins.

Schoolcraft was the more optimistic of his handlers and spent the downtime reading questions and attempting to elicit a response. "Maybe it was wise to keep him bottled up and out of the public eye. He won't stand up to Masterson and Conroy head to head, and it's too late to do anything about it. Those political ads are at least two years old, and he's sliding down a slippery slope to disaster," he confided to Cheevers. He stared at the raving madman and thought, "No amount of makeup will take away Blythe's glazed eyes and wobbly mannerisms." He pulled Cheevers into an adjoining room, and once they were outside of earshot, Cheevers blurted out what they were both thinking. "I didn't have the guts to confront him, to just walk in and shake him out of this. He should have been in rehab a year ago. But how would that have played with the press?"

He moved farther from the door, suddenly fearful of being overheard, then continued sharing his thoughts. "I can see it now. Scuperman would be sitting outside of the gates of the funny farm, and the press would be saying, 'It's the fourteenth day of the president's rehabilitation, and the course of therapy is progressing nicely, while Vice President Case has assumed his role as world leader during this emergency.'"

Schoolcraft nodded in agreement. "Let's get back to work—as if that will do any good." He flipped the lights off as he walked out of the room, leaving Cheevers standing in the dark.

Chapter Ninety-Six

Max stood at his assigned podium as the television crew scrambled to make last minute adjustments to sound and lights. He was early. He wanted to get familiar with the venue for the debate, and the audience would not be seated for another hour. By that time, he would be calmly waiting for the signal to take the stage with only Andrew Fox and Bill Staffman to keep him company. As he looked out over the empty seats, the feeling that his father was watching was unshakeable. Silently, he thought of the long journey that had begun when he was an infant and of the senator who became his father. If John Masterson had lived, he would have had the best seat in the house. If he had been able to give last minute advice, he would have told Max to stick with the plan he had crafted to get his son to that stage.

When the feeling diminished, Max walked slowly back to the room to Andrew and Bill for last minute advice. He would have preferred to have time to himself, but solitude is impossible during the last days of any political race. Andrew launched into his pep talk before the door closed.

"No speeches, right?"

"No speeches," Max replied.

"No messages longer than a sound bite, right?" Staffman chimed in, realizing that the time for preparation was long over for his young candidate. He had resigned himself to following the Maxims for so long that it was second nature, any new words would be a distraction.

"I'm sticking with the plan," replied Max. He walked over to a desk in the corner of the room. The lamp illuminated an envelope. The writing on it was familiar. The words were simple: Mr. President.

Max tore into the envelope as Andrew said, "Luke Postlewaite and mom are going to be in the audience tonight, and Luke gave me this for you." Inside was a copy of the original draft of the Maxims, along with a handwritten card. In his father's distinctive script, there were two lines:

Stick with the plan and release your fear.

You have taken the journey, now reach the destination.

Max stood at the podium, calm and perfect, dressed in a charcoal blue suit and red, white, and blue striped tie. His healthy tan was real, acquired on the ski slopes and beach trips he managed to use as backdrops for his many sound bites. He refused the assistance of a hairdresser or makeup artist. He didn't need anything.

Noticing activity to the side of the stage, he saw Scarlett surrounded by a swarm of assistants. They were busy patting and combing, all talking at once. Scarlett stood in the middle reviewing the flash cards she had trimmed to fit in the palms of her delicate hands. Until the cameras began broadcasting, Scarlett would remain in the wings, and take advantage of her unique ability to attract attention. She wore her trademark red politician suit, with a blue satin scarf. She, too, was perfect.

When the moderator approached his desk, the lights came on and so did the cameras, capturing every angle and activity in the room.

When she was certain that the broadcast of her image was imminent, Scarlett stepped onto the stage and began brushing her long auburn hair, then took her place behind the podium on the left side of the stage. The center podium remained empty, and nervous broadcasters began demanding reports on the whereabouts of the president.

Greg Scuperman sat at the back of the audience. He had wangled a pass from the League of Women Voters after threatening to sue the organizers for tackling him as he had tried to force his way into Scarlett's dressing room. He was sporting a hematoma on his hip the size of a softball, and he limped when he walked. The bruise on his left temple was still tender, but it could be covered with makeup now that the swelling had gone down. He wanted to be in the room when Blythe annihilated his opponents with his skillful debating. All electronic devices had been removed from members of the audience, and security was high. Scuperman felt naked and gagged, lacking the ability to ask questions. To compensate, he planned to do an immediate report outside of Wait Chapel, the debate venue at Wake Forest University, where his network had set up lights and sound. The fall foliage provided a colorful backdrop.

Accompanied by his team of assistants, Blythe appeared, strode confidently toward his place in the center of the stage, and smiled. If he had been scanned for electronic devices like the others present in the room, he would have had to forfeit the tiny microphone inside his ear canal. The president of the United States does not submit to security checks, and his calm exterior belied the fact that he would be fed answers from a secret location at the first sign that he was faltering. Inside the makeup, though, the inebriated man would soon face his largest audience, and his high-definition image would be viewed by everyone, everywhere.

"Good evening, ladies and gentlemen, please be seated. It's time to introduce our candidates," began Roger Forrestal, retired news correspondent for the now defunct CBS News. "The rules, as defined by a resolution of the League of Women Voters, are unchanged. For the benefit of the viewers who have not participated in our previous debates in this election, I will review them before we begin." He quickly read a summary of the rules, stressing that the questions for this debate had been submitted by viewers and the subjects had been changing on a daily basis for the past six weeks. "For the first time in history, the candidates have had no advance notice of the topics and no ability to propose or reject the questions. To ensure the integrity of this process, I have left them sealed in the envelope before me." With great drama, he tore open the envelope and extracted the contents.

Forrestal had been the default moderator since the start of the presidential race, and the rules defined by the League of Women Voters had not changed despite the efforts of the candidates to determine the questions to be asked in advance. Any candidate who could predict the questions would have a significant advantage. The ten questions to be asked were anonymously collected and guarded by the League, and to avoid corruption, they were changed constantly. The candidates could speculate, but they would lack the rote statistics that most annoyed the voters. Without advance preparation, there could be none of that. For the first time in a long time, the debate participants were in the dark.

The cameras panned the candidates. Max and Scarlett stood still, attentive to the announcement. Blythe, however, had his back to the podium, whispering loud enough to be heard by most of the others in the room. The microphones picked up the rest of his words, which were broadcast to the world. "Dammit! Where's my teleprompter? Cheevers! Don't just stand there like a retard! I'm not going to debate these two freakin' Independents without my notes! Get out here, now!"

Cheevers stood out of the glare of the cameras. Nothing short of a cattle prod was going to get him out on that stage, and he considered leaving the building before the president of the United States had a full meltdown in front of the world. Out of duty, he stood fast, but glanced around for the nearest exit.

Blythe realized that he had his back to the audience and turned, reaching for the podium. In his inebriated state, he missed his handhold by a good two inches, sprawling face first onto the hardwood stage. Immediately, Secret Service agents emerged from hidden locations and rushed toward the president. Trained to protect him from any perceived harm, they piled on top of him to protect his life from threats to his well-being. But no training could protect Blythe from himself, and it was several minutes before the pandemonium subsided.

Scarlett stood at her podium, covering her mouth with her hand, regretting that she had left her mirror in her purse and wondering whether they would be afforded an opportunity to freshen up. By the time Blythe resumed the podium, his hair was reminiscent of a Nick Nolte mug shot. His makeup had dissolved in sweat, and his face was red from exertion and self-abuse. Max was rock solid and waited impassively as Blythe continued to self-destruct.

"Let's continue, but first let me ask you, President Blythe, do you feel as if you are able to go on?" Forrestal was attempting to restore order, but it was a difficult task. He had no hope of erasing the start of this fiasco, and he knew that things could conceivably degenerate into pure chaos at any moment.

"Yeah, let's get this over with," replied Blythe, a droplet of sweat forming at the end of his nose. The cameras focused on the dangling drop and gave the viewers an unflattering close-up.

Back home in the real world, Bob, Phil, and Jerry remained glued to the big screen TV at Jesse's Tavern, which they had reserved for the occasion. Like other sporting events, they began betting on the only pending activity that could result in a winner or loser—that lone dangling drop on the end of the president's nose.

"I'll betcha five bucks that he'll never notice it, and I'll pay ya triple if it falls onto his podium," began Phil.

"Hell, I'll throw in another pitcher of Bud if it doesn't fall off before the first question," contributed Bob.

Jerry reached for another chicken wing and considered his wager. While the drop continued to cling to the end of the president's nose, he upped the offer significantly. "I gotcha all beat. I'll buy both of you dinner at Buddy's Steak House if he even leaves the stage on his own two feet."

Forrestal managed to maintain his own composure, and determined to get the show on the road, he scanned the first question. With a brief smile, he directed his gaze at Blythe. "Mr. President, the first question is for you, and you alone. The voters want to know, if you were given the opportunity to ask your opponents one question that defines their fitness to be president of the United States, what would you ask them?"

Blythe looked dumbfounded. In all the weeks of preparation for the debate, the possibility of him asking a question of Max Masterson and Scarlett Conroy, even one, had never entered his mind. In his condition, he reacted before he could regain his poise. "I haven't thought about it much, but what I really want to know is how these two goddamned Independents expect to beat me in this election. I have all of the experience, and they have none."

Cheevers and Partiman cringed from the sidelines. "This campaign is going down in flames," whispered Partiman.

Stunned, the audience was silent. Forrestal wasted no time in turning to Max. "Mr. Masterson, you will be allowed two minutes to respond." Max paused and directed his gaze into the cameras. "I won't need two minutes to respond. It's a simple question, and it deserves a simple response. Bad experience won't win an election. My ideas are fresh, and his are rotten to the core."

The audience erupted in loud applause as the cameras focused again on Blythe, who glared menacingly in Max's direction. The cameras resumed the close-up of Blythe's face. The droplet had tripled in size and fell from his nose, making an audible plop as it splattered onto his podium. It was quickly replaced on his nose by another one as his face took on a sheen that no amount of makeup could conceal.

The guys at the tavern were beside themselves. This was becoming real entertainment, and they laughed with delight at Max's direct jab at Blythe. They had long ago decided that Max was the candidate who would be getting their votes, but they clung to the precious few words he spoke, memorizing the simple messages. "I guess I'm paying for the beer tonight," said Bob. Phil knew he owed money to his two old friends, but they all knew that nobody would attempt to collect if Phil picked up the evening's tab. It was too early to predict whether Jerry would be buying them dinner, but the entertainment value of the event unfolding on the big screen made it all worth it.

"Senator Conroy, you will now be given two minutes."

Scarlett had waited for this moment all of her life. "Mr. Forrestal, I would like to start by taking this opportunity to thank all of the people who are responsible for tonight's debate, and especially the League of Women Voters, who have been so kind as to sponsor this event, a duty they have assumed once more for the benefit of all Americans." She launched into a prepared speech, touting her accomplishments as a politician and a woman. Where her resume was thin, she added the record of renowned women in history to hers, as if she had been there and done that; experience by affiliation. She was poised and confident, a supremely accomplished public speaker, and she filled the two minutes with well-rehearsed and packaged words. There was only one problem—she never answered the question.

While Scarlett spoke, Blythe tried to look past the bright lights into the dark recesses of the backstage area. If he had been successful, he would have realized that Cheevers and Partiman had stealthily made their exit for the less volatile comfort of a hotel bar in the Holiday Inn closest to the debate venue, safe from the wrath of the president, who was beyond the point of salvaging his last shred of dignity.

"Mr. Masterson, you have the next question. As you already realize, we are giving each of you the opportunity to ask questions of the other candidates before we go to questions composed by the voters, and this is an opportunity to inform America that each of you possess the integrity and vision to lead. Max Masterson, you're up," said Forrestal in his best announcer's baritone, energized by the path the debate was taking.

Max anticipated that he would be asking a crucial question, but he had to devise it so that he attacked Blythe's record and avoided boosting Scarlett's performance. Employing his characteristic economy of words, he turned to face the president. "I want to know how you are going to salvage America from the mess we are in and lead us to the prosperity that is our destiny." By addressing Blythe directly, he avoided having Scarlett respond before Blythe.

"Mr. Blythe, would you please address the question first," intoned the moderator.

The cameras zoomed in close, and Blythe's face filled the screen. In the age of high-definition imaging, no minor flaw could be hidden. Every pore could be examined in detail, and the president had managed by this time to smear his stage makeup with the back of his hand, and run his hands through his carefully coifed hair, giving the viewer the impression that he had just emerged from a barroom brawl. He puffed from exertion, despite the fact that he had been standing still the entire time. His eyes were glazed, and he wobbled slightly. He paused longer than was comfortable and glared once more at Max.

"You son of a bitch," he muttered in a low growl. "You think you are so smart, so perfect, so ready to lead." He launched himself from his podium and charged toward Max, raising his arm for a punch. Max calmly stepped left and feinted right as the president of the United States swung without the slightest contact. Blythe's momentum propelled him off the stage, his head ending squarely in the lap of Roger Forrestal. The veteran announcer managed to recover his poise almost instantly and proclaimed, "Ladies and Gentlemen, this will conclude tonight's debate. Thank you and may God bless America."

The lights were lowered as Blythe was extracted by Secret Service, his feet never touching the floor. Unaware that both of his assistants had left the building long before his outburst, he screamed, "Plan B! Plan B! Get Darkhorse on it immediately! Do you hear me?" His voice disappeared as he was carried through the heavy security doors.

From the hotel bar, Partiman and Cheevers turned to each other in astonishment. "I'll be damned. We still have a job, and he is still the president," proclaimed Cheevers. "Yeah, but what do we do now?" responded Partiman.

Chapter Ninety-Seven

At 4:30 p.m. on the day after the final debate, a hasty press conference was called at the White House. Press Secretary Wiley Talkinead read an official release and took no questions. Paper copies of the release, on official White House stationery, were distributed to all members of the press in attendance: "The conclusion of the final debate between President Warren H. Blythe, Scarlett Conroy, and Max Masterson is postponed until further notice. Regrettably, President Blythe has contracted influenza and will be unable to participate farther. Ms. Conroy and Mr. Masterson have graciously agreed to reschedule the debate at a time and place to be announced upon President Blythe's recuperation..."

The news of Blythe's withdrawal came as a surprise to the Masterson and Conroy camps. Not only were they not informed of the postponement, they also did not agree to the cancellation. Blythe's handlers had gambled that neither campaign would contradict the official announcement in an effort to deflect any negative public sentiment that would result.

Max went into a momentary scowl upon hearing the news, and then smiled. Andrew Fox and Bill Staffman waited for the inevitable Maxim that would come forth from Max. Instead, it was a question. "Bill, is the Kennedy Center reserved for tomorrow night? I want to make a speech."

Chapter Ninety-Eight

On the day of the speech, two days before the general election, Max fulfilled his pledge. He had vowed to America that he would not make any speeches during the campaign, but the campaign was over, and it was his last opportunity to get his message across before the vote. Unlike typical stump speeches, his was designed long in advance, by a man who was now long dead, and he now realized that he had been rehearsing it since he was old enough to speak. He knew the words by heart, which was the source of each syllable. He believed, and he wanted America to believe.

In response to numerous requests for speaking engagements, his staff had issued a press release that, finally, Max would be speaking on the day scheduled for the final debate before the election. This had the effect of delaying a substantial amount of early voting across the country in anticipation that this speech would be the one that would help people decide which candidate should become the next president of the United States.

Blythe and Conroy took the day before the election off from campaigning, as is the tradition. They were smug in their assessment of the polls. Projections for both the challenger and the incumbent showed close results, but with victories for each depending on which poll one chose to believe.

Blythe had developed a siege mentality in response to the serious allegations made by his Intelligence Secretary, who had not been seen since his visit to the White House, and was presumed by those not privy to the president's increasingly strange behavior to be recuperating.

The audience at the Kennedy Center paid for their seats, and the take was enough to erase the debt of the Masterson campaign. Big time luminaries treated the event like the Academy Awards and paid enormous sums for a pair of tickets, which were then surreptitiously sold to the highest bidder. They all wanted to be there, but billions of viewers had to settle for access over the Web.

There would be no commercials and no introductory speakers, and the crowd waited restlessly, murmuring in a low growl that seemed to grow as the 8:00 p.m. start time approached. Max was going to speak, and they craved listening him.

Security in black suits and hidden microphones lined the stage, identical dark sunglasses making them look like they had been manufactured on an assembly line. These were private security guards, although they looked like the Secret Service agents assigned to the candidates. Since Gunter Cover's disappearance, the Secret Service was only assigned to protect Blythe. They scanned the crowd and spoke to their central command in the sound booth.

The lights came on, and the crowd cheered, anticipating that Max would mysteriously appear on the stage and stand before the backdrop like a rock band. An opening appeared in the stage floor, and there he was, rising from beneath.

He was dressed in a black suit and red, white, and blue tie with brilliant white shirt for contrast. Every hair was meticulously in place. No wonder the networks chose to cover his campaign on Entertainment Tonight, "E," and the Entertainment Channel. If a president could look like a president, but double as a movie star at the same moment, it was Max. There were no props. No podiums to hide his image. Just Max in the middle of the stage with an American flag superimposed on the White House projected in high definition on the screen behind him.

The audience stood in unison, and he stood silently for ten minutes until the applause subsided below a roar, making no effort to quiet the crowd. The clapping increased with every facial gesture or body movement. He finally spoke in a loud and firm voice.

"I'm Max Masterson, and I'm running for president of the United States of America."

The crowd rose to their feet and the cheering beganagain. If it was possible, the noise was louder this time, but quickly diminished as the audience resumed their seats, eager to listen.

"I promised you that I would make no speeches during my campaign, but now the campaign is over. I am here today to ask you for your vote."

He shifted slightly, and the backdrop changed into a large ballot with a large red checkmark next to his name, which was larger and bolder than the other candidates' names. He looked serious, sterner than he had been portrayed in the many political cartoons of recent weeks. They liked to make him look like a carefree playboy or a baby in diapers to showcase his youth and inexperience, but now he looked older and more distinguished. His eyebrows peaked, forming a crease above his nose, and then he broke into his trademark smile, his dimples highlighting his handsome features.

"Many of you, particularly the press, and, oh yeah, that guy I'm running against, have been pestering me to make speeches on everything from what kind of underwear I wear to how I'm going to keep terrorists from sneaking in and blowing up the Statue of Liberty."

The audience laughed, almost in relief.

"I decided that if I'm going to run for president, I'm going to do it my way. Personally, I think that America is sick and tired of politicians."

The clapping began and cheers of support filled the room.

"I see what happens when politicians stand up and start talking by the hour. It happens to me, too. My eyes glaze over, my mind wanders, and by the time they are done droning on and on, I can't remember anything except the parts that pissed me off or made me think. Lately, there hasn't been much that has come out of a politician's mouth that has made me think."

A large man in the front row stood and yelled "Ain't that right!" blocking the view of the members of the audience for ten rows behind him, so they stood, too. He began clapping loudly, so they clapped along with him. In waves, the audience stood. He soon had a standing ovation for nothing more than the consensus that politicians create boredom.

He continued without a pause. "That's one reason why I'm not a politician. I'm just a man running for president."

The cheering began afresh, and he hadn't even begun to get into the important part of the speech. He raised his hands and achieved silence. "I have been telling you what I stand for. I have been doing it in sound bites, and I did it that way so the press wouldn't misrepresent what I said. I wanted you to remember me for what I believe, not for what they want you to believe." He paused, and the crowd settled down.

In the sound booth, the producer began to instruct the technicians to break to commercial, but then remembered that there were none scheduled. Max stood in silence, and the whole room became silent once more.

"I'm going to do a little experiment. When I tell you a subject, if you remember where I stand, tell me in one sentence. Ready?"

In homes all over the world, entire families waited for the impromptu civics test about to be broadcast. "Ready!" they yelled in unison, not realizing or caring that Max couldn't hear them. He heard the voices in the auditorium, and that was enough for him.

"The environment!"

"If you dirty it up, you make it cleaner than it was, or pay someone else to do it," they yelled.

"Jobs."

"Everyone should be able to make enough to support their family."

"Health care."

"All Americans are entitled to see a doctor when they are hurt or sick, and afford what it takes to keep them healthy."

"The elderly."

"Treat your elders as you want to be treated, to live a full life with dignity."

"Our children."

"We owe it to our children to protect them from harm, and to make their world better than ours."

"Education."

"The more you learn, the more you earn."

"Politicians."

"If you lie to the voter, we take note and you lose our vote."

This time, they broke into pandemonium, and it was several minutes before they composed themselves enough for him to go on. He stood patiently. When they settled down, he continued.

"Now, I want you to recite, word for word, what my opponent has told you about all of those things but leave out the lies."

In the midst of the laughing, the viewers at home looked at each other and realized that the incumbent president had lied to the American people on all of the subjects they had covered in Max's "speech," or that if he had told the truth, they couldn't remember what it was. For most, it was the first time that they clearly saw who they had elected to office and the serious choice they were about to make.

"I believe that Americans should have a clear choice when they decide who will lead them. I also believe that Americans should trust that they have made the right decision. The job of president should not be to deceive. It should not be a popularity contest. The true measure of a president is whether he can make clear choices, as unpopular as they may be at that moment, based on strong guiding principles. And when the decision is made, you should feel secure that it is right for America."

Max was settling into the speech he had rehearsed since childhood. He stood ramrod straight and solid, his hands emphasizing each point as the cameras zoomed to catch each facial expression. It was an intimate, personal conversation in tone, not preaching or loud, and he commanded their intense attention as he seemed to speak to each of them individually.

"I am one man. I am, above all else, a patriot. A patriot is an American who believes in and promotes American ideals. The next American president should be a patriot. I am not a Democrat. I am not a Republican. I am also not a liberal, a conservative, a communist, a socialist, a fascist, or a king. I am an American patriot."

"During the many months that I have been running for president, I have limited my words to clear messages so that you understand and remember where I stand on the issues. After I become your next president, my next important duty is to surround myself with other American patriots who are the best of the best, who will follow the maxims that define the way we will conduct the business of government."

Behind Max, the screen morphed into an image of the gold-embossed card that he carried in his pocket. He pulled the card from his suit and read. "These are my Maxims for America. They are the derived from the basic principles by which I conducted my campaign, and they are the principles by which I will conduct the office of president. I have modified them to deal with the task before us." The list transformed behind him.

The informed will of the people dictates what is right.
Maintain what is right, and right what is wrong.
Educate the people before asking them to decide an issue.
American interests must prevail over foreign interests.
Make Americans aware that they are a part of the world.
It is better to confess that you don't know than to lie.
Don't quote a statistic unless you can back it up with facts.
Persuade, don't deceive.
Combine strength with compassion.
Measure each decision by what is best for America.
Above all else, be a patriot.

"The time has come for us to take back America and take back our ideals. The days of 'My country right or wrong' are over. We are progressing to a higher rung on the ladder that is our legacy. We are progressing, right this very moment, toward the mutual goal of creating a nation of patriots. We are now, each one of us, Americans, and American patriots do what is right for America."

"When I walk away from this speech, I will be a rich man. Like my opponent, and all of the opponents I have faced and vanquished in this political campaign, I am wealthy. But the richness of my life that I have accumulated is the realization that I am no different from you, and you are no different from me. We are all Americans, and the United States of America is full of people who have mutual interests. We want America to succeed. We will succeed."

The response to his words was secondary to the response to Max himself. At that moment, he was the leader of the country, and no rebuttal by his opponents could refute the message that he had presented. As he stood, absorbed in the lights and applause, two men in identical black suits turned toward the stage and withdrew laser sighted machine pistols, aimed at Max's chest, emptied the magazines at 50 rounds a second, and fled as the shocked crowd surged forward. Screams filled the cavernous auditorium. Max remained standing, in the same position he had been in before the bullets flew in his direction. The screen behind him was punctured with black holes where the bullets had passed, but Max was unscathed. Two Secret Service agents lunged in his direction, trying to bring him down and protect him with their bodies, but they passed through Max and collided with one another. Max was not there.

The remaining Secret Service agents cornered the shooters just outside the door and hauled them out of sight. Darkhorse remained in his seat at the back of the auditorium, shocked at the failure of his suicide shooters to dispatch Max in front of a huge audience. He would have liked to get rid of him in a way that left doubt as to the cause of Max's death, but his employers were desperate. Masterson represented a threat to all that they sought to maintain. By the time the shooters had been detained for questioning, they would all be dead from poison capsules surgically implanted inside their mouths. Nothing would remain that would lead investigators back to the group that had devised this attempt to eliminate the man who continued to occupy the stage unscathed.

Max watched the monitor as his hologram was first shot, then tackled, and then immersed in running figures, all trying to protect him and bewildered about his lack of substance. "Hey, you guys!" His voice came from numerous speakers arranged to make the sound of his voice seem to come from his image. "I heard they were going to try this, so rather than dying, I thought I'd just make the speech from my house tonight. I hope you don't mind." He kept talking in front of the tattered backdrop, aware that his attempt at smoke and mirrors would never succeed a second time. "I have maintained all along that I am not a politician, and that's a good thing, because a guy could get shot being a politician."

The audience roared in laughter, partly out of relief and partly at the irony of the situation that had just played out before them.

The universal assumption was that the shooting was sanctioned by the president somehow, and whether that impression was accurate or not, Blythe had no time before the election to disavow all knowledge. Max did nothing to correct this perception, even though he knew that other forces were also responsible for his illusory demise. Blythe was finished, and so was his campaign. The press had gone wild posting the information that his Intelligence Secretary had leaked in features and editorials running on continuous feeds, fulfilling a lust for salacious scandal that threatened to engulf the issues of the election.

"You have probably been wondering, too, how I could run for president without announcing my running mate. I had planned on telling you about it during yesterday's debate, but the president came down with the flu and had to go back to the White House to rest. I'm sure that he's watching now." The image of Max turned to the right, the illusion of his physical presence shattered by the tattered backdrop that still displayed the Stars and Stripes behind the hologram. "So I brought her here, right here on this stage, to meet you."

As he spoke, the lights illuminated a small side stage, where Scarlett Conroy stood, red hair immaculate, beaming with vice presidential appeal. She took her position next to the spot where Max's image continued to appear, and spoke "Max will be here in a few minutes. After all, my dear voters, it's not reality, but the perception of reality we need to focus upon, as this evening's events have so clearly demonstrated. But here is a reality that you can count on."

"In a few short weeks, I will be a heartbeat away from the presidency."

Scarlett's comments struck a nerve with the audience, who stood to applaud, tears streaming down many cheeks. The sound of their applause prevented her from saying more, and her feeble attempts to settle the crowd were ignored. The cheering continued long after she surrendered to the emotion of the moment, and tears of joy trickled down her cheeks.

There was no way that she could have known, but the standing ovation was duplicated in households around the world.

Max boarded a helicopter to make the jump across the Potomac from Fairlane to the Kennedy Center. As he strapped himself into the passenger seat, it lifted off the landing pad and hovered briefly. His pilot turned to him for the first time.

"How did it go?" Rachel asked, guiding the chopper toward the monuments of the nation's capitol in the distance.

"It's too early to tell," he said. "But there's hope…"

The End

He paddled at full pull, using the foot-controlled rudder to maintain maximum speed around the turn. As the bow of the nineteen-foot surf ski rounded the narrow bend of the river, He passed into full view of the Mama Gator. The squeaks of her newly-hatched babies greeted his senses from the opposite shore. No sane person would intentionally come between an alligator mother and her babies , but his intrusion was unintended.

Max immediately realized his predicament.

He was about to get chomped.

The eleven foot long alligator slashed her body once, and lunged into the water. He paddled at full- tilt now, not bothering to turn his head to respond to the source of the splash.

He knew.

At the narrow bend, the river was no more than fifteen feet wide, with narrow sandy banks on each side. Beyond that gash of light, a thick cypress forest extended in either direction. If he wanted to live, he had to paddle.

Max could feel the bumpy scales of the huge gator as she swam beneath the fiberglass hull of the surf ski. It was nineteen feet long, but only extended three inches on either side of his hips. At twenty-nine pounds, it would be no obstacle to the five- thousand pounds per square- inch jaws of the ancient reptile. If he brought the man-powered speedboat to a full stop, it would tip him into the water, and at this point, stopping was definitely not an option. He saw the eyes and snout of the gator pop to the surface to his left ahead of him, and looked for the gaping mouth to open.

She was looking at him.

Max kept paddling. When he came abreast of the gator, he placed the blade of the paddle directly between her eyes, and hoped that the depth of the water would keep her from planting her powerful legs in the sandy bottom. If she was floating, he could sink her long enough to propel his watercraft beyond her jaws.

If she was planted on the bottom, she could have him for lunch.

Without breaking form, he propelled the surf ski as fast as his aching shoulders could go. A wake extended behind him, creating small waves that hit the sandy banks on either side. He imagined the eyes of the gator glowing yellow as she watched his retreat Fifty more strokes, and he came to a tree that extended its full length across the slave canal. A lush bush of poison oak covered the center section of the narrow passage. On the right, he saw light beyond the obstacle, and steered the rudder toward the hole in the foliage. Once beyond it, he turned and looked behind him. There was no sign of the gator, but he was not in a trusting mood.

He paddled for as long as his tired muscles would propel him, and then allowed the sleek craft to tip him into the water. It was cool and clear, and the invigorating wetness brought him back from exhaustion. Its spring-fed waters maintained a temperature of seventy-two degrees year-round, and he floated until his body temperature and breathing returned to normal.

"I wonder how frantic my Secret Service agents would be if they knew that the incoming President of the United States was almost eaten by a huge reptile on their watch," he wondered.

" I can only imagine the predators lurking in the Oval Office. And there are no corners to hide."

CPSIA information can be obtained at www.ICGtesting.com
Printed in the USA
LVOW081935111111

254639LV00002B/3/P